DRAFT SEASON

FOUR MONTHS ON THE CLOCK

BOBBY DEREN

PUBLISHING.COM

Copyright © 2010 by Bobby Deren

ISBN 0-7414-5756-3

Published by:

INFI(∞)ITY
PUBLISHING.COM

1094 New DeHaven Street, Suite 100
West Conshohocken, PA 19428-2713
Info@buybooksontheweb.com
www.buybooksontheweb.com
Toll-free (877) BUY BOOK
Local Phone (610) 941-9999
Fax (610) 941-9959

Printed in the United States of America

Published January 2010

CHAPTER ONE

A Better Life

There is only one sport in the world that generates a massive surge of adrenaline unlike no other. That surge is not only felt by its participants, but it can also be felt by the millions of spectators who watch from afar. Only one sport thrives on a savage brutality where grown men hurl their bodies into one another without any regard for their own safety. It is a game that has grown to epitomize the culture of American sports. It is also a game that has become a way of life for more than just its players. It is a game that interrupts the monotonous routines of people who do not make their living wearing a football helmet. And for a short time each week, people can take a break from their ordinary lives and lose themselves in the luster, exhilaration and intrigue that is the National Football League.

Throughout the entire football season, millions of people remain glued to their televisions watching human specimens perform at the most optimum levels. Prior to those games, those same people anxiously count down the seconds until kickoff. And when the football season is over, those people long for the return of that barbaric yet elegant game. However, for those extraordinary young men looking to make a career for themselves in the NFL, the most important season of their lives takes place while no other games are scheduled. Once those players have played the final down of their college careers, they immediately move on to the draft season.

For Florida Atlantic middle linebacker Frantz Joseph, that final moment came one day after Christmas. He looked up at the scoreboard at Ford Field in Detroit as his Florida Atlantic Owls held on to defeat Central Michigan by a score of 27-24 in the 12th annual Motor City

Bowl. Frantz took off his helmet and allowed his dreadlocks to breathe a little easier. His bearded face widened into a smile, knowing full well he was a major part of that victory. Frantz registered thirteen tackles and instilled fear into every Central Michigan player who touched the football. Frantz finished the season with the second-most tackles in the country and hoped that his college résumé would be adequate enough to land him a job somewhere in the NFL.

A job in the NFL would take Frantz down a road very different from the path that led him to this point in his life. Frantz was born and raised in one of the most dangerous and violent neighborhoods in Fort Lauderdale, Florida. Just making it this far had already been a monumental accomplishment within itself, but Frantz was looking to go even farther.

"My life is riding on making it to the NFL," said Frantz. "For me, it's now or never. If I don't make it now, I'm going back to the hood. And that means one of the most violent, drug-filled, non-opportunistic neighborhoods there is. There's no second chance and I'm going to do everything it takes to get where I need to be."

Frantz's journey to the NFL began long before he was named the MVP of the Motor City Bowl. At a very early age, Frantz was intrigued by the game of football, but wasn't always able to play.

"My mother never really had the money to put me into Pop Warner football," he explained. "I used to just hang out around the parks, looking and watching everybody else play."

So while other boys played the game of football, Frantz could only hope for the chance to join in. Frantz silently wished that he too could experience the same grandeur he saw spread across their faces. He wanted to feel what it was like to lower his shoulder and send a ball carrier to the ground with a bone-jarring thud. And he often wondered what it would feel like to cross the goal line with the football in his hands and a gang of defenders lagging a few steps behind.

But being able to afford football equipment was not his family's top concern. His single mother had struggled to make ends meet ever since Frantz could remember. His father had abandoned the family when Frantz was only three years old, leaving behind only faded memories of a few piggy-back rides that now seemed more like a distant dream. Frantz's mother was a Haitian immigrant who fled her native land in

2

search of a better life. But what Marie Clercius found in America was a constant struggle where five children depended solely upon her.

That struggle often left the family without enough money to afford some of life's bare essentials. Inside Frantz's home, there were many nights when candles took the place of light bulbs because an electric bill went unpaid. Frantz's homework was often done by candlelight and occasionally he had to keep wax from spilling onto his copybook. There were plenty of mornings when Frantz woke up and couldn't savor the luxury of a shower. Without enough money to pay the water bill, Frantz's mother would step outside and fill a bucket with water from a nearby hose. Frantz would then use that bucket of water to brush his teeth and wash himself as best as he could before going off to school.

"When I was a kid, I was embarrassed because I didn't have all the other things that other kids had," said Frantz. "They all had better stuff than I did. And I often wondered what it was like not to go to sleep with my stomach growling because there was no food in the house. It's very embarrassing when people know you're struggling and the lights are off and you can't pay the rent. But as you get older, you start to understand that life is different for everybody. You just have to understand your situation and live with it."

Frantz's mother spoke only a limited amount of English, which made it rather difficult for her to hold down a steady job. Still, she tried each and every day to do the best she could for her family. Every day, she would attend a local swap shop, where she would attempt to sell various items she had made herself. She also took on menial under-the-table jobs whenever she could.

"She's a Christian woman so she's not going to go out and steal, kill or strip for money," said Frantz. "She had to do it the right way. The hardest thing to see was that she couldn't make it happen. I can remember laying in bed as a kid and listening to her cry at night. But everything happens for a reason and, as you grow up, you start to understand that. But as a kid, that's something you don't understand. My life forced me to grow up faster than other kids."

As Frantz grew in years, so did his love for football. Whether it was watching from a distant bleacher or peering out from behind a tree, Frantz continued to sneak peeks at the game he so desperately wanted to play. But he wouldn't trouble his mother with the cost of equipment.

However, at the age of eleven, someone else noticed him watching from afar.

"I had a substitute teacher see how interested I was in football," said Frantz. "When he found out why I wasn't playing, he paid for me to play my first year. It was tremendous after having to sit and watch all the other kids. Just having the equipment on was like a dream come true! I finally had the opportunity to run around and play. I was just blessed. Ever since then, boy I just never looked back."

The more Frantz played the game, the better he became. At home, the financial struggles continued as Frantz and his family were forced to moved around quite a bit. Eviction notices were not uncommon nor was a late night move to avoid the actual eviction process itself. And while he was in high school, Frantz had to contend with even more problems. Friends of his began to fall victim to the many temptations that existed in his poverty-ridden neighborhood. As a young teenager, Frantz saw friends toting guns, selling drugs and resorting to robbery in order to line their pockets with cash. But Frantz never followed down that path.

"I had a lot of friends that messed up," said Frantz. "It was practically the whole neighborhood. I've had plenty of opportunities to make a bad decision. I could have went out and tried to steal when we didn't have any money or any food. But I got lucky because I had a mother that instilled great morals and values in me. And the guy upstairs led me down the right path."

Frantz's mother did not always have enough money to keep the lights on, the water running or the landlord from banging down the door. She did, however, provide Frantz with enough to keep him out of trouble.

"Without her morals and values, I wouldn't be here right now," Frantz said with heartfelt conviction. "I'd probably be somewhere in jail, God forbid, or maybe even dead. It was just the situation I was born in. I consider myself a pretty disciplined person because of the way my mother raised me. I grew up in a real, real violent neighborhood that presented a lot of distractions. But I really grasped the morals and values she instilled in me as a child. They stayed with me as I grew up."

Frantz also carried with him the desire and determination to get both himself and his mother far away from such a dangerous place.

"I've always had a determination in mind to get to a better place and get out of that violent, non-opportunistic neighborhood," said Frantz.

4

"Those things really kept me focused."

That focus was beginning to help Frantz stand out on the football field. He began his high school career at Dillard High, which had a history of turning out NFL players. Prior to Frantz's arrival, Isaac Bruce and Chris Gamble both played their high school ball at Dillard. Bruce went on to appear in four Pro Bowls while Gamble became one of the highest paid NFL cornerbacks in 2008. But Frantz wouldn't be able to follow in those exact footsteps. The family was forced to move once again and Frantz had to transfer from Dillard to Fort Lauderdale High School during his sophomore year.

It was there, as part of the Flying L's football team, that Frantz started to gain notice. No longer was he that same wishful kid who could only watch the game from a distance. Many eyes were now focusing on Frantz as he was blossoming into one of the best linebackers in Broward County. College coaches from all over the country began to travel down to Florida in an attempt to persuade Frantz to become a part of their program. The kid who used to just wish for the chance to put on the pads was now very high up on many coaches' wish lists.

A scholarship offer came locally from Central Florida, while others funneled in from faraway schools such as Vanderbilt, Connecticut, Colorado State and Boston College. Local powerhouses Florida and Florida State were also hot on Frantz's trail, leading him to believe that scholarship offers would be forthcoming. But after a late October visit to Boston College, Frantz wouldn't give any other schools the chance to vie for his services.

"Boston College had a great combination of athletics and academics," said Frantz. "They play in a big time conference and the education there is just a little below that of an Ivy League college. I was going to get the best of both worlds."

So, during his senior year of high school, Frantz ended his college recruitment on October 30th of 2003 by accepting a football scholarship from Boston College.

During his first year in Boston, Frantz practiced with the team but did not play in any games. That was a common occurrence in college football and is known as a redshirt season. Frantz did not play a down, but the upside was that he would still have four years of eligibility remaining.

Meanwhile, his mother's struggles continued back home. Frantz would talk to her on a daily basis, trying to lend words of advice, encouragement and assistance. Yet, words could only do so much. One night, as his mother was on the verge of being evicted yet again, Frantz returned home to help her vacate the apartment. And after he moved all of her stuff in the late hours of the night, he vowed not to return to Boston.

"My brother went away to the Navy and she was kind of down there by herself," said Frantz. "That led me back home. I wanted to be there for her not just financially, but emotionally too. When you're in a house by yourself alone, it gets tough on a person, especially at an older age. I've always pretty much been a strong foundation for my family."

Frantz could only be so much of that foundation from the New England area. The end result was a permanent trip back home and a transfer to Florida Atlantic University in nearby Boca Raton.

Florida Atlantic was dramatically different from Boston College. Its football program had just started in 2001 whereas Boston College had been around since the dawn of the 20th century. Even though Frantz knew it would be more difficult to make it to the NFL coming out of a small school like Florida Atlantic, he never thought twice about his decision. He also didn't take into consideration that no Florida Atlantic player had ever made it to the NFL. On the other hand, Boston College has seen almost two-hundred of its former players suit up on Sundays.

"Family comes first," Frantz stated. "I have no regrets at all. My brother was away in the Navy and the rest of her family is back in Haiti. It was just time for me to step up and be a man."

Once Frantz was back in Florida, he helped out as much as he could. Part of his scholarship stipend went towards his mother's bills and he would even try to find work whenever he could. He mowed lawns, cleaned churches and took on other various short-term gigs to help out with the bills. He did all this while carrying a full load of college courses in addition to playing college football.

Furthermore, Frantz was not the stereotypical football player who just cake-walked through a bunch of easy classes. He took on not one, but two majors; one in Business and the other in Marketing.

"Going through a class schedule and having to practice, then come home and study was tough," said Frantz. "Then, if you want to be a good player, you have to do film study. It was tough to get all that done. There would be days during the school year, I'd be going to sleep at three or four in the morning then wake up at seven or eight o'clock to get ready for the next day."

Transferring from Boston College to Florida Atlantic also meant that Frantz would have to sit out a year as per NCAA regulations. Whenever a player transfers from one Division 1 college to another, he must sit out a full season. That transfer essentially cost Frantz a year of eligibility. By the time Frantz was finally able to play again, it had been almost three full years since he had competed in a game.

Even when he was forced to watch from the sidelines, the reality of playing in the NFL always ran through Frantz's mind. It was a dream that never went to sleep, yet it wasn't until midway through his college career when that dream started to become a realistic possibility. During his junior year, Frantz began to emerge into a star. However, it wasn't just because of the way he played the game. It was also due to the passion that fueled him from one play to the next.

"When I was younger, I always had a passion for playing the game," said Frantz. "I had a passion for contact, that's why I became a linebacker. After I was playing for a while, I realized the opportunity was there to go to the next level. All those things made me want to make this my life."

In addition to realizing his boyhood dream, Frantz knew that the NFL presented an opportunity to rescue him and his mother from the utter poverty they had known throughout their entire lives.

"All my life, I've been there for my mother," said Frantz. "I never had a father to help us out. This really gives me an opportunity to put my mother in a position where she needs to be. But then again, you never know. This business is crazy. You're not guaranteed anything. There is nowhere in the blueprint that says Frantz Joseph is getting drafted just because of his college career. I've seen many guys in the past have great college careers, but not even get a shot at the next level."

Even if the NFL would not be part of his future, Frantz was confident that he could make his way in the business world. He needed to complete only one more college course in order to graduate with a coveted double major.

"I could really see myself owning my own business," said Frantz. "I always saw myself as a leader on the field and off the field. The leader is the CEO. I really feel like that's where I need to be in life."

Still, there was no guarantee that even a double major would land him a job.

"I know guys that graduated last year and two years ago that still can't get a job because how bad the economy is," said Frantz. "Not saying my education won't take me anywhere, but the way this economy is right now, you're not guaranteed a job just because you have a degree."

The almighty National Football League was even beginning to feel the effects of the current recession.

Indianapolis Colts general manager Bill Polian pointed out, "We have not yet seen the full effects of the recession in this industry. The wash-through of sponsorships and things like that has not really hit us yet. Of course, ticket sales are yet to be affected. Right now, it's sort of a murky picture. We know that the rest of the country is suffering badly. I'm worried as an American that everything is hurting and we're not immune to it."

The worsening economy forced many Americans to cut back on certain expenses in their daily lives. While this may have been a new concept for some people, it was nothing revolutionary for Frantz.

"I can remember times in the classroom when there were kids coming to school getting everything they wanted," said Frantz. "I didn't have that. At a younger age, I couldn't understand why I didn't have new clothes or the cool clothes that all the other kids had. Now that I look back, that's just the situation I was put in. But the Lord would never put somebody in a situation they can't handle. I feel as though he blessed me with a strong mind. And as I grew up, I took that to heart and it made me work harder."

Frantz's hard work enabled him to finish second in the nation with 154 tackles during his senior year. A year prior to that he piled up 131 tackles, giving him a whopping total of 285 over the last 26 games of his college career. Despite all his on-the-field accolades, Frantz believed that it was his work ethic that would allow him to make it in the NFL. Regardless of how many other linebackers would be competing against him for a spot on a NFL roster, Frantz was confident that he could outwork every one of them.

"I see a lot of guys with more talent and athleticism than I could ever imagine," said Frantz. "But they won't do anything with it because they don't feel like they need to. At the end of the day when they graduate college, they still have a two-story home that they're going back to. They still have parents that are well off. For me, it's now or never. It's do or die. If I don't make it now, there's no second chance."

A lifelong series of hardships seemed to hover atop Frantz like a dark cloud. Yet, if he had the opportunity to go back and alter the pages of his life, Frantz would not rewrite a single word.

"I wouldn't change it for the world," said Frantz. "The things I've been through molded me into the person I am today. I never take anything for granted, I never overlook anything and I appreciate everything. I wouldn't change that because I wouldn't want to be any other person than who I am right now."

That person was a hulking linebacker who sported a beard and long flowing dreadlocks. Watching Frantz play the game of football sometimes caused even spectators to cringe after each devastating hit he dished out. However, when he wasn't wearing a football uniform, Frantz was a soft-spoken, gentle, young man who almost always wore a smile.

"Plenty of times people look at the way I appear and make quick judgments," Frantz acknowledged. "A lot of times, it's the hair issue. They see a guy with dreads and automatically think he's a hoodlum or whatever the case may be. But I'm passed that. I don't worry about that. I'm a very caring person. I care for a lot of people and I like to help people because I've been through so much. And I know what it feels like to need help."

Frantz was the youngest of five children, but he was far from a baby. He had matured at an early age and grown into a confident young man. Still, there was a certain innocence about him. He looked at things with a sense of wonder and always seemed to have a curious question on the tip of his tongue. It was almost as if Frantz had seen some of the harshest realities of life, but would not let any of that adversity taint the way he saw the world. He possessed a rare combination of maturity and innocence. It was that combination that always seemed to put a smile on his face. As a result, people often referred to him as 'Smiley'.

Seeing Frantz interact in the everyday world made it difficult to tell that this was one of the most punishing linebackers in the nation.

Nonetheless, he was hopeful that such a reputation would be enough to keep his football career going. He had come from nothing and overcome so much to get where he was. But would it be enough to catapult him into the high-paying world of the NFL?

In just a few short months, the two-day extravaganza known as the NFL Draft would attempt to tell Frantz's future. Over the course of that weekend, 32 NFL teams would select 256 of the top college players to be part of its prestigious fraternity. Yet, Frantz could not just sit and wait for that day to arrive. He would soon face a season with a whole new series of challenges.

The draft season had finally arrived for Frantz Joseph. A successful draft season could mean a new life, free from the poverty, adversity and disappointment Frantz had come to know all too well. Conversely, a poor draft season could lead Frantz right back to the same violent neighborhood where he had spent almost his entire life. As soon as the last second expired on his college career, Frantz found himself on the clock that was ticking down towards the NFL Draft.

CHAPTER TWO

In the Maize

Of all the places to make a home across the continental United States, there may be no more perfect setting than San Diego, California. Never does it get too cold nor too hot and very rarely does rain ever ruin a day on the coast of Southern California. It was there in San Diego where Phil and Tina Trent celebrated the birth of their second son, Morgan, on December 14, 1985.

Long before that proud day, Tina was once an Olympic level diver and Phil played cornerback at the University of Nebraska. Both were elite athletes, which could only bode well for their youngest son Morgan. From the very first day Morgan enjoyed a breath of air, he was already well ahead of many of his peers.

As Morgan grew, he was able to enjoy more than just the gift of good genetics. Along with his older brother, Jarrad, Morgan was brought up in a comfortable, loving home where both parents served as role models. The Trents provided a comfortable life for their sons, but did not always enjoy such comfort themselves. As an inter-racial couple living in Nebraska during the late seventies, Phil and Tina had faced their share of adversity. During that time, it wasn't commonplace for people in that part of the country to see a long blonde-haired woman married to an African-American man. Living through that adversity only strengthened Phil and Tina's bond and, before long, they made their way to sunny California.

It wasn't long after that arrival when Morgan was introduced to the world. And it wasn't long after that introduction when both parents knew that Morgan was going to follow in their athletic footsteps.

"Both of our boys are excellent athletes," said Phil. "With Morgan, we knew early. It was very obvious that he was going to be something special."

Morgan started throwing a ball shortly after he took his first step. He then started to excel as soon as he began playing organized sports. However, Morgan did not start off on the football field.

"Back then in Southern California, soccer was the most important sport," said Tina. "All the athletes were on the soccer field. So the boys played elite soccer, it was like the highest level of soccer in the country. You can't try out for it, they pick you. The team travels all over the country and, for the coaches, it's their full time job."

By the age of six, Morgan was already starring on a team alongside kids two years older than him. And it was then when Morgan first experienced the pressure that came with being a top-notch player.

One day, after a losing effort, Morgan climbed in the car and told his mother in a very calm voice, "I lost us the game."

"No Morgan, you lose as a team," said Tina.

"Well, after the game, the coach made me stand up," explained Morgan. "And he told everyone to look at me. Then, he pointed and said, 'Morgan lost us the game today.'"

Most kids would have been devastated after hearing such words, but not Morgan. At the age of six, he took it in stride and refused to let that coach rattle him. It was also when he realized that expectations of him would always be higher than those of his peers.

Over the next few years, Morgan continued to thrive on the soccer field and also developed into quite an impressive baseball player. As far as basketball was concerned, he didn't play for any organized teams. However, he did begin collecting Air Jordans in the third grade. As long as he brought home straight A's and stayed clear of trouble, Phil rewarded him with a pair of those sneakers every time a new version debuted.

Life continued in the warm and cozy confines of San Diego up until Morgan reached the sixth grade. Then, all of the sudden, Southern California quickly became a place Morgan only used to call home. Phil was working for a national tire company and received a promotion to assistant vice president which required him to work out of Las Vegas. That meant that Sin City would now provide a new setting for Morgan's junior high experience.

Las Vegas also provided Morgan with a new opportunity. It was there that his parents finally permitted him to play football. And as soon as Morgan laced up his cleats and buckled his chin strap, he immediately became the best player on the field.

"I loved it right away," said Morgan. "There's no game like it. My dad wouldn't let me play up until then. Plus, I was sick of soccer. So I began to watch more football and really started getting into it. I started out playing quarterback. I couldn't throw, but I was fast. I just ran around all day. I come from such an athletic family, I'm used to being the best. My dad is extremely competitive and that was kind of instilled in me at a young age."

Phil also became involved in coaching to help Morgan along the way.

"Once you learn a bad habit, it's hard to break, especially with fundamentals," said Phil. "So I figured I'd be there to coach him and help him do things right."

Phil played four years of cornerback at the University of Nebraska, although the game had changed quite a bit since he waged war on the gridiron.

"When you played corner at Nebraska in the Big Eight, you were a glorified linebacker," Phil laughed. "They only threw on 3rd and 8. And back then, there were only about three pass patterns. It was a totally different game. It was a business, but nothing like the way it is now."

Phil's football career ended with his college graduation and Tina's diving career finished up shortly thereafter. However, Tina's decision was a more deliberate one.

"She sacrificed her career for all of us," Morgan professed. "She stopped diving so that she could have a family."

Tina did not say goodbye to the sport entirely. She became a diving coach and still coaches a couple of teams to this very day. With both parents helping him through the early stages of life, Morgan began to appreciate just how fortunate he actually was.

"When we lived in Las Vegas, the team I played for wasn't located in the best area," said Morgan. "So there were a lot of kids with single parents. I'm blessed to have both parents because, sadly enough, it's rare nowadays. They're the biggest support system there ever is. They're always there, they're my best fans. And they always tried to branch out to kids on my teams that didn't have both parents. We would constantly have them over our house and stuff like that."

That solid foundation was turning Morgan into a leader at a very early age.

"Even way back during recess, I was always organizing a game," said Morgan. "I was usually the captain picking the teams out and all that good stuff."

Being the best player on the field also helped Morgan develop the qualities of a leader. Yet, as good as Morgan was on the football field, it seemed as though his future may have lied on the baseball diamond.

"I had a real good coach when I lived in Vegas," said Morgan. "I was a real good pitcher. I actually had a Milwaukee Brewers scout come out and look at me when I was in the eighth grade. I liked baseball. But once I started playing football, baseball got boring to me. I look back now and see all the money these guys are making in baseball and maybe I should have stuck with that!"

Morgan had adjusted to life in Las Vegas and was getting ready to make the transition into high school when the family was suddenly uprooted once again. Phil's company decided that his presence was now warranted in the Detroit region. That led the Trents to a new home in Brighton, Michigan.

Brighton is a small town a little more than a half-hour drive north of Detroit. Instead of attending the local high school in Brighton, Morgan's parents sent him to a private school that was about an hour commute each way. It was there at St. Mary's Preparatory School where Morgan shifted his focus solely to football. He stopped playing baseball and emerged into a standout wide receiver and safety. During his first couple of years of high school, it was obvious that his playing days would continue well beyond graduation. At the age of sixteen, that talent and success led Morgan to Ann Arbor and into the office of Michigan head coach Lloyd Carr.

"I was sitting in Coach Carr's office and I was just kind of in awe," said Morgan. "It was Michigan. He offered me a scholarship so I committed real early. I was getting tons of letters from all these other schools, but I didn't even take any other visits."

And so it came to pass that Morgan would spend the next five years close to home in Ann Arbor. However, when Morgan arrived at college, he suddenly found himself in unfamiliar company. No longer was he the best player on the field. In fact, he did not even make it onto the field during his first year. Ahead of him at the wide receiver position was a group of players who would go on to make millions of dollars in the NFL. Braylon Edwards, Jason Avant, Steve Breaston and Adrian Arrington all caught passes that season while Morgan watched from the sidelines. He didn't play at all that year and it resulted in a redshirt season, which meant Morgan still had four years of college football left to play.

Depth at the wide receiver position eventually prompted Coach Carr to approach Morgan with the option of switching to cornerback. Morgan willingly accepted as he was eager to do whatever he could to get on the field. So after one full season at Michigan, Morgan found himself trying to adapt to a drastic change. He was learning a position he had never before played in his life. And it wasn't until his second year at Michigan when Morgan finally knew what it felt like to play college football.

"The first game I ever played was against Notre Dame," said Morgan. "I had no idea what was going on. It was a new position for me. But when you're out there, your body just kind of takes over. You're not really thinking, it's just happening. It's a little wild. You try to set in a little bit and get used to it."

Morgan tried to learn as much as he could, but four different position coaches in four years did not make things very easy. During his second year playing cornerback, Morgan received the eye-opening experience of playing against a pair of future NFL wide receivers when Michigan took on USC in the Rose Bowl.

"I had Steve Smith and Dwayne Jarrett lining up across from me and here I am a wide-eyed sophomore playing cornerback for the first time in my life," said Morgan.

USC went on to defeat Michigan by a score of 32-18 on the strength of 391 passing yards. Following that game, the Michigan fans never seemed to let Morgan live down those four quarters. Not much slack was given to Morgan even though he was still trying to learn the nuances of a new position while playing in one of the top conferences in the country.

Off the field, Morgan was getting acclimated to the college lifestyle. He was never much of a party-goer but rooming with tailback Mike Hart, Morgan attended his share of social events.

"Mike was the man on campus," said Morgan. "My freshman and sophomore years, I kind of went out now and then. I wasn't wild compared to a lot of the people out there. I was never much of a drinker, so drinking anything was a big deal for me. I think I had enough of the partying while I lived with Mike."

Morgan had his taste of the college life, although he didn't represent the cliché of a typical football player.

"I grew up in the church but when I got to college, I really found out who the Lord was for myself," said Morgan. "Everybody has to find the Lord for themselves and I definitely did that. I knew I wasn't doing what I should be doing, but that only lasted so long."

During his final two years of college, Morgan began to lead a lifestyle very different from most kids his age. Morgan moved off campus to share a home with his brother, sister-in-law, niece and nephew. On many mornings when most college kids attempted to sleep off a hangover, Uncle Morgan would baby-sit his niece and his nephew.

Of course, no matter how quiet a life Morgan tried to lead, there was still a certain mystique that came with wearing the blue and maize. Many young men all across the country played football for various colleges, but being a football player at the University of Michigan was something different. There was a tradition and allure that transcended other colleges.

"It carries out a power," said Morgan. "There's a lot behind it, but you don't realize it until you're out of it. You see how people react when you walk around in Michigan gear. People say, 'Wow, you went to Michigan!'"

Nevertheless, Morgan was never one to run towards the spotlight.

"I would go to class, go to practice and go home," said Morgan. "I was never at the places where most people get recognized. I like to go home, spend time with my family and just relax. That was cool for me."

Enough people around town were still able to pick Morgan out of a crowd, but that never became a problem.

"You wear a helmet all the time so people really don't know who you are unless you say something about it or unless you're wearing something with Michigan on it," said Morgan. "But that's not my thing. I'm not going to tell anybody I play football. Sometimes people have asked me if I played and I've lied and said no. It just depends. It's cool to

16

be noticed, but it is what it is."

Morgan maintained his role as a starter through his sophomore and junior seasons, but was hit with some unexpected news prior to his senior campaign. Coach Carr was retiring and would hand over the coaching reins to former West Virginia head coach Rich Rodriguez. That also meant another new positional coach for Morgan.

Morgan's final year in Ann Arbor turned out to be an unexpected one both on and off the field. He and his girlfriend Liz got engaged after a year of dating. They had agreed to wed in Cabo San Lucas exactly one week before the 2009 NFL Draft. The two met while at the University of Michigan, however Liz had already graduated and was living and working in Los Angeles.

"We've been doing the long distance thing for a while and it's worked," said Morgan. "It's only tough if you make it tough. But we don't have to struggle with a lot of things other relationships do. I don't go out to the clubs and neither does she. She's also extremely supportive of what I'm doing. She understands she's going to leave her job after I get drafted and that's a sacrifice she's going to make. It's exciting and I think we'll make it happen."

As Morgan's life flourished off the field, he was forced to watch Michigan suffer its worst season in 129 years. The coaching change combined with a roster laden with youth set Michigan up for a miserable campaign. Rodriguez had installed a defensive system that was scrutinized by experts and media across the country. The offensive-minded Rodriguez took a lot of criticism for the defense's poor performance during his first season in Ann Arbor. Unimaginable losses turned into reality week after week. After starting off the season with a 2-2 record, Michigan would go on to lose its next five games.

"When I committed to Michigan, I never thought something like that would be possible," said Morgan. "It was a long season, but I went out and gave it my all on every play. I always gave everything I had out on the field."

Morgan also never envisioned the final game of his college career playing out the way it did. As a raucous Ohio State crowd celebrated the final few minutes of a 42-7 drubbing, Morgan took a seat on the bench.

"I just sat there and looked around," Morgan said in a very profound voice. "It's crazy how many people are there. I got to play in front of millions of people every week. You have to enjoy the atmosphere, that's for sure. And after all these years, I still get a rush every time I go out on the field."

Morgan finished his career at Michigan tallying 41 starts, 149 tackles and 7 interceptions. He had a solid college career, but his best football may have been yet to come.

"They still haven't seen what's on tap," said Phil. "Some college players are better pros and I think that's exactly what Morgan's going to be. We had mixed emotions at the end of the year because the season was such a catastrophe. I was sad that during his senior year, Morgan couldn't go to a bowl game. But we were just happy he came out of the season healthy."

Following that final game, Morgan also had mixed emotions as he entered the locker room for the last time as a Wolverine.

"I felt for guys that I knew would never be part of a team again," said Morgan. "That was the last time they would ever put on a helmet and go out there and be a part of something like that. It's sad. I felt the same way in high school. There were guys who I knew would never play in college and they took it that much harder. But I knew that I would play again in the NFL. And for that reason, I felt as though I was truly blessed."

CHAPTER THREE

A Southern Superstar

Not every state is home to a professional football team, but that does not mean that the people of those states do not love their football. What often happens in such places is that a local college takes the place of a NFL team. Fans of those nations sometimes show more dedication, support and passion than some NFL fan bases. The University of South Carolina is one such place. It is a place where the NFL finishes a distant second behind Gamecock football. That also means the South Carolina players are elevated to a status beyond that of the average college football player. Players are put up on a pedestal and heralded as heroes before they are even old enough to buy a beer.

Over the years, there have been more than a few memorable players who have worn the garnet and black colors of South Carolina. Former Heisman Trophy winner George Rogers, ex-NFL head coach Dan Reeves and receiving legend Sterling Sharpe are all part of the brotherhood that is Gamecock football. One of the latest and greatest players to join that prominent list of names is the school's all-time leading wide receiver Kenny McKinley.

Kenny endeared himself to the South Carolina faithful with his dynamic play and personality. On the gridiron, Kenny was a flashy human highlight reel with quick moves and great instincts. Outside of football, Kenny also made a lasting impression on all those he encountered. He was a light-hearted kid who always wore a smile and seemed to have a genuine love for life. He also loved being a part of South Carolina football. He loved the notoriety that came with being a standout on the football field. Most importantly, he loved to play the game. And there was no other place he would have rather played his college football than in Columbia, South Carolina.

"It was the best four years of my life down there," said Kenny. "It's a college town so anytime you're doing good, they love you. They treat you with so much respect. They don't have a pro team, but they treat us like pro athletes. They love the Gamecocks and that's the thing they love the most."

The South Carolina fan base showed their love by selling out Williams-Brice Stadium week after week. Williams-Brice Stadium, also known as 'The Cockpit', holds more people than most NFL stadiums. Usually, not many of its 80,000 seats remained empty on game day.

The competition Kenny faced in 'The Cockpit' was among the best in the country. In 1992, South Carolina joined the Southeastern Conference which gradually developed into the nation's top collegiate football league. Four of the last six national champions all hailed from the SEC.

"I always said there's only two real conferences, the SEC and the NFL," said Kenny. "That's how people in the SEC feel. We play elite competition week in and week out. It's a step right under the NFL. You have to bring you're A-game week in and week out. When you know you're playing a SEC team, your preparation has to be perfect because anybody can beat anybody any week. Even the worst team in the league can upset the best team. I feel like four years of that tough competition really prepared me for the NFL."

In the southern part of the country, football is more than just highly competitive. It goes beyond the realm of being just a game. Fans are extremely passionate and they take college football very seriously. While that intensity is present each week, the instate rivalries of the south elevate that intensity to another level. The Alabama vs. Auburn rivalry may be atop that list, but not far behind is the heated battle between South Carolina and Clemson.

"In South Carolina, we got two teams," said Kenny. "We split the state up. There's Clemson and South Carolina. Half the people go with Clemson and half the people go with South Carolina. Fans get really crazy. My sophomore year, we beat Clemson at Clemson and one guy killed his friend because they had a bet on the game. That's how you know it's real serious. The fans of every team in the SEC are crazy. We done had fans throw stuff at our bus and say all kinds of nasty things. It gets crazy, but I love playing in it though. I love the fans in the SEC."

Intense competition and overzealous fans may have gotten Kenny ready for life in the NFL, but they were not the only two components that prepared him.

"The fame was there in college so I don't think that will really bother me when I get to the NFL," said Kenny. "I'm still young. I'm still going to live my life, but I can't get outrageous with it. Columbia's a football town so I had women coming up to me and all that type of stuff, but it prepared me for what to deal with in the NFL."

Kenny was able to make the most of his time in South Carolina both on and off the field. Now that those days were behind him, he had quite a few fond memories to take with him.

"I was a little more wild in college," said Kenny. "I went out a lot and spent a lot of time with my friends. We used to barbecue a lot, and then I'd get up with my girlfriend. I'd go out Saturday, go out on Thursdays and have a couple of drinks or what not. College was fun, it was a great time."

Individually, Kenny went out with a grand sendoff. Before his senior year concluded, he managed to break all of Sterling Sharpe's receiving records at South Carolina.

"If you asked USC fans, the old time fans will probably still tell you that Sterling Sharpe is the greatest receiver in USC history," said Scott Hood, a senior writer for GamecockCentral.com of the Yahoo Sports network. "But I think the younger fans would all say Kenny McKinley was the best and I think the numbers prove it."

Kenny wasn't the biggest player in the world, but he never shied away from contact. On his best day, he was lucky if he cleared the six-foot plateau and he usually carried about 185 pounds on his wiry frame.

"Size has never been an issue," said Kenny. "I got heart that makes up for it. I'm going to take the hits and keep on ticking. There's a lot of heart about me."

As successful as Kenny was at South Carolina, he had never played receiver before arriving in Columbia. He was a lifelong quarterback who first started playing at a very young age in his hometown of Atlanta, Georgia.

"I was four years old when I first started playing and I played in a six year-old league," said Kenny. "I didn't know what I was doing out there. I was like a chicken with his head cut off. But when I started playing with my age group, I was pretty much better than everybody else."

Superstar status came very early for Kenny. He quickly grew accustomed to being the best player on the field and that continued all the way through high school. His constant devotion to the game of football also helped him steer clear of the everyday dangers that lurked in the city of Atlanta.

"Football is something that keeps people out of trouble," said Kenny. "If I wasn't playing football, there's no telling what I'd be out there doing. Football was everything. I'd be at practice til' seven o' clock. After that, I would go home. During that time after school, I could be out there doing the wrong things. I had a lot of friends who didn't play football and wound up getting into some kind of trouble. Football gave me a chance to go to college and explore the world. Football is a beautiful thing."

Like many superstars, Kenny received a lot of recruiting attention when it came time to choose a college. He had quite a few schools urging him to become a part of their program. But when it came down to it, choosing South Carolina was a no- brainer. Kenny explained why.

"Steve Spurrier. He's got a great offensive mind and he's just an offensive genius. He told me I could play receiver. Coming from Steve, if he says you could be a great receiver, that's a great accomplishment. He put a lot of them in the league. I just left everything up to him and he turned me into a pretty good one."

Kenny started out his career at South Carolina in the shadow of future second-round NFL Draft pick and current Minnesota Viking Sidney Rice. As a first-year receiver, Kenny followed, watched and studied Rice's every move.

"Sidney was the man before I was," said Kenny. "He's like my big brother. We used to room together at South Carolina and he still calls to check in on me. He even flew me out to Minnesota and I saw how much the hard work paid off. It just made me want to work that much harder. I think knowing people in the league puts me a step ahead."

Kenny went on to make steady progress through his first two years of college. He caught 25 passes as a true freshman and then doubled that performance with 51 receptions during his sophomore campaign. But it wasn't until the last game of his sophomore year that Kenny began to emerge into a superstar at the college level.

"Kenny's breakout moment was the fourth quarter in the 2006 Liberty Bowl against Houston," said Hood. "He caught two long touchdown passes. Up until then, he was just Sidney Rice's understudy. But I think that kind of set the tone for the next two years."

The following two years paved the way to superstardom for Kenny. He earned All-American honors his junior year and eventually set the record for most receptions and receiving yards in school history. Kenny might have racked up more records had it not been for the hamstring issues that plagued him during his senior year. Kenny missed three games because of a pulled hamstring and was less than one-hundred percent for most of the season.

"I would get down a little when I couldn't play," Kenny admitted. "I was always off to the side just chilling. I don't let anyone see my emotions like that. I always felt that if you keep working hard and fight through it, something good is going to happen. I believe that. Being positive just comes natural."

Instead of giving Kenny more time to heal, the coaching staff rushed him back out on the field, needing every superstar they could muster in the highly competitive SEC.

"I think they should have done more for my injury," said Kenny. "They tried to rush me back and I pulled it again. They were basically just putting ice on it and trying to let it heal naturally."

For most of the season, Kenny played through the pain and dealt with the situation as best as he could. Following strenuous afternoons of practice, which were becoming all too common, Kenny longed for a trip to the trainer's room. But before he could take a dip in the ice tub or get some additional treatment, there was always a large media contingent eager to ask him some questions.

"There was always a lot of media covering the team," said Hood. "This is a college football state. The players here are treated like Gods almost. They get a lot of media attention, a lot of face time on TV and all that stuff. Kenny was always very good with the media. He was one of the more enjoyable players that I got to work with on a day-to-day basis. He always had a smile on his face and he always seemed to enjoy playing football."

Yet, behind some of those smiles was a kid who could not fend off the lingering pain that comes with a hamstring injury.

"Sometimes, I would have a bad day and not feel like interviewing," said Kenny. "But I would always say a little something even if I didn't feel like talking. I understand it comes with the territory. That's just my character, I like talking to people."

On the strength of a very frail hamstring, Kenny helped lead the Gamecocks to a 7-5 season and a trip to the Outback Bowl on New Year's Day. That led South Carolina fans to Tampa, Florida where Kenny would play the final game of his college career against the Iowa Hawkeyes. Shortly before kickoff, the crowd cheered as Kenny joined his teammates for one last trip out of the tunnel.

Not too many people are able to experience the rush that comes with performing in front of 80,000 people. There aren't many people whose simple movements can bring an audience of that size to its feet and command them to applaud, cheer, scream and rejoice simultaneously.

"You kind of get accustomed to it, but every time I come out of the tunnel, I'm like wow," said Kenny. "Every game, I always have a little bit of butterflies. But once you get that first hit on, you're ready to play."

Regardless of how many fans jammed into a stadium, Kenny could always spot his family.

"I could always pick them out because they always brought an 'I love Kenny' sign. My father hasn't missed one of my college games. He's been very supportive. My family comes to as many games as they can. They've been very supportive ever since I was a little boy. They keep my head straight and I feel like I owe them all."

Similar to every other game Kenny has played, he took the field wearing his game face. Unfortunately, some of his teammates did not have the same look. The result was a miserable first quarter for the South Carolina offense. They ran a total of nine plays and managed only two first downs. Coincidentally, those first downs came courtesy of Kenny on receptions of 15 and 17 yards.

South Carolina continued to struggle through the next two quarters and went on to face a 31-0 deficit heading into Kenny's final quarter of college football. At that point in the game, the Gamecocks' fate was pretty much sealed.

"I'm a competitor so going out like that put a real bad taste in my mouth," said Kenny. "When we went to the Outback Bowl and didn't perform that well, it hurt me just to know that the fans came out and spent all their money to watch us. I'm real passionate about the game. I like doing things for the fans and it's rewarding when we win."

As the last quarter of Kenny's college career started to wind down, he was able to distract himself from the game's unfavorable outcome. His mind suddenly became filled with thoughts that were very new to him.

"Towards the end of the game, I started thinking about me," said Kenny. "I was thinking, 'I don't need to be doing anything crazy and getting hurt because the game was out of reach.' I didn't want to go out and get injured in a game that was already out the window. I was basically thinking about the future. I was thinking that I have a chance to go pretty high in the draft. That kept going through my mind."

Those thoughts did not just sprout up out of nowhere. Furthermore, Kenny wasn't worried solely about his own future. A few weeks before the Outback Bowl, Kenny became a father after witnessing the birth of his son, Keon. Throughout his whole life, Kenny knew what it was to be a superstar on the football field. Now, he had the opportunity to be a different kind of superstar.

"It's already kind of maturing me," said Kenny. "I feel like I have to make it to the NFL for my whole family. I love my family and I love my little boy. That's what I live for now. My mamma's working two jobs right now to help pay for my sisters to go to college. I told her 'hold on because help's on the way!' Hopefully, I can be the support person to help out along the way. That's why I don't need any distractions now. My birthday's coming up and I'm fitting to be twenty-two years old. I had some great times in life and I'm fitting to have some more. But I think I'm becoming mo' cool laid back Kenny instead of the wild guy party animal. I got a family now and a lil' boy I got to look after."

After a grueling 31-10 defeat in the Outback Bowl, Kenny's college career had come to an abrupt end. The carefree days of enjoying the college lifestyle were also a thing of the past. As some of the seniors hung their heads, Kenny held his high because he knew he had plenty of football left to play. He knew that he had a chance to make a career for himself in the NFL. But making it in the NFL would require a resolute commitment on his behalf. Kenny would have to put his partying days behind him if he planned to make a living playing professional football. Hailing from the always entertaining city of Atlanta, there would be plenty of opportunities for Kenny to experience quite a bit of nightlife in the coming months. Still, the road ahead was paved with possibilities. It was now up to Kenny to move forward and ignore any obstacles that might serve as a detour.

When the final second ticked off the clock in Tampa, time seemed to expire on more than Kenny's college football career. The boy who had played four years at South Carolina would now have to become a man in order to make a future for himself in the National Football League.

CHAPTER FOUR

Necessary Evils

A necessary evil is commonly known as something that possesses undesirable qualities, yet has to exist for one reason or another. The death penalty, nuclear arms and even federal taxes could all be classified as necessary evils. In the world of professional football, many close to the game will contend that there is more than one necessary evil. In some conversations, agents are even whispered as being one of those necessary evils. Yet, it's hard to imagine that a single man can house the same capabilities as the death penalty, nuclear arms or federal taxes.

Every year, college players who are on the cusp of becoming millionaires are forced to find an agent before they can close a deal that will enable them to cash a seven-figure check. It is usually during that search when players learn why certain agents are whispered to be necessary evils.

The top college players get their first introduction to the world of agenting long before the draft season begins. As soon as players start to emerge into college stars, a bull's-eye is immediately placed upon their backs. Agents waste no time shooting in and trying to strike a deal with those players. However, that is all part of the game.

The NFL Players Association certifies roughly 1,000 agents who have the right to negotiate player contracts with NFL teams. Without that certification, an agent cannot do business with the NFL. An agent must also negotiate at least one contract every three years or else that certification is no longer valid. With many high-powered agents having long lists of clients, the vast majority of agents are left battling for the few players that remain.

Being an agent may seem like a glamorous lifestyle, but more than sixty percent of NFL certified agents have one client or less. Agents also have a cap on how much they can make off a player's salary. Three percent of the contract value is the highest amount an agent can collect. That leaves many agents hungry to sign new players each year. That may also explain why such extreme measures are taken as these agents scour the country in search of new clients.

Being a superstar introduced Kenny to the world of agenting rather early in his college career. Following a junior year in which he caught 77 passes and 9 touchdowns, Kenny entertained thoughts of leaving college early for the NFL.

"I thought about it," said Kenny. "But I needed to get surgery on my toe and I wanted to come back and refine everything. I didn't have the senior season I wanted to because of the injury, but I'm happy I came back. I had another fun year in college. You never get that year back."

Agents are not permitted to contact underclassmen before they declare for the NFL Draft, but that didn't stop them from approaching members of Kenny's family.

"After my games, they'd always try to come up to my daddy," said Kenny. "One game, they even tried to go up and sit with my daddy and talk to him during the game. They're everywhere, like vultures."

As Kenny's college career wore on and the NFL started to become an inevitability, agents grew more persistent by the day.

"There was a dude that used to call me and my daddy five times a day," said Kenny. "I just stopped picking up the phone. He used to call so much that he kind of pushed himself out of the picture. Then, when I stopped taking his phone calls, he started e-mailing me every day; me and my daddy. Then, he started calling my girl. He was like a stalker. Finally, I just went and got my number changed."

With so many agents constantly trying to contact Kenny, the situation felt much like the one he faced when having to choose a college.

"It felt like it did when I was in high school being recruited by a lot of colleges," said Kenny. "It's a tiring process. Some of them are like car salesmen, but I guess that's their job."

The common sales pitch Kenny often heard was the promise of a better life in the NFL. Although Frantz attended a much smaller university, he was not exempt from hearing the same pitch.

"Guys have offered me money and the New York life so to speak," said Frantz. "I've had guys promise me that I would get drafted. I've had guys come at me downplaying other agents. It's kind of crazy. Everybody is trying to tell you the same thing. They promise you all these things. After a while, they all sound like a recording saying the same things over and over."

Many agents targeted Frantz's family as well.

"I'd have guys pop up at my games and wind up sitting next to my brother and my mother," said Frantz. "And I wouldn't have even spoken to these guys before. Out of nowhere, here they are at my game."

That pursuit did not stop once the bleachers had emptied out.

"There would be times I'd be on Facebook and five guys would come at me out of nowhere," said Frantz. "It could be two or three in the morning. I'd wake up and check my Facebook and guys would send me a quick instant message. In the middle of the night, it's kind of scary."

Morgan also found his computer routinely clogged with e-mails from various agents.

"I got more e-mails and phone calls than actual people stopping by," Morgan said. "After games, I would get a few people hanging around. But it's more phone calls and e-mails. I really didn't deal with it too much. I just forwarded it all to my parents and they kind of screened all of them."

With the help of Phil and Tina, Morgan narrowed down the long list of agents who were actively seeking him out. As a family, they selected ten finalists and set up meetings with all of them over a four-day period.

"Morgan's mother is the publicist," said Phil. "She set up every single meeting. But at the end of the day, we knew what Morgan was looking for."

Instead of meeting at a public place or inside some stuffy office, the interviews were conducted right inside the Trents' living room.

"There were two reasons for that," said Phil. "Morgan has both parents here and they're not going to flatter him with material things. We also wanted to understand their character. I wanted to see what they brought to the table as opposed to all the flattery."

It didn't take long for Morgan to form his own opinion.

"As soon as they walked through the door, I would know in the first five minutes," said Morgan. "Some of the meetings were rough because then I'd have to sit there and listen to them go on for the next two hours. It gets repetitive."

It wasn't so much everything the agents said, but rather the rapport they were able to develop with Morgan.

"Your agent is someone you have to feel comfortable with," said Morgan. "It has to be someone who's real. I can see through people pretty quickly. If I didn't feel comfortable, I knew it wasn't going to work."

Once all ten finalists had spent some time in Morgan's home, he was pretty sure which agent he would choose. Morgan opted to sign with Doug Hendrickson out of Octagon Sports Agency. The agency was very reputable and already represented over sixty current NFL players. But Morgan had further insight beyond that of his parents.

"My agent represents a lot of my friends as well," said Morgan. "He reps Leon Hall who plays for the Bengals, Marlin Jackson who plays for the Colts and LaMarr Woodley for the Steelers. They told me what a great guy he is and what he's done for them."

Yet, as important as it was to have a top-quality agent, Morgan knew that his representation could only take him so far.

"A lot of players told me that agents don't do much. They can't take you from the fifth round to the second round. You have to do that yourself. But it does help to have someone in your corner that is respected in the league, someone that can really get in the GM's office and do something for you."

Morgan's friends in the NFL also explained to him how an agent's role begins to wane as time passes.

"Once you get in the league, you kind of do your thing," said Morgan. "Your agent is there if anything's going down, but he's really there for your contract negotiations. When it comes down to getting your second contract, that's what your agent does. It's really just someone in your corner. They're not going to do too much. Getting you in the league, yes. But once you're there, you're there. They can't go out and play for you."

In contrast to Morgan, Frantz had no former teammates to turn to for advice. However, he had witnessed some of his former teammates fail in their quests for the NFL. In those cases, Frantz believed the agent had something to do with their missed opportunities.

"They were different situations, but a lot of the time the agents had an effect," said Frantz. "They were slick talkers who promised the world. I tried to stay away from those guys. I tried my best to stay away from all those agents during the season. Realistically, they won't stay away from you whether it's through e-mail or whatever the case may be."

Nevertheless, Frantz had become quite familiar with slick talkers and hustlers over the years.

"Growing up in my situation, I had a lot of run-ins with hard pressing people," said Frantz. "I'm used to it. Some of those agents couldn't even look me in the eye. I caught on to the fast talkers and slick talkers. Those are the guys you can tell are B'Ssing. It just comes down to character. You have to figure out who is the best character person. Who can you call at four in the morning if you need him?"

Both Frantz and Kenny finally signed with Metro Sports, an agency based out of New York City. Metro wasn't just an agency filled with men in suits who had never seen the inside of a huddle or the first round of a draft. Former first-round NBA Draft pick Eric Murdock was one of the founding partners and former NFL player Latish Kinsler serves as the director of player development in addition to being both an agent and mentor to the players.

A former standout defensive back at the University of Cincinnati, Kinsler had a brief foray through the NFL which included stops with the Pittsburgh Steelers, New York Jets and Philadelphia Eagles.

"I understand the full gamut of being a free agent, of having to train in between teams and things of that nature," said Kinsler. "I'm able to give the guys a realistic viewpoint. It doesn't matter if you are a first-rounder or a priority free agent, this time period of going from college to the NFL is key for every player. And these kids want to be able to know what's ahead of them. A lot of kids may have a preconceived notion of what the league is like. I think they feel more comfortable being able to talk to someone who has been through it."

Kinsler's experience from both ends of the spectrum helped him to understand the true nature of the business. He even recalled an instance from his playing days that influenced the way he conducts business now.

"I was with a mega-agency at the time and I was released by the Jets," said Kinsler. "The first thing I did was call my agent because I wanted to know which direction I should go from there. When I called, his assistant picked up the phone and I could hear my agent talking in the background. He was talking to another one of his clients who was a first-round pick. It turns out, this other player was having car trouble. The assistant told him I was just released and I heard my agent say, 'Get off the phone with him. We need to take care of this guy's flat tire.'"

Kinsler's experience in finding an agent also influenced the way he approaches potential clients.

"When trying to secure a client, a lot of agencies will do some unethical things that aren't in the best interest of the clients," said Kinsler. "Sometimes, if you are young and impressionable, it's hard to see past that. People always have this perception that agents have to be cutthroat and they're always throwing money around. But you can have a successfully run agency without any of that stuff."

Through the entire process, Frantz made a firsthand discovery of the illicit tactics practiced by some agencies.

"Frantz had about twelve other agencies pulling at him," said Kinsler. "He could have been unethical and taken money from those other agents. But to not act in that manner and not utilize his star power for financial gains, I have so much respect for him. His situation was dire and he could have used that money to help out at home, but he didn't take advantage of it in that way."

Even when players signed with an agent and left that process behind, others agents still hunted them.

"Even now, Kenny and Frantz are still getting calls from agents after they signed with us," said Kinsler. "It just never ends. Even when you sign a player, the other agents are still out there competing. It's rough at times. But to have young men like Frantz and Kenny with such genuine hearts, it's so unusual in this profession. Now, with the media and the internet, there is so much information available about these athletes. A lot of times, it boosts their egos. But to have Frantz and Kenny just so grounded, it's really unbelievable. They're not looking for any handouts."

With an agent secured and the NFL Draft only a few months away, the players could now shift their focus to doing everything possible to secure a spot on a team. However, one necessary evil would remain throughout the entire draft season; it was a necessary evil none of the players even wanted to acknowledge. What would happen if they didn't make it in the NFL?

"If it wasn't for football I don't know what I'd be doing," said Kenny. "I have no clue honestly. My whole life revolves around football. This is what put me into college and this is what gave me an education. I love the game. I do everything for football. It's a big part of me. If I got an injury and football didn't work out, it's hard to see where I would be. It's hard to see myself without football."

For Morgan, an alternative profession was something he could not even fathom. So what would he do if he could not make a living playing professional football?

"It's a good question," said Morgan. "Maybe it's bad that I don't have an answer. I really don't. This is what I've been preparing for since I've been in sixth grade. Should I have a backup plan? Yes. That's where my degree from Michigan comes into play. That's the good thing about going there. You've got the biggest alumni base in the world. I've met enough great people in my life to branch out and do something else if necessary."

But to Morgan, entertaining such thoughts was like getting ready to hoist a white flag in surrender.

"If you've got a backup plan, you're thinking that it might not work out," said Morgan. "That's not my mindset. I know it's going to work out. That's just where I'm at and I'm surrounding myself with people that feel the same way I do. It's not about a backup plan, it's about going out and making this thing happen."

Frantz was also without a backup plan, but he was just one credit shy of earning a degree with a double major. He had already learned the value of a quality education. He had also learned some important lessons that couldn't be taught in a classroom. He had waded through some grim situations and treaded through some very turbulent times. And he knew full well that a life in the NFL would enable him to paddle away from those oceans of adversity.

"I feel like going to the pros gets me a good start in the real world," said Frantz. "All I can I ask for is to get to somebody's camp. If I don't get drafted, it is what it is. I just need to get to somebody's camp and show what I can do. Right now, it's life or death for me."

CHAPTER FIVE

Just Over the Mountain

Inside every man who has ever played a game of football, there lives a young boy who has always dreamed of catching a pass in the NFL. Those little boys often long to hear the sound of a capacity crowd explode into a thunderous frenzy as they cross the goal line on a Sunday afternoon. Within schoolyards, empty lots, quiet streets and living rooms across the country, boys of all ages spend hours pretending to be a NFL player perfecting their very own touchdown dance. Long after those little boys have grown into men, there still lives a burning desire to make a living while wearing a helmet and a pair of shoulder pads. However, only a select few can actually live that childhood fantasy.

On Sundays from September to February, there are 1,696 grown men who make their living playing the game of football. Yet, the journey to the NFL is anything but an easy one. Just being able to break into the league requires a mountainous climb that entails years of sweat, sacrifice and hard work.

With the start of every new season, the top college prospects face an uphill battle regardless of how much talent has carried them that far. Even when those players finish their college careers, there is still more work to be done before they can relive the rapture of playing in front of thousands of screaming fans.

Towards the end of every February, the NFL invites approximately 330 of the top college players to attend its annual Scouting Combine in Indianapolis, Indiana. The NFL Scouting Combine is a six-day event where players are put through a series of tests, drills and interviews in front of NFL scouts, coaches and general managers. The results of those tests, drills and interviews often play a key part in where a player gets drafted. A good showing at the Combine can boost a player's stock while a poor outing will usually cause a player's value to plummet. That could mean the difference of hundreds of thousands of dollars, perhaps even millions. Where a player is selected in the NFL Draft has a significant effect on his first NFL contract and how much he will take home during his first few years of work. The NFL Scouting Combine started back in 1982 and each year it has become more and more of a telling factor as to where a player will be picked in the draft.

"It's amazing how the Combine has grown at every turn," said New England Patriots head coach Bill Belichick. "The media, the agents and the players and the preparation for it. All these guys spend months getting ready for it."

The combine events are very different from what takes place on the football field. Thus, the training for these events changes drastically. With so much riding on the results of those combine events, players must be adequately prepared when their time comes to take center stage in Indianapolis. Players are tested in events such as the forty-yard dash, the bench press, the three-cone drill, the shuttle run, the vertical jump, the broad jump as well as various positional drills. The players also undergo extensive interviews, psychological and aptitude tests and are subjected to rigorous medical examinations. NFL teams take into serious account the results of every one of those tests.

"Our position on the Combine is that it's one element to the bigger process of the evaluation," said Houston Texans general manager Rick Smith.

Players who are not invited to the NFL Scouting Combine still have the opportunity to perform in front of NFL scouts, although it will not be on such a grand stage. Just about every Division 1 college holds a Pro Day on its campus. During these Pro Days, players participate in the same events that are run at the Combine. NFL scouts from every team are also invited to attend. The number of NFL scouts that gather for a specific Pro Day is usually determined by how many legitimate prospects will be performing. The players who participate in the NFL Scouting Combine also perform at their respective Pro Days. Yet, if those players are content with their performance at the Combine, they will generally just run through a series of positional drills during their Pro Days. More often than not, most players rest on the numbers they post in

Indianapolis. But if a player is not happy with how he fared at the Combine, he will have a second chance to redeem himself at his school's Pro Day.

Both Morgan and Kenny received invitations to attend the 2009 NFL Scouting Combine. But despite finishing second in the nation in total tackles, Frantz's invitation did not even have the chance to get lost in the mail. He was snubbed by the selection committee, which consisted of a small panel that determines who has earned the right to go to Indianapolis.

In preparation for the upcoming NFL Scouting Combine and subsequent Pro Days, players were faced with another critical decision. They have to decide where to train for the two-month period leading up to those important dates. There are a handful of facilities throughout the country that specialize in combine-specific training. In order to gain a step on the intense competition, players continually look for any possible edge. That leads players to spend the months of January and February training at these various facilities. The training facilities also make arrangements with nearby housing communities, which provide the players with a place to live during their training. Once these players finish their final game of college football, they flock to a faraway city where home becomes a different place for the next couple of months.

Many of those training facilities are located in warmer climates such as Arizona, California, Florida and Georgia. However, in the heart of Central New Jersey, there is a facility that specializes in helping college football players realize their dreams of making it to the NFL. Before Morgan, Frantz and Kenny could climb into the NFL, they would spend the next two months living and training just over a mountain in Martinsville, New Jersey.

Although New York City was only an hour away, Martinsville did not look anything like the Empire City. It was a small, sleepy town with a hilly landscape. For the inhabitants of Martinsville, hats were common while gloves and scarves were rarely left crinkled up on a closet shelf. The wintry air forced human breaths to take on a smoky form making it feel like a late season playoff game. Much like the rise and fall of emotions during one of those heart-stopping contests, those traveling into Martinsville had to motor up to the summit of a small mountain and then descend into the town.

On the other side of that mountain, a host of businesses provided some necessary services for the people of Martinsville. And just beyond the deli, bank and doctor's office, there was one of the town's newest buildings. Parked cars decorated the lot of this facility, a facility that welcomed some of the nation's top athletes for two months every year.

That facility is TEST Sports and it is owned and operated by Brian Martin, a former college football player who takes on the role of trainer, mentor and friend to a band of NFL hopefuls every year. Martin has put together one of the most comprehensive training programs in the country for college athletes looking to make a splash at the NFL Combine and their subsequent Pro Days. With the aid of former NFL players and some top flight trainers, Martin spearheads the TEST Football Academy.

"I've been training football players for fifteen years," said Brian. "But this Combine business has just evolved. It's become a cottage industry that has become very tight. There's only about five groups out there that are very reputable and a lot of other guys trying to get into it."

Nearing the latter part of his thirties, the 5-foot-9 Martin doesn't look like a NFL player, but he knows what it takes to become one. He was a former special teams player and backup linebacker at the University of Delaware where he relied on hard work and determination to carry him through his football career. Incidentally, those two components have become a major part of his training philosophy. And it was just that philosophy which helped two players sneak into the first round of the 2008 NFL Draft. Boise State offensive tackle Ryan Clady and Delaware quarterback Joe Flacco became the 12th and 18th overall picks after completing their pre-combine training at TEST.

In spite of TEST's proven success, a lot of big-time NFL prospects flee to warmer climates. Many of the facilities TEST must compete against are located in more temperate regions of the country.

"We lose out to the sunshine sometimes," Brian acknowledged. "But the guys we get here are our kind of guys. They're grinders. They understand what things need to happen. They're not out chasing the thongs in Arizona or Orlando. They're not worrying about the strip clubs in Atlanta. We attract the kids that want to work and don't care about being in the cold. They just want to get better. Those kids who have agents that are going to pay for a two-month vacation, we don't want those guys."

Although Brian has a soft spot for his players, it is still a business. Therefore, a player's agent usually foots the bill for the expense of training. The agent also pays for the player's housing while training at TEST. The theory behind that is that a much more lucrative payday will benefit both player and agent after such training. In such a highly competitive profession, just about every NFL hopeful finds somewhere to train before the draft. This competitive industry forces Brian to spend much of the year touring the country in an attempt to draw some of the top college prospects to Martinsville for their pre-combine training.

"I believe we have the best program in the country," said Brian. "The combination with what we do with the speed, the strength, the medical, the power and the nutrition, nobody does it better than us. But a lot of kids don't want to come to the cold. So we lose out on a lot of first-round picks and that kind of stuff."

It didn't take long for Morgan to decide that he wanted to make the trip just over the mountain. He developed a strong rapport with Brian a few months prior to the start of the draft season.

"Brian came to the house and I thought he was going to make Mo do push-ups right there on the living room floor," joked Morgan's brother Jarrad. "I told Mo right away, this dude knows what he's doing. After we saw the facilities, we all knew it was the best place for him. Brian's a really good dude and he knows what he's doing."

Morgan may have been partial to the warmer weather that existed in his home state of California, but that did not factor into his decision.

"I chose TEST because that's the best place to train," said Morgan. "I could care less about the weather. These are critical months. I don't need to be somewhere where it's nice outside and I'm going to relax. I'm here to do a job and get it done. I'm not here to relax."

Morgan's father even compared the training to that of a fictional east coast underdog.

"Morgan took the Rocky approach," said Phil. "He didn't want to go out and look at girls in bikinis on the beach after he worked out. I'd rather him be out there with Brian because I know how it is out in Arizona and California."

Before Frantz decided on training at TEST, he took some time to size up other facilities across the country.

"I definitely looked at a bunch of them," said Frantz. "From just

38

comparing TEST to other places and doing the research, this puts you over the top. It not only offers speed training, but it also offers weight training and definitely has a great, great rehab facility. Those three components really put it over the top."

While Kenny valued all that TEST had to offer, he needed to find a place where he could focus solely on his future.

"Where TEST is located in New Jersey, there's nothing really to do," said Kenny. "I kind of need that being from Atlanta. I need to get away from the city, get away from friends, get away from all the distractions and just get ready. If I was in Florida where it's nice and hot, I might want to be out on the beach every day. I might be going out in South Beach and partying it up. All the ladies, man there's so many distractions! Arizona is the same way. Up here, I don't have any distractions. I don't even have a car so I won't be able to go anywhere. When I'm finished training, I'll just go to my apartment, rest up and get ready for the next day. That's what I need right now. I have the rest of my life to kind of goof off and have fun. If I can't sacrifice these next eight weeks for the good of my career, then I don't deserve to be in the NFL."

Throughout the fall, Kenny wasn't burdened with the worry of where he would be spending the months of January and February. After multiple visits with Brian, he made a decision before his season ever finished.

"I wanted to pick a place to train early," said Kenny. "I came up in the summer and checked it out. I also checked out a couple other facilities. Brian is a great trainer/inspirator/motivator. He's one of the reasons I came here."

With the bowl season stretching out over a three-week span, the college season finished on different dates for different players. However, for the thirty-two players who would comprise the TEST Football Academy class of 2009, their new season would begin on January 5th. That didn't give Kenny much time to rest up after finishing his college career in the Outback Bowl on New Year's Day. Three days removed from that game, Kenny was settling into his new apartment in Martinsville. The first thing he noticed was the drastic change in climate.

"It's real cold up here," Kenny remarked. "It's something you got to get used to. I have to go out and buy a bigger coat as soon as possible. It might be thirty degrees outside, but it feels like it's damn near fifteen degrees out there!"

Hailing from the south, Frantz was also forced to adapt to a sudden drop in temperature.

"It's not Florida with all the cold and snow, that's for sure," said Frantz. "But I'm really glad I came here. It gets me away from all the distractions and gets me to a place where I can focus on what I need to get done. It also lets me think a lot about life. Whereas if I were in a place where there was a lot of distractions and things of that nature, I wouldn't be as focused. Putting myself in this position allows me to visualize what I need to get done."

Frantz also took the opportunity to put in some early work prior to the New Year.

"My bowl game was on December 26th and, on the 27th, I was on a plane to Jersey," said Frantz. "I didn't want to waste any time. The clock is ticking."

All of the sudden, college was nothing more than a memory for these players. It was now time for them to go out in the working world. But their workplace would consist of a field 120 yards in length and 53 1/3 yards wide. It was also a workplace where millions of spectators looked on, ready to point out the tiniest of mistakes. And the wrong amount of mistakes could quickly lead to the search for a new job.

"My friends who play in the league tell me the NFL is great, but it's a business," said Morgan. "You're still part of a team, but it's not the same. It's not the same love like it was in college. It's a new season in my life. College was five years, but it went by fast. Now, this is the first time I'm not part of a team. And I'm not employed. This is like a big job interview I'm getting ready for. It's an interview for a great job right out of college. There are very few jobs in the world where you can make millions of dollars coming out of college and it's playing a sport that you love. It's a blessing just to have this interview."

Football had carried these players to this point in their lives. Football had also paid for college and had the capability of lining their pockets with sizeable incomes. But football had taught them some other lessons along the way.

"Football taught me accountability," said Frantz. "On the field, if you're accountable for the A-gap, then you have to be in the A-gap. That translates into real life. Off the field, you're accountable to write a paper, to pay a bill, to be at a meeting or to take care of your mother. You'll get those things done because you know what it means to be accountable. For me, this game is not only becoming a job, but it has also helped me out in life."

It may have been just a game, but Frantz couldn't shake the notion that there was more than one parallel between football and real life.

"Football to me is what I've been through in life," said Frantz. "There's always going to be a time on the field when adversity comes at you and you just have to react. It's similar to life. When adversity comes up, how are you going to react and what are you going to do? On the field, I never think that a situation will come up that I can't handle. I don't think anything is impossible to overcome."

For Kenny, football also played a major part in the way he saw the world.

"This game is just like life," said Kenny. "When things don't go your way, you can't dwell on it. The only thing you can do is get better. There is a lot of pressure on you in football just like there is in life. But I thrive under pressure. I always have and I always will. In big pressure situations, I want the ball in my hands. I don't get rattled."

Since the sixth grade, football had also been a big part of Morgan's life. Yet, it didn't define who he was as a person.

"Football is not who I am by any means," said Morgan. "It's what I do at times. I want to say I am a man of the Lord first. I want to say I am a great son, a great brother and a great fiancé. After that, I would say I am a great football player, but it's not what defines me by any means. I play football because the Lord blessed me with the talent to play. It's not what I chose to do, I think he chose it for me. That's what I do and I enjoy it. But football could be done tomorrow. If I couldn't play tomorrow, then I guess that's what the Lord had planned for me. You have to try to live in the Lord's will and if football's not the way, I can't be upset about it. If it's not football, then I'll find out what it is."

Many young boys grow up playing, watching and loving the game of football. That love of the game stays with many of those boys as they journey into adulthood. Throughout the winter and autumns of their lives, many weekends are spent in front of a television or packed in a stadium watching world-class athletes fight their way into an endzone. But the farther away a man gets from his childhood, the less time he will spend actually playing the game. Only the best of the best can make their living playing a boy's game. Frantz, Morgan and Kenny were hoping to join that privileged group. The sun had set on their college careers, but a future in the NFL was just on the horizon. However, there was still one more mountain to climb before they could realize their childhood dreams. For Morgan Trent, Frantz Joseph and Kenny McKinley, the draft season was about to begin.

CHAPTER SIX

Training Begins

There's a lot more to playing professional football than what fans see on the field every Sunday afternoon. It takes years of hard work and dedication just to make it through each quarter of play. Even when the last second has ticked off the clock, the game does not end. Training is a year-round event for those men lucky enough to be employed by the National Football League.

It was a little past 8:30 on a cold, gray Monday morning when the TEST Football Academy officially kicked off. Brian addressed the players inside the warm confines of TEST's large indoor field.

"Right now, it's a fight to get as much money up front," said Brian. "You have to get drafted as high as you can. It's not just for the money, but it's for what I like to call sticking power. The more money teams invest in you, the more likely they are to keep you around."

The NFL Draft is split up into two days. On the first day, which always falls on the last Saturday of April, sixty-four players are selected in the first two rounds. Then, on the following day, approximately 190 more players are selected through five more rounds. The work that ensues over the next few months would culminate during that all-important weekend.

Following a short pep talk from Brian, school was now in session. The players were immediately introduced to various training routines that were geared toward improving their times in the forty-yard dash. The forty was the most critical and highly publicized event at the NFL Combine.

"That's what they decide is important," said Morgan. "Someone decided that's how you find out who's fast. I can't complain about it.

Until they change that, it's the thing. I just have to go out there and do my best. We're going to spend most our time here working on that. That's where the money's at. So if you run a good forty, you shoot up in the draft. It could mean millions. A 4.3 and a 4.5 aren't even close. It's wild."

For Morgan, posting a good forty time at the Combine was critical in boosting his draft stock. Already working against him was the poor showing from the Michigan defense during the previous season. Being part of the team that suffered the worst record in school history was not going to bode well for any of the Wolverines looking to break into the NFL. There were also those who had some reservations about the strength of Morgan's game film.

"Scouts kind of have a love-hate relationship with Morgan," said draft analyst Scott Wright, who owns and operates DraftCountdown.com. "There's some who think he could be a mid-round pick and there's some who think he could be an undrafted guy. I think he is a draftable prospect, but I think he's going to end up going in the late rounds. I see him as a sixth-round pick, but I wouldn't be completely shocked if he went as early as the fifth."

It may seem a bit drastic, but Morgan's future could hinge on a mere tenth of a second. But he wasn't the only one in that position. Kenny could also help himself a great deal by posting a good time in the forty.

"I want to be a first-day pick," said Kenny. "In order to get that done, I need to get my speed up and that's one thing they focus on here. I didn't need to go anywhere where there's going to be a thousand guys and it's hard to get one-on-one contact. To be a first day pick is my biggest dream right now."

As much as Kenny felt as though he could sneak into that first day of the draft, not everyone shared that belief.

"McKinley's kind of interesting, he's quicker than fast," said NFL Network draft analyst Mike Mayock. "He catches the ball really well. He'll be a second day guy, I've got him in my fourth (round), late four to mid-five."

Predicting where players would go in the draft had become a popular hobby throughout the draft season. For some, it had become their livelihood. But no matter how many draft gurus projected Kenny to be a mid-round pick, he was determined to turn them all into liars.

"I take it as motivation," said Kenny. "I always want to prove my critics wrong. There's always going to be critics. But hopefully, I can go out there and prove all of them wrong. People might have forgotten about me, but my junior year I led the SEC and was an All-American. Hopefully, I'll go into the Senior Bowl and light it up. I want people to know I'm still the receiver that I was my junior year. I just want to remind them."

While many experts expected Kenny and Morgan to be second-day picks, there were mixed reviews regarding Frantz. Many questioned his linear speed and whether or not he had enough quickness to keep pace with NFL running backs.

"He doesn't have that elite stopwatch speed," said draft analyst Rob Rang of CBS Sports' NFLDraftScout.com. "But if you watch this kid on film, he has the ability to make it in the NFL. Unfortunately, I see him falling late; possibly sixth, seventh round or even as an undrafted free agent. Historically speaking, linebackers do drop on Draft Day, especially one with the perception of being slow. But as a run-plugger, I think he can play in the NFL and contribute on special teams."

Over the final two seasons of his college career, Frantz had done everything he could to endear himself to NFL scouts. He played the game like an old-school middle linebacker and was among the top tacklers in the nation. Now, his future in the NFL might depend on how fast he runs a forty-yard dash while wearing a pair of shorts. But it was much too early for Frantz to even think about Draft Day.

"I'm not looking at that day specifically," said Frantz. "I'm just looking at one day at a time and taking it one rep at a time. I need to make the most I can out of today because if I dwell on the future, I'm going to lose what I got going on right now. If you don't grind, you're not going to be able to shine. You got to put in the work to get the results. It's all the same whether it's in football, in the business world or even if you're writing a book. The work you put in is what you're going to get out of it."

Frantz not only started putting in work right away, but he was also relentless with his questions. He wanted to know at what angle he should come out of his stance when running the forty. He wanted to know why he was supposed to hold his breath for the first ten yards of the forty. He also wanted to know exactly how he should move his arms during that 120-foot stride.

There was a lot more to running a forty than just speed. To achieve the most optimum times, players needed to learn the proper and most efficient techniques. Once the players received an in-depth introduction to the forty, they began learning about the three-cone, also known as the L-Drill. This drill required players to maneuver around three cones spread out in the shape of an L.

"What that is about is short area quickness and the ability to change directions, drop your hips and bend your knees," explained Mayock. "You're trying to change directions several times. You're trying to weave around the cone and the way you do that is by dropping your hips and bending your knees. It's important to almost every football position there is. But if you're a linebacker or defensive back especially, you want to see if that guy can change directions, stay on balance, make a turn without touching his hand on the ground and keep balance just in case he has to make a tackle. And it's really a good way to compare a small defensive back versus a big defensive back. Typically, a lot of corners that are tall don't move as well in the L-Drill. If you get a tall defensive back that moves well in the L-Drill, you know you've got a guy that's not just a straight-line speed guy."

Cleveland Browns general manager George Kokinis explained how NFL teams use those drills to evaluate players.

"You match it to the tape, you match it to the film, you match it to his competition. And then you try to project it against NFL corners and safeties and linebackers."

But the NFL is about more than just speed. It is also about power. The vertical jump and the broad jump are both indicators of a player's power. In separate tests, players are required to jump as high and as far as they possibly can.

"If you're talking about broad jump or vertical jump, what you're looking for is lower body strength and explosion," said Mayock. "And that can translate differently based on position."

Yet, the most telling test of power would come on the bench press. At the Combine and at each player's Pro Day, they would attempt to bench press 225 pounds as many times as they could. In preparation for that, TEST had a detailed itinerary that was guaranteed to improve a player's performance in the bench press.

Heading up the strength program at TEST was Skip Fuller, a former standout defensive tackle at West Virginia. Once upon a time, Skip had come very close to realizing his dream of playing in the NFL, only to see it snuffed out from under him. After a solid career at West Virginia, where he played in the 1988 national championship game against Notre Dame, Skip was invited to the Miami Dolphins rookie camp. Two weeks into camp, Skip blew out his knee and would never put on a football helmet again.

"It wasn't a crushing blow," Skip said while wearing his all too familiar smile. "I just kind of woke up and got on with my life. I just kept moving. I always roll with the punches. Life throws you bones here and there and you have to deal with them. After my football career was through, what I really wanted to do was help young athletes get to where they wanted to go."

Skip went on to become a strength and conditioning coach at Rutgers University before coming to TEST. Skip's past also provided him with a firsthand view of how much the draft season has changed over the years.

"Back then, they had twelve rounds and now it's cut down to seven," said Skip. "The numbers are everything now. If you're fast and you can run a forty and you have big numbers, you're probably going to get drafted. Back then, they looked at athletic ability, they didn't really look at the numbers. I think it's come tenfold. A lot of the stuff now is movement based. It's a little bit of everything."

The bench press may seem like a simple exercise, but Skip began teaching the proper techniques which would lead to a higher number of reps. Daily workouts were also geared towards strengthening the muscles needed to increase a player's performance in the bench press. While Kenny participated in every drill, he planned to forgo the bench press at the upcoming NFL Combine. Each year, many of the smaller receivers forfeited the chance to bench press and it rarely ever wound up hurting their draft status. Nevertheless, strength was always an important factor in the NFL. Minnesota Vikings head coach Brad Childress mentioned the upgrade in physicality as being one of the most important challenges any rookie wide receiver will face.

"There's a lot of things as a rookie wide receiver, probably the first thing being the physical nature that confronts you at the line of scrimmage that you have to get by," said Childress. "In other words, the holding, the grabbing, things that maybe you don't see in college football. I think that's probably number one."

Kenny and the rest of the players spent that morning learning the nuances of various techniques that would help them improve in each drill. When morning spilled over into the afternoon, the players went on to do positional work with some former NFL players.

"We're training them to be track stars for the forty, but we're teaching them athleticism and mental focus," said Brian. "We also put positional work in there because we never lose sight of the fact that they're football players."

During that first week, players were also tested in each of the combine events. The TEST staff did not disclose those results, but did film each player through every drill. Each player then had individual sessions with the staff where they would go over each minute detail. Specialists broke down the film, explaining what each player did wrong and how they could improve their times.

Morgan got a head start on the rest of the players as he tested before Christmas. After a thorough analysis of his performance, he could already notice a difference in his times when he tested again during that first official week of training.

"It's crazy how far you can come using small techniques," said Morgan. "That's with only two weeks of work. We got a lot more. I don't want to let myself get caught up in that, but it's in the back of my mind. That's great that I made my improvement, but I can do better."

A nutritionist was also on staff to make sure the players were fueling their bodies with the utmost precision. Meals were planned and provided as was an endless supply of protein and recovery drinks. Massage therapists and physical therapists scheduled daily sessions with the players to make sure their bodies were in proper working order. The players also took part in Yoga and Pilates classes a few days a week.

"We did Pilates in college so it was something similar," said Kenny. "Yoga is good for the flexibility, but it gets you pretty sore. It used to be a little weird, but now people are doing that stuff everywhere."

One of the most important parts of that first week came on the third day of training. Specialists were brought in to find out just how much wear and tear the players had on their bodies. These young men had been playing the brutal game of football throughout most of their lives. Regardless of how many pads protected them, the experience left the majority of them battered and bruised.

"This is a violent game," said Frantz. "You're going to have bumps and bruises. It's either you're hurt or you're injured. If you're hurt, you can go. If you're injured, that's a different story. I never had any serious injuries through college. But the day after the game, sometimes it's hard to walk. That's just the nature of the game."

Healthy didn't have same meaning for football players as it did for ordinary people.

"It's a rough, tough, physical sport and you're going to get banged up," said Morgan. "No one's playing healthy. You just want to get banged up as little as possible. Come mid-season, it's tough. It really is. As long as you don't have any knees torn up or anything, you consider yourself pretty healthy."

In order to find out the extent of the wear and tear on each player, a series of individual examinations were conducted by a pair of medical doctors, a foot doctor, a chiropractor, a physical therapist and an orthopedist. When all of those players were finished being examined, those specialists gathered for a round table meeting to discuss each player's individual case.

Back issues were common as were ankle and shoulder problems. A significant amount of players even suffered from something called 'turf toe'. It was very rare for a player to be free from some type of ache, sprain, strain or other lingering issue. One of the specialists remarked on how a couple of the players had hip issues that resembled that of a seventy year-old man. Another specialist commented on how another player could even manage to walk, let alone play football with such severe foot problems. In the most unique case, one of the players actually suffered a stroke a few months prior to his arrival at TEST.

The round table of specialists identified Morgan's shoulder problems and also discovered a lower back issue that somehow slipped pass the medical staff at Michigan. Frantz still showed signs of wear and tear, however, there were no major concerns with his health. But one of the doctors winced when he read Kenny's medical report.

Looking into the thick folder that held Kenny's diagnosis, he said, "I don't know about this kid. This one is going to be tough. He has severe issues."

With determination guiding his voice, Brian stated, "Well, we have to make him right for the Combine. He might be one of the best guys we have here. So let's get it done."

Prior to that round table meeting, the players were also put through a Functional Movement Screening to further diagnose any issues. The screening was a seven-step process where players were asked to perform ordinary exercises such as a deep squat, a straight-leg raise and an in-line lunge. From these simple tests, TEST rehabilitation specialist and co-owner Kevin Dunn was able to identify more health concerns.

"Everyone's body is as different as a fingerprint and we all compensate differently," said Kevin. "To me, the Functional Movement Screening is a way to forecast the future on injury potential which is why they now adopted it at the Combine. This will be the first year they will be doing it at the Combine, but we've been doing it ever since we started. After the screening, we put them through corrective exercises based on that screening. Some of it is Yoga based, but they are specifically designed and prescribed to correct these specific movement patterns. What that does is help these guys move efficiently at high speeds. Right now, they're just moving at high speeds on their natural gifts."

The Functional Movement Screening combined with the extensive medical evaluations provided Kevin with a clear view of Kenny's injury problems.

"Kenny was just beat up," said Kevin. "He had three pulls in his right hamstring and two pulls in the left. He should have been shut down. On a pain scale of one to ten, right now he is an eight or a nine. It's just a bad scene. His feet are a mess. He had turf toe so bad, he has an actual screw in the bone that still needs to come out. His turf toe was so bad that when he was trying to press off his foot, he was getting tremendous pain in the second joint of his big toe. And because it hurt to push with his toe, he started to push with his hamstring. So instead of activating his glute and his quad to extend at the hip and the knee, he was actually planting his foot and pulling through. That's the number one reason why his hamstrings went down."

Kevin was a former Atlantic-10 diver of the year as a junior at Rutgers University. Being so dedicated to that sport, he had an excellent understanding of the human body, which complimented his academic prowess in exercise science.

"My whole thing was about proper body alignment, proper body mechanics and being judged every single time I was on the board," said Kevin. "For me, this type of thing is a passion because I get it. I know what proper alignment and perfect posture is because I did it for so long."

That led Kevin to take a special interest in Kenny's case and the two had been corresponding ever since the season.

"We were trying to rehab him from afar even during the season," said Kevin. "We'd go back and forth and when we heard about his hamstring, our advice was to shut it down. But he didn't want to and he was getting all kinds of injections in his hamstrings just to get him through. It was a lot of pain."

That left Kenny's hamstrings in a very fragile state heading into the draft season. And it was now, only in hindsight, that Kenny could see clearly into the past.

"I should have started looking out more for myself back then," said Kenny. "But I've always been a team player. I wasn't thinking about the NFL back then. I was just thinking about going out and doing what I could to help my team win. But it would have been smart to take some more time off and make sure I healed up right. If I did that, this probably wouldn't be happening now."

Even though Kenny's hamstring issues could threaten his draft status and potentially cost him hundreds of thousands of dollars, he bore no ill-will towards the South Carolina coaching staff.

"I have no animosity," said Kenny. "Down there, they're worried about their job and they want to put the best people out there. That's how it is. That's what they had me there for, to win football games. I have to worry about myself, so I can't fault nobody but me."

Following that long day of medical evaluations, Kenny's biggest hurdle was now just getting healthy for the NFL Combine. The TEST staff would have six weeks to correct a severe problem that had been lingering for nearly two years. And they knew full well that any signs of injury at the Combine could drastically affect Kenny's place in the draft.

Through the first few days of training, the entire experience was very new to the players. For the first time since these young men were small boys, they were not enrolled in school during the month of January. It was a completely new time in their lives. However, it still had a very reminiscent feel to it.

"It's like the first week of school," said Frantz. "There's new faces, new people to get used to. You're starting all over again. You're not the top dog anymore. Everybody's good, everybody's strong, everybody's fast. It really brings you back to the environment of that first week of school."

Nevertheless, the setting was quite a different one for Frantz. Aside from the drastic change in climate, TEST was a significant upgrade from anything he had ever seen down in Florida.

"There's nothing down there as detailed as this, nothing even close to this," said Frantz. "My school didn't have this many resources. We just started the football program in 2001. We didn't have as much as the Florida's and the USC's with alumni giving back. We had to deal with a smaller weight room, less staff and less resources. This right here is a great experience for me."

Morgan, on the other hand, was used to the best of the best after spending five years at Michigan. But through the first week of training, he quickly noticed a change in his lifestyle.

"I wake up every morning and I eat healthy all day long," said Morgan. "I've never eaten this healthy before. I'm doing speed work and I'm lifting every day. It's already getting repetitive and it will for the next month, doing the same drills over and over. But that's what I got to do. It's such a big deal and there's so much emphasis on this Combine."

Kenny was now far away from any distractions that might have derailed his progress. He became fully aware of that fact when he spoke with some of his friends who were training in warmer parts of the country.

"I talked to some other guys this week and they were going out a lot," said Kenny. "I told them they shouldn't, but they're grown men. I'm glad I'm up here with really nothing to do. If I was down there, it would be tempting. All the beaches in the south and the women and the partying, I would probably slip up. I made the right decision to be up here and I think it's going to pan out."

For Kenny, Frantz and Morgan, that first week was unlike any semester they had ever spent in school, nor was it similar to any football game they had ever played. Although they put in a lot of work, they were not getting paid for a single drop of their sweat. But the more they sweated, the better their chances were of landing a job in the NFL.

CHAPTER SEVEN

Back on a National Stage

In life, there is one certainty that people can always count on. They never know what is going to happen next. That is also one of the certainties that makes the sport of football so exhilarating. The game continuously keeps us on the edge of our seats as we anxiously await the next play. For some, it is a gut-wrenching experience that causes the heart to burn, the hands to shake and the mind to run wild. For others, it is a welcomed experience that revivifies the soul and makes Saturdays and Sundays worth living. But for Morgan, the game was something different altogether.

"When I'm playing, I try not to think about it too much and I try not to put too much pressure on myself," said Morgan. "I just try to go out and have fun."

In the uncertain game of football, there was one certainty that Morgan faced week in and week out. He would take the field for four fifteen-minute quarters and, at the end of those sixty minutes, the team with the most points would be declared the winner. Now that he was heading down to Houston for the 84th Annual East-West Shrine All Star Game, winners and losers would be judged on a different scale. The outcome of the game was pretty much irrelevant, but never before had one game been such a critical part of Morgan's future.

Every NFL team sent scouts, coaches and executives down to Houston for the entire week leading up to the East-West Shrine Game. Those influential eyes would watch every practice and also spend a great deal of time getting to know the players. Morgan had been part of many all-star teams since he first started playing sports, but he knew this experience would be unlike any other.

"This is a whole different deal," Morgan noted. "I just have one game to play my best. When you're younger, you want to do your best for your team. Now, it's different. It's more of a selfish thing. I want my team to win but, more importantly, I have to do well. It's my last college game ever."

The East-West Shrine Game was the first of three post season all-star games that featured the top Division 1 athletes in the nation. The Senior Bowl would take place the following week in Mobile, Alabama and was considered the best of the three all-star games. Morgan had been passed over for the Senior Bowl and was not at all happy with his exclusion.

"Personally, I think I should be in the Senior Bowl," said Morgan. "That's my belief. The Senior Bowl is kind of the bowl you want to be in. Sadly enough, there's politics involved. I know that with our team going 3-9, that hurt me. That's just how it is. But what can I do? I can't stress over it. All I can do is go to this game and show why I should be there."

Brian accompanied Morgan down to Houston and the pair arrived on a cloudy Saturday morning. Coming from the University of Michigan, which has produced so many great NFL players over the years, Morgan had plenty of friends who briefed him on what to expect in the coming weeks.

Leon Hall of the Cincinnati Bengals told him, "It's a long but quick process. It gets repetitive. You're going to get sick of it, but you got to do it."

Braylon Edwards, the third overall pick in the 2005 NFL Draft, advised Morgan, "You want to get paid and this is what you have to go through. Regardless of where you get drafted, it won't be soon enough."

It was helpful to have advice from players who had previously traveled down the same path. Nevertheless, every bit of advice was nothing compared to the lessons taught by experience.

During his first day in Houston, Morgan went through an expected round of orientation, but the next day would be full of surprises. That Sunday morning included a round of testing, the likes of which Morgan had never experienced. He was given a psychological test that covered everything away from the realm of his football acumen.

He looked curiously when he read the question, "Would you rather be a dog or a cat?"

Morgan also raised a brow when he saw another question asked a few more times in three different ways. He even scratched his head when he was asked to distinguish what he saw in a picture that was nothing more than a bunch of incoherent shapes garbled together. When that testing period was finished, Morgan welcomed the chance to move on to something else.

"I wasn't expecting those tests and I also wasn't expecting how long they actually took," said Morgan. "There were a few of them and man they were long!"

That afternoon, the players were slated to visit the Shriners Hospital in Houston. Since the game's inception, it has not only brought together some of college football's top athletes, but it has also raised quite a bit of money for the Shriners Hospital for Children. There are twenty-two Shriners Hospitals across the United States that treat children with orthopedic conditions, burns, spinal cord injuries and other deformities. Morgan welcomed the chance to pay these children a visit, but braced himself for a grim setting where he expected to see a sadder side of life. When Morgan arrived at the hospital, the reality of what he saw differed immensely from what he had envisioned.

Morgan didn't walk into a quiet hospital room housed with an unfortunate child trying to recover from a life-threatening injury. Instead, he walked into a party. There was a DJ playing music, some kids had already started singing karaoke, other children were getting their faces painted and games had been set up all over the room. While Morgan surveyed all the fun, a basketball rolled over to him and bounced off his foot. He watched a group of young children scramble for the ball, not acting like sick kids. No more than a few seconds later, a young girl with severe burns on her face came running over to Morgan. She stopped in front of him and allowed some words to pass through her innocent smile.

"Hey, do you wanna sing some karaoke with me?" she asked.

Morgan grinned and didn't even have to articulate his compliant answer.

One day very soon, many of the players in that room would go on to make millions of dollars in the NFL. And there will come a time when those players will be spotted by fans in their respective cities. When that does happen, grown men will turn into little boys and ask for autographs in voices filled with awe. But in the eyes of these children, the players were something different. They were simply a gang of new playmates who would help them enjoy a Sunday afternoon. The girl with the burns on her face had no idea that Morgan Trent was the starting cornerback at the University of Michigan. She wouldn't remember a game-changing interception or a fourth down tackle just shy of a first down marker. But she would remember the words to the numerous songs Morgan sang with her that afternoon.

After a few hours in the company of those children, Morgan and the rest of the players left the hospital. A week of practice would follow as the East and West teams would square off against one another on a daily basis. However, those battles now seemed rather trivial. Protected by helmets and pads, football players were often heralded as heroes and placed atop a pedestal. Many people across the country knew Morgan's name in addition to the names of many of the other players who would take part in the East-West Shrine Game. But not many people knew the name of the little girl with the burns on her face. None of them knew about her daily battles and what she already had to contend with at such an early age. Her story would not make the front page of any newspaper nor would it be aired on any television show. Yet, before Morgan left the hospital, he went over and gave her a hug. He thanked her for singing so many songs with him and made sure to call her by name. He left behind a smiling little girl, enamored by a day of fun. In the days to come, there was a very good chance that little girl would remember Morgan's name. But it would have nothing to do with the fact that he played football.

As much as the game did for the Shriners Hospital, football was the main reason so many decision makers from the NFL assembled in Houston. The hometown Houston Texans did not have to make an arduous journey as the week's events would take place right on their own stomping grounds.

"We're fortunate to have it in our backyard," said Houston Texans head coach Gary Kubiak. "I put a lot into it, how they practice, how they handle themselves. We've gotten a couple of kids out of that game that played very well for us."

On Monday, Kubiak joined other NFL coaches on the Houston Texans practice field for the first day of practice. Morgan hustled out on to the field and was instantly amazed at just how many scouts had gathered.

"There were so many more scouts than I expected," said Morgan. "But I had to shake it off because if you're worried about the scouts, you're not going to play well."

For Morgan, the surprises had only just begun. He didn't expect the scouts to evaluate every single part of practice. But that fact quickly placed a distant second to adjusting to the new field. The NFL field was the same width and length as a college gridiron, however the hash marks were located in different places.

"The NFL field is very different," said Morgan. "It takes some getting used to. It's different from what I'm used to. Playing corner, that's a big deal. In college, the hashes help out a lot. That was the thing that really helped me out with the receivers' splits and where they were on the field. On the NFL field, it's different. There's so much space, the hashes are closer and the numbers are closer. You're out there on a smaller island than usual."

The pace was also much quicker than what Morgan had seen in college.

"I think that surprised me the most," said Morgan. "It was my first experience with any of that. I didn't expect how fast the practice was going to be. It was a lot faster paced than college. It went by fast and it was also at a NFL pace, it was a lot faster."

Morgan's day did not end at the conclusion of practice. Scouts hung around and requested fifteen-minute interview sessions with the players throughout the evening. Morgan traveled from room to room meeting scouts from all over the NFL.

"I thought it was just going to be practice," said Morgan. "But when I'm done practice, I have to sit down with the scouts and do interview after interview. It's crazy. I'm losing my voice from doing some many interviews. They want to know everything from your home life to your girlfriends. They ask you stuff about everything."

With so much activity monopolizing his time, the first day flew by for Morgan. Before long, he was already halfway done his second practice of the week. Morgan checked out of the lineup and hurried over to the sidelines to grab a drink of water. A short older man in a cheap suit with only a smidgen of hair on his head immediately rushed over to him.

"Morgan, Morgan Trent," he yelped. "I'm a financial advisor and I really think you should consider working with me when you get to the pros. I can make you all kinds of money."

It wasn't clear exactly how this man gained access to the field, but it was evident that Morgan wasn't the first player he pestered. As Morgan brushed off the folliclely-challenged man, Brian was on the opposite sideline oblivious to what was happening. That is because his attention had shifted to a young boy in a wheelchair.

"The kid couldn't really move around at all," said Brian. "He had cerebral palsy very severely. I was in the middle of talking to some scouts and agents and I felt a magnet to this kid and his mother. So I went over and I spent like thirty minutes talking to them. The kid could barely talk. He can't move his hands or legs, but he's got straight A's in school. The kid wants to be a scout for the NFL."

There remained a vast array of agents, scouts and future NFL players on hand, yet Brian spent the better part of that day in the company of this young boy. Perhaps it was because the boy's situation hit very close to home.

"I have a son with cerebral palsy and another who is on the autistic spectrum," said Brian. "One is probably never going to walk unless we get some kind of miracle. My son survived after weighing only eleven ounces at birth. For about eighteen months, me and my wife lived in the hospital. My kids are my inspiration. My kids have given me a drive and strength. They love being around the guys and it really brings out the best in our athletes. It's a unique blend and the athletes know I'm not faking it. They can feel it."

Following that day's practice, Brian was helping Morgan with some weight training when a few scouts gathered around and took an interest. They watched Morgan bench press 225 pounds sixteen times before putting the bar back on the rack. Then, a scout from the Minnesota Vikings walked over and introduced himself.

"That was very impressive," he said. "I didn't expect you to be so strong. You look like you've bulked up a bit. How much weight have you put on?"

"About ten pounds," said Morgan.

Brian then proceeded to boast about all the progress Morgan had made over the last month and just how much of an asset he would be to any NFL team. When he spoke about Morgan, there was a sense of pride in his voice, almost as if he was speaking about a member of his own family.

"After all the negative stuff I've seen, I'm able to channel my energy into something positive," said Brian. "In a way, these athletes are kind of running for my son."

The week of practice seemed to fly by and Morgan was quickly learning that he was always under a microscope. It seemed as though scouts and coaches took an interest in everything the players did that week.

"I saw a lot of those kids just walking throughout our hallways in the stadium when they would get dressed for practice and visit with a couple of them walking over to the field," said Kubiak. "Then, I'd go watch them compete in that environment. I went out to dinner one night and saw three or four of them at a restaurant. It's funny, throughout the week, you really run across a bunch of those young men."

That weeklong experience also made Morgan question just how much stock was placed into the actual East-West Shrine Game itself.

"The scouts are gone before the game happens," said Morgan. "They'll get film of the game and watch it, but they want to see what you can do four days straight. They want to see what your practice is like and what your motor is like."

Finally, on a pleasant Saturday afternoon, game day had arrived. As the countdown to kickoff came to an end, there were still plenty of open seats in Robertson Stadium, home to the University of Houston Cougars. Morgan's parents made the drive from Michigan to watch their son play one more game, but Tina had trouble spotting her son.

"At first, I couldn't find him because he had a different number," said Tina. "But I really had trouble because his body just transformed so much."

Morgan was getting more muscular than he'd ever been. He was also hard to distinguish because he covered his Michigan helmet with stickers from other teams. At the East-West Shrine Game, it was common for players to distribute decals from their respective schools to the friends they made over the course of that week. Placing another school's emblem on one's helmet was simply a sign of camaraderie and respect. It was basically just one more way for these young men to enjoy themselves during their last week of college football. However, it wasn't the array of stickers on Morgan's helmet or his bulked up frame that made him stand out midway through the second quarter.

With Morgan's East squad already leading 14-3, the West faced a 3rd and 3 from its own 37 yard-line. Central Washington's Mike Reilly dropped back to pass and Morgan read his eyes perfectly. Morgan jumped the route and stepped in front of Oregon State wide receiver Sammie Stroughter to make a textbook interception.

Morgan then felt his momentum take him right to the ground. But he had the presence of mind to pop up and run being as though NFL rules were in play and no opponent had touched him. Morgan would go on to gain 19 yards before he was tackled, giving the ball back to the offense on the West 18 yard-line. That led to a field goal which put the East up by a score of 17-3. Halftime followed shortly thereafter with Morgan already having himself a memorable afternoon.

Unfortunately, the first part of the second half did not go as well for Morgan. Early in the fourth quarter, he was beaten for a 35-yard touchdown by Rice wide receiver Jarett Dillard. The all-star game rules did not allow press coverage, which put all the defensive backs at a distinct disadvantage. Yet, Morgan offered up no excuses.

"I was mad cause I got scored on," said Morgan. "I gave up a touchdown that I shouldn't have. It wasn't like me, but it happens. You can only run man or cover-3 so it's kind of easy for the offense to pick you apart."

Morgan didn't let that play have a lingering effect. He came right back on the next play and broke up a two-point conversion that kept his East squad leading by a score of 24-19. His opportunities wouldn't end there.

The West squad would later drive down the field and threaten to take the lead towards the end of the fourth quarter. Facing a 4th and goal with exactly two minutes left on the clock, Reilly tossed a pass in the endzone. As the ball came down, Morgan was right there to break up the play and help preserve a 24-19 victory for the East.

The game ended and Morgan didn't forget to wave to his parents before walking off the field one last time. As he headed into the locker room, he felt a bit torn. He was happy with the way he played through most of the game, yet he was very disappointed that he had allowed a touchdown in his final quarter of college football. He silently wished for one more chance to get on the field and make one last impression.

Morgan returned to New Jersey about twenty-four hours later and spent the next day just trying to get his body to feel normal again. Not many people realize how much of a beating players take over the course of a season.

"After a game in the Big Ten, your body is going to be beat up regardless of who you play," said Morgan. "Teams like Iowa and Wisconsin run the ball like fifty times a game. Your body gets beat up. Last year, I had a nagging shoulder injury through the whole season. I would get a shot before each game to try and take away the pain. On the day after the game, I couldn't even lift my arm up in the air."

A week of practice followed by the Shrine Game was just like a regular game week for Morgan. Therefore, he made it a point to take it easy that Monday and planned on heading to bed at a relatively early hour. Just as Morgan was about to hop into the sack, his phone rang. Noticing that it was his agent, Morgan quickly answered the call.

"Morgan, someone got hurt at the Senior Bowl and you're in," said his agent. "They offered you a last minute invitation."

"You're kidding!" Morgan replied.

"Pack a bag and your helmet because you're going to Alabama for the week!"

A few hours later, Morgan was on a plane headed for Mobile, Alabama. He would now have one more chance to showcase his skills before heading out to the NFL Combine. His wish to play one more game had not gone unheard as Morgan had just been granted four more quarters of college football.

CHAPTER EIGHT

The Senior Bowl

A few hours of sleep on a late night flight painted a bit of red in Morgan's eyes as he trotted out onto the practice field in Mobile, Alabama. None of the other players had to take a similar early morning flight after spending the previous week at another all-star game. Morgan was one of only four players to be invited to both the East-West Shrine Game and the Senior Bowl. Although that invitation took a while to get to him, Morgan made no qualms about having to trek through more adversity on his way to Mobile. As he glanced out at the star-studded cast of NFL coaches, scouts and general managers, a surge of adrenaline suddenly wiped away his fatigue.

"It's a different gear out in Mobile," Morgan stated. "Not to take anything away from the East-West Shrine, but the Senior Bowl is on a whole different level. The Senior Bowl is where you want to be. It's taken more serious, more GM's are here, more head coaches. I realized that as soon as I stepped out on the field."

Morgan took his place with the best of the best in college football and proceeded to stretch out in the cool southern air. Although the Senior Bowl would be broadcasted in front of the entire nation at the end of the week, the next few hours are what the NFL brass really came to see. It was during the week of practice when the real evaluations were made.

Some of the coaches in attendance had a closer view than others. The North and South squads were each equipped with a NFL coaching staff. The Cincinnati Bengals staff coached Morgan's North squad while the Jacksonville Jaguars staff was in charge of Kenny's South squad. Morgan's head coach for the week would be Cincinnati's Marvin Lewis. Throughout the week, Lewis would do more than teach simple x's and o's. He was also there to evaluate the talent and take a long, hard look at who he might want to see wearing Bengal stripes next season.

"The week leading up to Mobile, I was able to take a lot of video with me," said Lewis, who watched everyone with a very close eye. "I've had a chance to look at them on video, but the week in Mobile is very, very helpful to me."

While Lewis sized up this impressive group of prospects, Kenny took full advantage of every second during warm-ups. He wanted to make sure his hamstrings were as loose as they could possibly be. Those muscles were a grave concern, yet the look of determination on his face showed no signs of worry. Kenny was determined to go out and make an impression on the scouts by making a mockery out of anyone who tried to defend him.

A few plays into the action, Kenny picked up where he left off on the preceding day. He exploded off the line of scrimmage and quickly left his defender reaching for air. On the strength of two questionable hamstrings, Kenny tore down the field and widened the gap between him and the cornerback who now lagged a few steps behind. He looked up and saw the spiraling football start to become bigger and bigger. The Alabama wind then pushed the ball towards the sideline, forcing Kenny to readjust his stride.

Kenny quickly looked over his other shoulder, repositioned his body and leapt up in the air. The ball fell into his hands as he came back down to earth only inches away from the sideline. The defender finally caught up to Kenny and bumped him to the ground. By then, it was too late.

Kenny popped up off the ground without even realizing that he was running on two flimsy hamstrings. He was about to celebrate and let the defender know just how badly he was beaten. Instead, he held his tongue.

"I wanted to celebrate, but I told myself to keep my mouth shut," said Kenny. "I wanted to make a good impression on all the scouts. All that talking is gonna come later when I'm playing in the NFL."

Kenny made quite an impression through the first couple of days as many scouts walked away from the practice field holding the University of South Carolina's all-time leading receiver in very high regard. Meanwhile, Morgan was trying to grasp the intricacies of the various defensive schemes.

"My first day there was the biggest practice of the week so I kind of stepped in on the most important day," said Morgan. "The defense is more in depth at the Senior Bowl and I just had to go in there and learn it as I went. I just did my best and tried not to worry about all the scouts out there."

At the conclusion of practice, teams requested interviews with players that lasted late into the night. Each team was allotted a fifteen-minute interview session with every player. Those interviews were conducted in small rooms with scouts trying to delve deeper into the psyche of each player. Questions from the scouts ranged from the ordinary to the obscure.

In one cramped room a scout asked Morgan, "Tell me about your family life and what it was like to have two top athletes for parents?"

In another room just down the hall, another scout asked Kenny,

"What can you tell us about that fight in the nightclub you were involved in two years ago?"

"I wasn't involved in it," Kenny bluntly replied. "I was there, but I didn't fight anybody."

That particular question was one Kenny would hear more than once that week.

Former Detroit Lions and San Francisco 49ers head coach Steve Mariucci explained why such questions are asked.

"With so much draft coverage and people leaving no stones unturned, there's so much said about every individual. The longer this goes, the more dirt we dig up it seems. It's unfortunate for some of these kids. As coaches, we're optimistic human beings and we look to the good side of all of these kids."

As time ticked down on each interview, some scouts would rush through their list of questions. Morgan had no problem maintaining the same cool demeanor through each interrogation. One particular scout just continued to rattle off question after question.

"What kind of music do you have in your iPod?" he asked.

"A lot of Gospel," Morgan answered.

"What kind of clubs do you like to go to?" the scout continued.

"I don't go to clubs. I'm not a partier."

"If you were on a TV reality show which one would it be?"

"Top Chef."

"What's one of your most favorite hobbies?"

"Fishing."

"Any others?"

"I like to play chess."

Then, Morgan heard one of the most popular questions of the day.

"Have you ever been in any kind of trouble?"

One of the reasons Morgan remained so calm throughout each interview was because he could answer that question without any hesitation or trepidation.

"I don't have anything to hide so nothing can really creep up on me," Morgan later revealed. "If you don't have anything to hide, it's easy."

The next day would play out in a similar fashion for Kenny. He made it a habit of burning defenders, running crisp routes and making some highlight reel catches. It was obvious to all those watching that he would be one of the main attractions at the Senior Bowl. And with Georgia wide receiver Mohamed Massaquoi bowing out of the game with a sprained ankle, more of the focus in the passing game would shift towards Kenny.

As Kenny left the field after that third day of practice, he walked over to Brian who had been watching from the sidelines.

"Great job out there," Brian said with a wide smile.

That smile quickly vanished when Kenny inched closer and spoke in a low tone of voice.

"B, my hammies are killing me," he confessed.

"How bad?" Brian asked.

"It feels like they're going to snap."

Brian then quickly placed a call to Kevin, who got right on the phone with Kenny.

"On a pain scale of one to ten, where are you?" asked Kevin.

"Right now, I'm a nine and it feels like it's going to pop when I'm running," said Kenny. "And when I'm sitting down it's at about an eight."

"Pain is your body telling you to shut it down," said Kevin. "You don't want to risk an injury right now. You've already shown what you can do on the field when you are quasi-healthy."

After a brief discussion with Kevin, Brian turned to Kenny and said,

"All right, I'll tell them you can't stay here any longer. You don't want to jeopardize your NFL career just so these guys can sell more tickets. You showed the scouts what they needed to see. Everybody's been buzzing about you all week. We'll get you out of here and get those hammies right."

While Kenny headed off to the locker room, Brian approached the Senior Bowl staff to inform them of Kenny's decision to leave. In a fraudulent tone, one of the bowl representatives said he understood, but requested a quick meeting to go over the particulars. Brian obliged and met Kenny outside the locker room a short while later. Then, the two of them were directed down a long, narrow corridor which led into a small room where a couple of empty chairs awaited them.

Kenny and Brian stepped inside the room where the pungent odor of stale air made for an oppressive environment. A bright light shone down upon them as they looked over at a pair of faces that were not tinged with the slightest touch of friendliness. Even the two men's succinct hellos had a cold air to them. The large, smug-looking man with the beady eyes was Terry McDonough, the director of player personnel for the Jacksonville Jaguars. Seated next to McDonough was Senior Bowl president and CEO Steve Hale. Hale's graying hair was peppered with hints of black, his face salted with a look of disapproval. Hale wasted no time starting the interrogation.

"So what's this I hear that you're not going to play on Saturday?"

"Yeah, I'm sorry but I have some stuff I have to take care of," Kenny answered in a polite tone of voice.

"Oh come on," McDonough barged in. "We know you're leaving because you think you're injured."

Just at that moment, the door flew open and in staggered a middle-aged man with a crooked smirk on his face. The man's hair was a bit unkempt and he looked as though the taste of whiskey was still fresh on his tongue. Apparently, this man was one of the doctors overseeing a lot of the medical issues at the Senior Bowl.

Hale looked over at the disheveled man and stated, "This is Kenny McKinley. He wants to go home because he thinks he's injured."

"I've looked over your case Kenny and you're fine to play," the doctor said in a raspy southern drawl.

Before Kenny had a chance to respond, McDonough hurled in his two cents.

"You have to play in this game Kenny, you have to."

"Why does he have to?" Brian intervened.

"Because no one thinks he can run. You should hear what everybody's saying about you, Kenny."

"I know I can run," Kenny firmly responded. "I just have to do what's best for me."

"Oh come on," McDonough said in a sarcastic voice.

"Hold on a second," said Brian. "What business of yours is it if he wants to go?"

"Because we invited him here and he needs to play. It's the only way he can help his draft status," McDonough snarled.

"We invited you here, so the least you can do is honor that and play in the game," Hale added.

"I'm sorry, but I can't do that," Kenny said in a calm voice.

It was as if that simple response triggered an angry nerve inside of McDonough.

"Well then everybody's going to know that you got no heart. You hear me Kenny? You can't go over the middle and you're slow!"

"This is your only chance to show everyone that you have any kind of speed," Hale followed up.

Kenny sat quietly wearing a look that bordered on insult and anger.

"Were these guys serious?" he thought to himself. "They want me to risk my career for a damn all-star game? It didn't make any sense. I understand they want to sell tickets. But if a guy's hurt, you can't force him to go out and play. It's not like it's my team or we're playing a championship game. I have a future to consider. I haven't made it to the NFL yet. I'm just trying to get there."

Kenny didn't have the chance to voice any of those thoughts because Brian beat him to the punch.

"You can't force him to play just because you want to sell tickets," said Brian. "Just because the receiver from Georgia left yesterday, you think that Kenny leaving is going to hurt your precious ticket sales?"

"That has nothing to do with it," said Hale. "Nobody thinks he can go over the middle and scouts are questioning his heart."

"Man, just turn on my film and watch me go across the middle," Kenny returned. "I'll run those routes all day!"

McDonough's voice suddenly mutated into a cocky one as he bellowed, "Yeah right, you can't run. I don't even know why you were invited here. It's just a big waste of everybody's time."

The doctor was then able to push a few words past the frog that seemed to be lodged in his throat, "If you play, you won't hurt your hamstring any worse than it already is."

"How do you know what's best for me?" Kenny came back. "Nah, that's it. I'm done. I made my decision and that's the end of it. I'm done."

"Well you should leave," said McDonough. "You can't do anything out on the field anyway. You can't run and you got no heart Kenny, you remember that. You don't have the speed to compete at the professional level."

By this time, the color on Brian's face had boiled into a bright crimson.

He stood up, stared directly at McDonough and growled, "When he runs a 4.3 at the Combine, I want to call you and I want you to pick up. Then, I want to tell you I told you so. Kenny doesn't need to prove anything by playing in this game."

McDonough tossed his business card on the table and smeared an arrogant grin across his face.

"Call me on Draft Day when he doesn't even get drafted," said McDonough. "I'm always up for a good laugh."

Brian swiped the card off the table and maintained his fiery glare.

Kenny then rose out of his chair and said, "Come on B, let's get out of here. I'm done with this."

Kenny continued to maintain his cool just as he did when the trio across from him attempted to push his buttons. Here were three grown men attempting to bait Kenny into playing in a game that really didn't matter. And why? Because the South Carolina fans might purchase more tickets and boost the game's attendance if Kenny played.

These men had walked the earth far longer than Kenny had, but it was this kid on the verge of celebrating his twenty-second birthday who displayed more maturity and poise than any of them. Brian and Kenny headed out of the small room, leaving all that antagonism and negativity behind.

"Don't listen to any of that," Brian advised as they walked down the long corridor.

"I'm not," said Kenny. "I can't believe those guys. If I go out there and get hurt in the game, then what? Then, I'd be really screwed up. Those guys are just looking out for themselves. Now I just can't wait to get to the Combine and prove those guys wrong. They're trying to question my heart and my speed? That's all right, it's just more motivation to take to the Combine. I can't wait to get there!"

"And I'm going call that jackass as soon as you run that 4.3!" Brian confirmed.

In a few short hours, Kenny fled that southern hospitality and was on a plane bound for New Jersey. When he stepped off that plane, he carried more motivation to go out and put on a stellar performance at the Combine. But, as he walked, he could still feel the tightness in both of his hamstrings. Hopefully, that tightness would not allow McDonough's predictions to come true.

Meanwhile, Morgan remained in Mobile and finally caught up on some much needed sleep. Unlike some of his teammates, Morgan didn't waste his final nights in Alabama by accepting an invitation to explore the town's nightlife.

"Guys were going out to the strip clubs and going here and going there," said Morgan. "I just went back to my room. I would just go back and relax, but that's what I enjoy doing."

Although Morgan declined the offer, a few other players asked him more than once. But Morgan would not be swayed.

"I'm not here to impress anyone so I don't care what anyone thinks about me. I have no problems saying that's not what I do. I won't fall victim to peer pressure."

A few nights of rest had a positive effect on Morgan as did a week of instruction from NFL coaches. Following each day of practice, he watched film with Cincinnati defensive backs coach Kevin Coyle as well as head coach Marvin Lewis. Coyle was entering his seventh year as the Bengals' defensive backs coach. It was quite a change from the coaching he received at Michigan where he went through four different position coaches in four years.

"The Cincinnati coaches were all down to earth," said Morgan. "I really like Coach Lewis. He's a cool dude. You can talk to him. I also like Coach Coyle and the way he teaches. He's not really a screamer and he seemed like he really cared."

Those coaches continued to lend their tutelage during the 60th annual Senior Bowl where Morgan continued to excel. During the game, Morgan was on the field for about half of the defensive plays and not once did a ball come his way. His tight coverage forced West Virginia quarterback Pat White to continually look in another direction. Morgan wound up finishing the game without one pass thrown in his direction. For a cornerback, that is a game well played.

As Morgan left the field, he looked up and saw his parents who had made the long trip from Michigan to see their son play one more game.

"Since Morgan was five years old, we were always those parents in the stands and that's never going to change," said Phil. "Not going to one of his games wasn't an option, that's just the way it is. We do whatever we have to do. For the Senior Bowl, I had to shuffle some meetings and Tina had to get someone to cover her coaching. We drove all the way down there and we wouldn't have missed it for the world. It was an honor to be there. There's only a certain amount of kids who get to wear that uniform. Just being there was great."

Far away from Mobile, Kenny was busy icing down his hamstrings and clinging to the hope that they would heal by the time the Combine rolled around. Kenny also had the opportunity to talk to his parents that night and shared his thoughts on the entire week.

"The Senior Bowl helped me a lot, but it might have hurt me physically," said Kenny. "Being out there in front of the coaches, I tried to go extra hard. That could have been a week where I could have been toning it down and trying to get my health right. But I guess you gotta do what you gotta do and I think going down there was something that I definitely had to do. It was an opportunity to make a name for myself."

It was also an opportunity to do more damage to an injury that should have been attended to a long time ago. Now, more than ever, Kenny's hamstrings could mean the difference between making hundreds of thousands of dollars and standing in an unemployment line. The only thing that would truly heal Kenny's hamstrings was time. With the NFL Combine rapidly approaching, time was one luxury Kenny couldn't afford. As he limped into bed that night and closed his eyes, all Kenny could see was his son. He envisioned his son growing up with all the things he never had. That vision carried him off to sleep as he winced from the pain left behind by the Senior Bowl.

CHAPTER NINE

Frantz vs. The Nation

The last of the three Division 1 all-star games was the Texas vs. The Nation game. In only its third year of existence, the game was considered to be a notch below the Senior Bowl and the East-West Shrine Game. Nevertheless, many NFL scouts traveled to El Paso, Texas to take in a week of practice. Each year, the game was gaining more momentum and seeing more of its participants selected in the NFL Draft. In 2008, Eastern Kentucky cornerback Antwaun Molden parlayed a strong all-star game showing into becoming a third-round pick. Richmond running back Tim Hightower also boosted his stock and ultimately became a steal in the fifth round for the Arizona Cardinals. Frantz was hoping to follow down that same path and become the next great find in the Texas vs. The Nation game.

From the time Frantz boarded the plane, he already seemed to be wearing his game face. He didn't think of the fact that it was only the Texas vs. The Nation game and not the Senior Bowl. He didn't care that he wasn't selected to play in the East-West Shrine Game and he wasn't concerned with the fact that his NFL Combine invitation never came. He was just honored to have the chance to play one more game of college football.

"It's the opportunity of a lifetime," said Frantz. "Every play, every rep I get, I'm just going to make it happen. And I'm not going to just try, I'm going to make it happen. If you just try, you're not doing enough."

Some players might be happy with a good showing in front of the conglomerate of scouts, but not Frantz. He wanted more.

"I want to be the best player to come through there," Frantz professed. "I want to be the meanest, most physical player on the field. I want to be the MVP. I want to go there and show everybody that what they're saying is wrong. That's my goal and I'm not going to stop until I get there."

Frantz was referring to the numerous critics who had questioned his ability to play in the NFL.

"He's strictly a two-down linebacker who doesn't have the timed speed that they're looking for in the NFL," said draft expert Rob Rang. "But he has football speed and great football instincts. I think it's an absolute travesty that he wasn't invited to the NFL Combine, especially considering the lack of talent at the inside linebacker position in this year's draft."

Frantz did all he could during the 2008 season to show that he deserved a Combine invitation. Evidently, finishing second in the nation in tackles was just not enough to endear him to the NFL Combine selection committee. Nevertheless, Frantz did not let that snub affect his demeanor.

"In life, you can't look at things you can't control," said Frantz. "I'm not really worried about the Senior Bowl or the Combine. Everything happens for a reason. It'd be an honor to go to those events, but I've been an underdog my whole life. I went to a smaller high school and a smaller college. I'm used to this road. I'm used to being overlooked. What I always do is just take every opportunity I can to shine."

In the eyes of many people across the nation, Frantz still had more to prove. At this particular all-star game, he would be representing the 'Nation' squad. But much like he had done his whole life, it seemed as though Frantz would be fighting an entire nation of doubters and cynics.

Similar to the other all-star games, the week of practice in El Paso was probably more important than the actual game itself. Frantz knew this as he latched up his shoulder pads in the locker room at Sun Bowl Stadium. The smiling, warm-hearted, sensitive Frantz Joseph was now transforming into a linebacker who was known by many other names. On the field, some people called him 'F-150' because he hit like a truck. Others referred to him as 'Savage' because he tried to destroy everything he could. And there were those who referred to him as 'Killer', which basically speaks for itself. No matter which nickname people opted to use, Smiley was not among them.

The locker room wasn't filled with much noise prior to the first practice of the week. Frantz contributed to that quiet as he taped his wrists and listened to his iPod with a mean look plastered across his face.

"I listen to a couple of tunes, but I try not to listen too much because it kind of wears you out," said Frantz. "For me, I get inside myself. What I mean by that is I get inside my mind, my heart and my soul. I know what level of physicality I have to get to. You can't just snap and play this game. I gotta get pissed off is what I'm saying. I gotta get mad. When I get inside myself, I accomplish that and I really feel like there's nothing in my way."

The closer it got to the start of practice, the deeper Frantz got inside himself. When the time came to take the field, the gentle, caring young man who was wearing number 56 shed all remnants of a smile and began to wreak havoc. Frantz thwarted nearly every blocker that came his way and dished out some numbing hits. Running backs who tried to maneuver through the second level of the defense received a painful greeting when they met Frantz Joseph. He laid one smack after another and continually introduced players to the unforgiving artificial turf.

"I have an understanding of how this game is supposed to be played," said Frantz. "This is not a nice guy game. It's not a game where you're supposed to be friendly. I have a lot of friends on the offensive side of the ball. But on the field, they hate me. It's just a mindset you have to get into. You have a job to do and that job never gets done by being nice. It's a mean state of mind type of thing."

While Frantz took a break from laying people out, the Nation offense took the field. One of the offensive players who managed to stand out did not touch the ball a single time. Yet, Lydon Murtha always stood out. Even on a field crowded with all-stars, he towered over just about everyone. Standing 6-foot-7 inches and tipping the scales at 310 pounds, it wasn't too difficult for Lydon to get noticed. The offensive tackle from the University of Nebraska received a late invitation to play at the Texas vs. The Nation game after a college career that was haunted by injuries.

Lydon came to Nebraska as one of the top fifty recruits in the country and looked forward to a future filled with possibilities. But shortly after he arrived in Lincoln, a dark cloud hovered over him and began to rain down injury. Shoulder problems, a broken toe and even a

Staph infection limited Lydon's time on the field. Heading into the draft season, Lydon was without an invitation to any of the three all-star games as well as the NFL Combine. His Texas vs. The Nation invitation came late, however he was thankful to have one more chance to put on the pads.

"Some people say it's only the Texas vs. The Nation and it's not the Senior Bowl, but I didn't care," said Lydon. "It's still an opportunity that was given to me and I know I have to take full advantage of it. My main focus is that I need to stand out somehow. Just because I was injured last season and played a couple of games hurt, there may have been a stereotype that I was soft or that I might not be able to cut it with really good players. So when I got the invite, it was the perfect opportunity for me to show that I can compete against some top athletes."

Following that first day of practice, Lydon was feeling very good about his performance. He went through a round of interviews that evening and came away feeling equally as good. However, another thought played through his mind as he tried to drift off into a peaceful sleep.

Lydon had been informed that he was one of the thirty-one players under consideration for a late invitation to the NFL Combine. The NFL formed a committee which would choose exactly who was awarded those late invitations. That committee had already convened and, on the next day, Lydon would know his fate. He tried not to think about what it would be like to actually get the chance to go out and perform in Indianapolis. Yet, that thought continued to arrest his slumber.

When Lydon finally awoke, he checked his phone and was disheartened to see that he had not received a call. He checked it again before he ate breakfast and a couple of more times in between his second and third helpings of food. Then, Lydon started to receive text messages from a few of his friends who were also on the bubble. They had informed him that they had received their Combine invitations. As the day wore on, Lydon would receive no such news.

Once practice had ended, Lydon hurried into the locker room to check his phone again.

"It was like three in the afternoon and I didn't get a call," said Lydon. "I had to face the fact that I didn't make it. But what could I do? I just had to do well at the all-star game and hope that could help me for my Pro Day."

Just at that moment, Lydon's phone finally rang. He quickly answered the call only to learn that it was his agent.

"So, did you make it?" his agent asked.

"I never got a call," said Lydon.

"Why don't you call them?"

"Because that's kind of stalkerish."

"Why not, what's the worst they can say?"

Lydon followed that advice and dialed the number to the NFL committee office moments after he hung up with his agent.

"Hi, I was wondering if you could help me," Lydon began.

"I'll certainly try," a woman returned in a pleasant voice.

"My name is Lydon Murtha and I was just calling to see if I received one of the late combine invites?"

"I can check on that for you. What did you say your name was?"

"Lydon Murtha," he said with a gulp.

"Hold on, I'll check."

Silence ensued and it suddenly seemed as though time slowed down for Lydon. Each tick of the clock moved at a snail-like pace while Lydon's heart continued to accelerate. A simple yes or no answer could mean a world of difference. He knew he could boost his draft stock with a good performance at the Combine. All he needed was a chance.

"Everyone always said that I was going to test out really well at the Combine," said Lydon. "I've been hearing that for the last three years. So when I didn't get invited, I felt like I let down all those people."

While Lydon waited for an answer he said a quick prayer, pleading for the chance to go to Indianapolis. That plea to a higher power wasn't the first time he asked for help in getting to the Combine. Before he could finish with a heartfelt Amen, the women's voice rang out.

"Lydon?"

"Yes, mam," he said with much more quickness.

"As a matter of fact, we called your number and it was not available. But congratulations are in order. You're coming to the NFL Combine."

Lydon smacked himself in the forehead as he remembered that he had recently changed his phone number. It turned out that the NFL was trying to contact him through his old number, which was no longer in service. Lydon's prayers had been answered! He had received a late invitation to the Texas vs. The Nation game and now a last minute invitation to the NFL Combine. Lydon thanked the woman profusely and, before he hung up, he made sure to give her his new number. He then called his wife who was back home in Lincoln to share the news. She responded with tears of joy as Lydon was one step closer to realizing his dream of playing in the NFL.

With a couple more practices remaining before the Texas vs. The Nation game, Lydon couldn't spend too much time rejoicing. He had to get right back to work, but seemed to do so with an even sharper focus.

"Getting the Combine invitation kind of helped spark some motivation to really play hard and stand out and complete the whole package," Lydon said.

Lydon tried his best to do just that, yet it was Frantz's name that came from the lips of just about everyone who attended each practice. And after every practice, scouts scrambled to spend some time with him.

"The scouts were always writing down notes and talking to different guys," said Frantz. "I talked to so many of them. A lot of them asked about my family history, whether I ever got in trouble or not and things like that. They asked me about my strengths and weaknesses. They were pretty straightforward in general. But then a few asked about my girlfriends. I wondered why they asked questions like that? They would ask if I had a girlfriend or if I was married. I don't know what difference that makes."

Frantz spent a great deal of time that week talking to scouts. But when it came time to take the field, the scouts were the furthest thing from his mind.

"I don't think about the scouts that are out there," said Frantz. "It definitely gets away from the mindset of playing football. If something good comes out of it, good. If it doesn't, it doesn't. I just go out and play the game. This was my final chance to play at the collegiate level so I was going to leave it all out there. Every day coming out on the practice field, I didn't take anything for granted and I didn't take a single play off."

The week of practice led up to game day and, once more, Frantz turned into the not-so nice guy who was pissed off as he took the field. Frantz not only had one more chance to play a game, but he also had one more chance to play for his college coach. Florida Atlantic head coach Howard Schnellenberger had been selected to coach The Nation squad. Schnellenberger had a reputation for being a no-nonsense rather cantankerous man, but also possessed a great football mind.

Before taking over as head coach of Florida Atlantic when the program debuted in 2001, he had prior head coaching stints at the University of Miami, Okalahoma University, the University of Louisville in addition to the Baltimore Colts. Since Schnellenberger took over at Florida Atlantic, he has led the Owls to two bowl victories and a Sun Belt conference championship. But he wasn't an easy coach to play for.

"He's old school," said Frantz. "Through training camp, we always had three-a-days. We're probably the only school in the nation that had three-a-days. And during the season, it was always full pads. Practice was never just in shorts and helmets, he didn't care how hot it was. But it helped me. Linebacker is a tough position to play, mentally and physically. Going through those hard times helped me. I didn't understand why he was doing it at the time. But now, as I sit back and speak to these other guys at other schools, it makes sense why we were wearing out teams in the fourth quarter. We were tougher guys for it. It was a privilege to have one more opportunity to be coached by him here in Texas. The way he practices and his mentality is old school football. He really understands how the game is supposed to be played and I appreciate that. I really feel like it was a privilege playing for that man throughout my career. He made me understand how to play this game."

Once the 3rd annual Texas vs. The Nation game kicked off, it was Frantz who showed people how to play the game. He played with a controlled violence that was reminiscent of some of the game's greatest linebackers. It was also no coincidence that some of those tough, hard-nosed players were his boyhood idols.

"I grew up admiring guys like Mike Singletary, Ray Lewis and Dick Butkus," said Frantz. "I try to model myself after those guys, just coming downhill and being very physical. I really feel like that's how the game was meant to be played."

In today's version of college football, the spread offense has managed to take away some of that physicality. That trend showed up once again as the Texas squad reverted to a more pass-oriented attack.

"A lot of the new type of spread offenses do not allow the linebackers to be as physical as the older linebackers might be," Frantz said.

Nevertheless, Frantz dropped back into pass coverage and was able to keep up with running backs that were supposedly too quick for him to handle.

As the first quarter was winding down, Frantz found himself back in pass coverage once again. And once again, he made liars out of those who suggested he was only a two-down linebacker. Frantz found his way over to the ball moments after Western Michigan tight end Branden Ledbetter caught a pass. Ledbetter took a pop and the ball escaped from his hands. Frantz quickly scooped it up and took off in the other direction. Suddenly, the Texas offense turned into the defense as Frantz went from an attacking linebacker to a scurrying tailback. He scurried down the field as the Texas players chased him past the 40, the 30, the 20 and finally managed to bring him to the ground when he reached the 10 yard-line. It's too bad Frantz didn't stay in the game and carry the ball another couple of times. The Nation offense could have used him as it could not advance the ball any farther. The end result was a short field goal, which boosted the Nation's lead to 6-0.

Frantz continued to wreak havoc on the Texas squad through the next few quarters. His play helped the Nation cling to a 20-17 lead with just under twelve minutes remaining in the game. Once more, Frantz stared down the offense as the ball rested on the Texas 42 yard-line. The moment the ball was hiked, Frantz dropped into coverage on a 2nd down and 10. Virginia Tech's Sean Glennon dropped back and fired a laser over the middle of the field. The ball bounced off the hands of a Texas receiver and popped up in the air. And there was Frantz, right there to cradle the ball as it soared downward. He tucked it away and then took off down the sidelines. This time, Frantz was only able to gain twelve yards before he was pushed out of bounds.

That play allowed Lydon to return to the field with the offense and help clear the way for another Nation touchdown, which put the game out of reach. Lydon put on a solid performance, but offensive tackles are rarely featured in any highlight reels. Ironically, offensive linemen whose names are not mentioned throughout the game are often the ones who are most productive. Fortunately for Lydon, the announcers did not have the chance to utter his name too many times that afternoon.

As the final seconds ticked off the clock, Frantz turned back into

Smiley. He crept up behind Coach Schnellenberger with a bucket of Gatorade in his hands and a wry smile on his face. Then, very stealthily, he turned the bucket upside down and gave his coach an unexpected bath. Schnellenberger turned around and took a few moments to muster what could be construed as his best impression of 'Smiley'. The result was half a grin and a horizontal nod of the head. From the looks of it, Frantz may have been the only player on the Nation sidelines who could have gotten away with such an act.

Following the Nation's 27-24 win, Frantz was announced as the game's MVP. He had done exactly what he had set out to do. He came down to Texas and was the best player on the field for the final sixty minutes of his college football career. Frantz continued to play the part of Smiley after the game, but he knew this was just one small step on the path to a much greater goal.

"The reality is, it doesn't mean anything," said Frantz. "A lot of guys are MVP's. The reality is that even if I do get drafted, I have to go through camp and make the team. This all-star game is nothing to get me hyped up about. After the game, a few scouts came up to me and told me they were impressed with my knowledge of the game and how I play. But it really doesn't go that far. I can't get overwhelmed about it and think that I made it just because I got some compliments and was named the MVP of an all-star game. It's just a step forward and now I have to work even harder. Where I'm coming from and how I was brought up, there's nothing that I've done so far that could make me satisfied. If anything, I'm starving and I want some more. I can't stop grinding because the minute I think I made it, someone else is going to outwork me. There's always someone else out there who's hungry. I want more and I have to get more. And in order to get more, I have to work harder."

Frantz boarded a plane later that night and flew back to New Jersey so that he could resume his training. He had left his mark on the game, but more importantly, he left an impression on the NFL scouts. Yet, Frantz had taken on more than just an opposing team that week in Texas. He had taken on quite a few skeptics who questioned certain aspects of his game. Frantz won the latest round, but he knew there would be more battles to fight in the future. Ever since the time he was born, it seemed as though Frantz was constantly fighting a nation of adversity, so why should that stop now?

CHAPTER TEN

Monster of the Midwest

Two days after the Texas vs. The Nation game, TEST welcomed a new addition to its Football Academy. When Lydon Murtha walked through the facility for the first time, just about everyone turned to stare. Lydon dwarfed almost everyone he encountered. However, he wasn't just tall. Large muscles popped out from every part of his body. To say that Lydon Murtha was a physical specimen would have been a tremendous understatement. Still, his hulking stature did not earn him an initial invitation to the Combine. But after learning that he was one of the last of the official invites, Lydon knew it was time to step up his training.

"I was training at Nebraska, but there's a lot of stuff I need one-on-one attention with," said Lydon. "I looked at a lot of places and saw what they had to offer. But when I met Brian, I felt very comfortable. TEST was somewhere I could go and compete with a lot of good players and refine a lot of my techniques. I knew if I came here, it would help me a lot. I'm pretty far behind at this point. I have to recuperate from the all-star game and train at the same time. But the facilities here are just amazing. It's everything I could ask for. "

Brian was just as excited to work with one of the more impressive athletes he had ever encountered.

"He's got a chance to break records out at the Combine," said Brian. "He could be the fastest lineman ever at the Combine!"

Linemen are not generally known for their straightaway speed. Offensive tackles rarely dip below the 300 pound mark. As a result, their forty times rarely dip below the 5.0 second mark. Since 2000, only ten offensive tackles have posted times under a 5.0 at the Combine and just one of those players ran under a 4.9. Of those ten, only one tackle went undrafted while the other nine were selected in the top four rounds.

"If you get a chance to go to the Combine, it's like your ticket, your golden ticket," said Lydon. "It's one of those deals that if you get invited, it's either going to help you or break you. Not a lot of people go there and just stay the same. They're either going to raise their stock or lower it. Every event counts."

Lydon had always envisioned himself playing in the NFL while growing up in the small town of Hutchinson, Minnesota which is located about sixty miles west of Minneapolis. He was born in Homestead, Florida but didn't spend too much of his life in the Sunshine State. The Murthas headed north when Lydon was only six years-old, although he always had the pedigree to play football. His father played college ball and his uncle enjoyed a short stint in the NFL and USFL. Football was in his blood, as was possessing the gift of size. Both his father and uncle were massive men who also played on the offensive line.

"Football's everything to me," said Lydon. "Football's all that I know. People get their degree and they get stuck not knowing what they're going to do. I don't even want to think about that. The NFL is where I want to be. How nice is it to receive an income and take care of your family for the rest of their lives playing a game you love? That's everything to me. Wherever I get drafted doesn't matter, I just need to play."

There was once a time in Lydon's life when football nearly disappeared altogether. As a young boy, Lydon watched his mother fall victim to the disease of alcoholism. He was forced to painfully watch his church-going mother become seduced by the bottle. That addiction forced his parents to divorce and began to lead Lydon down an undesirable path.

"There was a point in my life when I didn't want to play football anymore," said Lydon. "My parents got divorced and I had a rough relationship with my mother. There was a point in my life when I said 'I'm done with football.' I got in fights with my coaches, it was a huge battle. This happened from fifth grade all the way through tenth grade. Everything was just going against the grain. I just didn't like sports and I started hanging with the wrong crowd."

Then, at the age of sixteen, Lydon deviated from that path which seemed to be leading to nowhere.

"My life-changing event was building my relationship with God," said Lydon. "That was my junior year of high school. And from that point on, it's been a one-hundred eighty degree difference. From the minute I accepted him in my life, it was a complete change as far as me wanting to play football."

For the next two years, Lydon channeled all of his positive energy out on the field. By the time he graduated from Hutchinson High School, his accolades included being a three time All-Conference selection, two time All-Metro and a two time All-State selection. Following his senior season, he was named an All-American and the Gatorade Player of the Year in the state of Minnesota. At that time, he was the number two ranked tackle in the nation. Looking ahead to the future, a place in the NFL seemed inevitable.

Lydon decided to attend the University of Nebraska and was all set to start at tackle even though that was a rarity for a true freshman. Everything seemed to be falling in place, that is until the final week of training camp. Lydon was running a drill in which players crawl underneath a long chute. As Lydon reached the halfway point of the drill, a pin snapped and the chute collapsed.

"The whole thing tipped over and landed on the back of my leg," said Lydon. "I couldn't feel my leg at all. Afterwards, they were sticking pins in there and I still couldn't feel it. It turns out that a nerve had gotten severed and it took about three months to recover."

The injury forced Lydon to sit out the entire season as a medical redshirt. But that wasn't his first or last run-in with injury. For Lydon, injuries dated back to when he first started playing football.

"I broke my femur in fifth grade and the doctors said I might not ever play football again," said Lydon. "The break went through my growth plate. I couldn't even get around without anyone's help. I can actually remember sitting on the couch and soiling myself because my mom left me alone to go out for a drink. I couldn't even get up to go to the bathroom. But it healed up okay. Then, later on, I had surgery on my nose. Someone face masked me and turned my helmet completely around and it just snapped my nose. My septum was severed and completely cut off. They had to go in, realign it and shave it all down."

Lydon's femur never gave him problems again, his nose eventually healed as did the severed nerve in his leg. But he was reintroduced to injury almost a year after that chute came down on his leg. This time, a motorcycle accident forced him to undergo shoulder surgery and miss even more time.

"It was a struggle," said Lydon. "People expected me to come in and be the stud and I wasn't. I had fans telling me I sucked and I wasn't good enough. That was a struggle because no one really believed in me. But there was still always that relationship with my family and God that I could always lean on."

Lydon's shoulder eventually healed, but injury struck again during his junior year.

"I was just starting to put together a good season when someone got pancaked on the back of my foot," said Lydon. "It actually split the bone in my toe. At first, the school doctors gave me the choice of having surgery on it or not. They told me that the bone would grow back together and I could play in a bowl game later that year. But if I went to the NFL, I'd almost be guaranteed to have major problems because it wouldn't have grown back normally. If they did surgery, I'd be done for the rest of the season, but I'd never have problems with it ever again."

Lydon wasn't given much time to mull over a decision.

"The surgeons came right back to me and said I have a real good chance of playing in the NFL and this will be a big problem if I don't get it fixed right. The NFL looks badly upon injuries that are going to be a prolonged thing. Because of that, all my coaches urged me to get the surgery and I did. Now, my toe is perfect."

The doctors did an excellent job fixing Lydon's toe, but he knew it wasn't his endearing personality that compelled them to steer him in that direction.

"If it was just a regular guy, they would have just let it heal without the surgery," said Lydon. "They're not going to waste all that money, time and rehab for a surgery that isn't necessary. For probably ninety-eight percent of the team they wouldn't do the surgery. They were kind of straightforward in that they kind of told me what they were going to do. It wasn't like they were going to let me sleep on it and get back to them. They wanted me to have the surgery because they knew I was going to play in the league."

With his toe fixed, Lydon was hoping to have his best season as a fifth-year senior. Yet, that dark cloud of injury continued to hover over him. Lydon suffered a Staph infection in his leg just before the start of the season and missed the first two games. A foot sprain sent him to the sidelines for two more games later in the season, although he did manage to start nine games in his final season of college football.

All of those freak injuries not only marred his college career, but they also affected his draft status. Draft experts and teams across the NFL set up draft boards, which ranked the top few hundred players in the nation. On many draft boards, Lydon was considered a free agent prospect who was not likely to get drafted.

"His college career wasn't what people expected coming out of high school," said draft expert Scott Wright. "He was a phenomenal recruit, one of the top fifty players in the whole country coming out of high school. He didn't necessarily live up to that billing."

After an unfulfilled career at Nebraska, Lydon now had the stigma of being an injury prone player. But that wasn't the only stigma he had to fight off. Lydon's massive size forced more than a few people to question whether or not he used any kind of illegal substances to reach that point.

"People ask me a lot if I ever used steroids, but it doesn't bother me at all," said Lydon. "Truth is there's quite a few athletes who use illegal substances. There's always kids trying to find ways around it. But the benefits you're going to get from it aren't worth the risk of getting caught. Being into nutrition and taking classes, I've learned about all types of steroids. It's a million-dollar mistake if you're a good player. I understand there's a lot of kids that do it, but they're usually the kids that aren't starting. Prohormones is the fad now with high school kids trying to make it to college and college kids trying to step it up a notch. It's a quick fix and the benefits are so minimal. Your body doesn't have time to adjust to them. If kids have to do that, they're cheating themselves and cheating kids who are working hard and doing things the right way."

Lydon claimed that so many people are uninformed about training the proper way that they automatically assume anyone with his kind of size must to be injecting himself with something.

"Most people who say that don't know about nutrition and don't know what it takes to shape your body or work hard," said Lydon. "It's ignorant, misinformed people. They see anyone who's lean and muscular and they automatically think they're taking something. It'd be easy for me to eat whatever I want and take steroids and be a good player. But that's the easy way out. Training hours a day, having your diet so perfect and actually working for it is so much more satisfying."

Not too many people could maintain the strenuous training regimen Lydon put himself through on a daily basis. But it's very likely that many people would have more of a problem emulating his strict eating habits.

"I kind of made a decision going into my junior year of high school that I was going to change how I was eating," said Lydon. "I didn't do it for the fact that I wanted to look good or play sports better. I did it because I knew how I was eating was not healthy. I wanted to change that lifestyle. When you change the way you eat, it's incredible how your body can change. If people just do that, they can literally see a change in their body in just two weeks. People can work out every day and their body won't change because it all has to do with diet. It was then that I realized how much of a role diet plays in your performance. Not a lot of people know that, not even athletes."

Lydon also had some help at home in the nutrition department. He married his high school sweetheart, Natasha, just before his final year of college. Natasha also shared the same philosophy when it came to diet.

"My wife is going to be a fitness model and she is going to be in a competition in May," said Lydon. "That helps a lot too, having a spouse eat better than I do. And I eat as clean as anyone I know! When you have someone that can do it with you, that's a huge help."

While Lydon was training, his diet not only consisted of quality, but it also consisted of quantity.

"I wake up at 5:30 and have a protein shake," said Lydon. "Then, I go back to bed and wake up two hours later and have another protein shake, dry oatmeal, 2 cups of milk and glutamine on training days. On my off-days, I'll have seven eggs, only two yolks, a cup of cooked oatmeal and OJ. Two hours later, I'll have a Myoplex shake. In another two hours, it's lunch time. Three times a week, I'll eat large quantities of red meat, always lean. Sometimes, I'll sit down and eat a pound of lean hamburger meat. And sometimes I'll have natural turkey on whole grain wheat bread with a side of vegetables. Two hours later, I have another Myoplex shake. Two hours after that, it's dinner. That's usually my smallest meal. Usually, it's two chicken breasts and a lil' green beans or something like that. Then, two hours later, I have another protein shake. I try to eat between 6,000 to 8,000 quality calories every day. I never eat any fried foods, no sugars and no saturated fats. It's a science and it takes big time dedication. You have to plan it all out every day."

But even Lydon indulged himself every once in a while.

"You can't eat the same thing every day or you'll go crazy," said Lydon. "And if you eat good every day, you'll go crazy. So, once a week, I'll have a nice big cheese steak or a large pizza or some cheesecake. I eat healthy all week, but I look forward to that one day when I can just splurge."

It still takes a great deal of will power to resist the temptation that comes with the smell of bacon sizzling on a stove or the aroma of a freshly cooked pizza that has just come out of the oven.

"When I go out with my buddies, they might have a pizza and I will have to say no. They'll say 'come on, you're taking it too seriously. You've got to enjoy yourself.' Well I do enjoy myself, once a week. Some people think I'm crazy. But to be a top athlete, you got to eat right and train hard."

Training hard was never a problem for Lydon. However, with only two and half weeks left until the Combine, training was not Lydon's only concern. His final game as a Cornhusker had come in the Gator Bowl on New Year's Day where he helped his Nebraska team hand Clemson a 26-21 loss. Almost a month later, he finished out his college career in the Texas vs. The Nation game.

"I'm like sixty or seventy percent because I didn't have a lot of time off," said Lydon. "I was just starting to feel good and then I got invited to that all-star game. That's a huge deal because the exposure is just as critical as the Combine. But that's a sacrifice you have to make. Hopefully, I can get ready in two and a half weeks. It's definitely stressful. If anyone says it's a breeze, they're lying. It's a very, very stressful thing."

All those events led this big kid from the Midwest to new and unfamiliar territory. New Jersey was a very different world from what Lydon was used to. Nonetheless, he focused on the task at hand and was determined to put on an impressive display at the Combine.

"I really have to loosen up my hips and really refine my techniques," said Lydon. "My speed is there, but all the stuff we're doing now is really helping; being able to sink my hips and doing the little things which takes care of the big things. That's where training with Brian comes in. I needed a little more one-on-one attention."

On day one of Lydon's TEST experience, Brian and his staff provided some extra individual attention for their newest arrival. And when Lydon's first day of training wound down, he found solace in listening to his wife's voice on the telephone.

"She's everything to me," said Lydon. "It's almost emotional because everything is just falling in place for me; from getting married to finishing out and having a good bowl game, to getting invited to the all-star game to the Combine and now to training at TEST."

The latest chain of events seemed to be pointing Lydon toward the NFL. All those occurrences had furnished him with a fresh outlook. For Lydon, it was now the NFL or bust.

"A lot of kids think what am I going to do if the NFL doesn't work out?" said Lydon. "I think that's kind of a distraction. If you just think about football all the time and put all your effort into it and know you're going to make it, there's no chance you're not going to make it. I know I'm going to make it."

Those thoughts sweltered through Lydon's mind as he lay down that first night and tried to grab some sleep. With his feet dangling off the bed, Lydon envisioned himself at the Combine. He pictured himself posting a forty time better than any other lineman who had ever attended the Combine.

"When I go to bed, I almost shake a little bit because I am so focused," said Lydon. "I keep telling myself, what if I run this time or maybe I will run that time. Just because I'm an O-lineman, why can't I run a 4.7?"

Chapter Eleven

Swagger

It takes more than blazing speed to make it to the NFL. It also takes more than Herculean strength to earn the right to call oneself a professional football player. Wide receivers who run the most precise routes, quarterbacks with pinpoint accuracy and running backs who bounce off tacklers like a human pinball all need something more. Linebackers who literally knock the snot out of people and cornerbacks who run stride for stride with the fastest of humans must also have a little something extra. Offensive linemen who possess the ability to move small pickup trucks and defensive ends who have reinvented the term athlete cannot do without this most integral feature. Any young man who attempts to complete the journey to the NFL must carry a swagger to that destination.

Swagger is a term quite common among professional athletes. It is also a prerequisite for making it in the NFL. There are different types of swagger, but all fall under a similar definition.

"A guy who has swagger is someone who is cool, calm and collected," Kenny explained. "I have swagger because not too much phases me. I'm pretty confident in my craft of being a receiver. When you're confident, you kind of walk with a swagger. You got to have swagger to play this game. I tell them boys down in South Carolina all the time, 'you gotta have some swag'."

Kenny's swagger seemed a little louder than any of the other players at TEST. From the way he walked to the way he talked to the way he played, his swagger practically screamed out, 'I'm something special.' It was hard not to notice Kenny when he stepped into a room. However, his swagger shouldn't be confused with being cocky. He wasn't conceited, arrogant or condescending by any means.

"I think I might have more swagger than most people," Kenny said with a grin. "I think it has to do with the way I came up. I'm from Atlanta, so you got to have it growing up. Coaches in Atlanta teach you swag. Your mamma, your daddy, your sisters, your cousins, everybody from Atlanta grew up with it."

Kenny's football swagger had grown into what it was from making so many extraordinary plays on the field. He was the type of player whose moves dazzled spectators and frustrated defenders. As a result, Kenny was often the focus of many highlight reels. In fact, his college career earned him the right to have his number 11 retired. It was the first number to be retired by the University of South Carolina since Sterling Sharpe received the honor twenty-two years earlier. Kenny had just learned of that tribute while he was training at TEST.

"Coach Spurrier called me and told me they're retiring my number," said Kenny. "It's a great accomplishment. It's awesome. Sterling got his retired in '87, so it's been over twenty years since anybody got their number retired. It's a big deal down there. It really hasn't hit me yet."

Kenny not only used his swagger to gain respect on the football field, but his swagger also demanded respect when he took off the pads. And it was his swagger that helped him deal with potential problems that surfaced in his everyday life.

"Coming from Atlanta, you got to have swag just to make it through the day," said Kenny. "When you go places, you can tell which people got swag. Certain places in America, people don't have swag. They ain't used to it. But in Atlanta, you gotta have swag."

While Kenny's swagger may have been more pronounced, Frantz developed a quiet swagger. He wasn't as outspoken as Kenny and exuded his swagger a little differently. Frantz was the type to use less words and more action. Much of his swagger on the field came from laying people out with thunderous hits.

"I'm not one to blow my own horn," Frantz began. "But I feel like I have a little swagger in me. Sometimes, you need a swagger to get you where you need to be. Guys misunderstand the meaning of swagger, it's not a cocky thing. It's just a confidence you have about yourself, about what you do and what you're going to get done. All of that comes with preparation. If you have great preparation, you're allowed to have that swagger because you know you're going to get the job done."

Throughout Frantz's college career, he squared off against many players whose swagger had morphed into blatant arrogance.

Frantz went on to say, "Coming from a smaller school, basically every game we played we were the underdogs. Whether it was Texas or Florida, we'd always feel like they were a little cocky because they were a bigger school. It gets under my skin a little, but I don't say anything about it. I just go out and get the job done."

Many times, Frantz's opponents would launch verbal attacks against his team, particularly when they played on his home turf. Florida Atlantic University was not equipped with a football field and was forced to play its home games at Lockhart Stadium, which had been built for two local high school teams. Frantz knew the lay of the land because he had graduated from Fort Lauderdale High a few years earlier and played all of his high school home games on that same field. The stadium held a capacity crowd of 20,450 people, although it was quite a stretch from playing at places like Clemson, Michigan State or even a short trip up to Gainesville to do battle in 'The Swamp'.

"It was like playing on the beach," Frantz chuckled. "When you run, you could see the sand coming out of the ground. In the beginning of my career, I kind of looked forward to away games. But it was my high school field so, as I got older, I started to cherish playing there. It had become very special to me."

That field was also a far cry from Boston College's Alumni Stadium, which Frantz had left behind. Yet, each time Frantz returned to his high school field, he did not carry an ounce of regret.

"It is what it is," said Frantz. "But you have to remember, BC has been around for over a hundred years and Florida Atlantic just started its program in 2001. We're getting there."

Throughout most of Frantz's senior season, Florida Atlantic was heralded as the underdog heading into quite a few games. The Vegas odds makers often stacked the deck against Frantz and his newly formed college football team. However, Frantz has always embraced the role of the underdog.

"The underdog is all about motivation," said Frantz. "People always say you're not good enough or you can't do this or you can't do that. I don't know about other people, but when somebody downs me, I really step up to the challenge and show them what I can do."

Being a perpetual underdog is one of the contributing factors that helped Frantz choreograph his own swagger. A quiet swagger had carried Frantz to this point in his life and remained with him through the draft season.

Swagger was not something that was taught at TEST, although there was plenty of it to go around. Tad Kornegay, one of the trainers at TEST, put his swagger on display every day. He had a loud swagger that was noticeable every time he stepped into a room. And it didn't take long before his swagger became audible. Tad wasn't the tallest guy in the world, but he was never short on words. Tad was one of the nation's top Division 1AA cornerbacks while at Fordham University in 2004 and a consensus first team All-American. He trained at TEST for his Pro Day and performed exceptionally well. Yet, when the 2005 NFL Draft came around, Tad was unusually quiet.

"I prepared the hardest I ever had in my life," said Tad. "I thought I was a competitor in college. But when I prepared for the draft, I tuned in and was the most focused I've ever been. I cut out all the negative stuff because I really wanted to make it. But then I started to see all these other guys get drafted ahead of me. I started to get really down and then it was real depressing when the draft was over and I didn't hear my name called. I was really down."

Following that 2005 draft weekend, not one invitation from a NFL team came Tad's way. Discouraged and disheartened, Tad was forced to consider the unthinkable; that his football career had come to an end. Three long, torturous weeks passed without a peep from anyone and then a light finally brightened the dark tunnel that seemed to be eclipsing Tad's football career. An opportunity of a different kind suddenly arose. The Hamilton Tiger-Cats of the Canadian Football League offered Tad a contract. He immediately signed and then the hands of time played a cruel trick on him. About seventy-two hours after Tad had signed that contract, he received an invitation to the Buffalo Bills rookie camp. Having already signed a contract, Tad honored that commitment and took his swagger up north.

"I could have went to Buffalo, but I believe everything happens for a reason," said Tad.

Five years later, Tad is still playing in the CFL as a defensive back for the Saskatchewan Roughriders. Tad also has a Grey Cup Championship ring on his finger.

"There's a lot of people out there that would love to have this opportunity," said Tad. "Going up to Canada, I thought I was going to be better than all those guys. I pumped my swagger up to like the twentieth power. I mean, I was supposed to be in the NFL! But you go up there and there's some real talent. They're all college stars who just missed the NFL or guys that came from the NFL. The money isn't like the NFL, but you're getting paid to play professional football. And if you establish yourself up in Canada, you can make close to six figures."

For the last five years, Tad has spent June through December up in Canada making his living playing professional football. He returns to New Jersey during the off-season where he works at TEST helping college players prepare to make the leap to the NFL. Tad is one of the fortunate college players who found an excellent alternative to the NFL. And every time Tad returns to the Canadian tundra, he makes sure to pack his swagger, especially being a defensive back.

"As a DB, you can never question yourself," said Tad. "You always have to believe you're the better player no matter who you're going against. I don't give a damn if it's Randy Moss or Terrell Owens. You always think you're a champion and you never settle for number two, you always want to be number one. The way I see it, number two is the first loser so I always want to be number one. And you can't back down from any challenges. That's what sets a swagger to me."

Cornerbacks are basically out on an island of their own and sometimes a swagger could mean the difference between a sixty-yard touchdown pass and an interception. No cornerback wants to be posterized behind a receiver as he glides into the endzone. That simple fact would mean that Morgan may have needed more swagger than any of the other players.

"Morgan has a confident swagger," Tad pointed out.

It was a swagger that wasn't quite the same as Frantz's, Kenny's or even Tad's. Morgan's swagger seemed to be powered by confidence and it was with him both on and off the field. But Morgan admitted that he gained his off-the-field swagger at an early age, whereas his football swagger had to develop over time.

"I have always been a confident guy," said Morgan. "I don't believe in peer pressure. I never did anything to impress people. I've always had my own way about me. I've always had a swagger about myself, but not when it comes to football. That's something I had to build up. I had to find it. Once you get comfortable and start making plays, you kind of develop your own swagger."

Part of the reason Morgan was able to develop such a confident swagger was because of the high level at which he competed. From the time Morgan first started playing sports, he always competed in a higher age bracket.

"That helped mold him into being an elite player because he was always head and shoulders above everybody else," Tina noted.

Also factoring into Morgan's heavy dose of confidence was living up to the same heights his parents had reached.

"Being that Morgan's mother and I were such high-level athletes didn't make it easier on us because our expectations were higher," said Phil. "It would be easier if we weren't such high-level athletes because we expect a certain level of performance. Expectations are at an elite level and we know what it takes to get there. When you're at that level, there's no in-between. You get used to it and that's all you know."

Those expectations were not forced upon Morgan in an oppressive way and his parents were far from the stereotypical mom and dad whose every thought placed Morgan on the highest possible pedestal.

"We've been able to show him that there are other things in life," said Phil. "As long as Morgan did well in school, he got what he wanted. And I always told him you can get a million degrees, but the best degree you can have is one in common sense. That's one I pull out of my pocket and use every day."

Yet, even at a very young age, Morgan seemed wise beyond his years.

Tina explained, "He's always been an old man. He told me at six years old, he disapproved of my parenting style. But Morgan is amazing because he's extremely humble and extremely grounded. He gives glory to God for all the gifts he has. Few people will say that it's a gift they've been given."

Having lofty expectations thrust upon him at such an early age also forced Morgan to play with confidence.

"You have to have that swagger," Morgan said. "That swagger will do a lot for you. That's what people want to see. You have to believe in yourself. People respect that. That's one thing I learned playing corner. You're out there by yourself. You're on a team, but you're by yourself out there so you have to have a swagger and confidence. If not, you'll get killed out there. They can see it if you're walking around scared. If you got swag and you get beat, it's like so what. You come back and do something else."

Perhaps the most unusual form of swagger at TEST was evident in Lydon. Through Lydon's first week of training, his swagger really started to show. He came to New Jersey completely focused and was a mold of concentration. But, as time went on, more of his personality began to surface.

Lydon's swagger was made up of many ingredients and was a tribute to his versatility. For instance, he would walk through TEST shirtless, causing people to gawk and stare at his massive frame. But he would then find a secluded spot and pray for a short while before his training. He would remain very focused through his training and listen to every word of instruction with the utmost seriousness. Then, once the training concluded, he wouldn't hesitate to spend some time clowning around.

"He even has his own little dance," said Brian. "He calls it the Murtha dance. I like that. What I like about him is he's intense and he's focused, but he's loose. He's definitely got swagger. I think the combination of his meanness, his focus, his work ethic and being a little goofy is a major plus for him. He's very unique. But I think in the NFL, it works well."

Lydon attributed his swagger to much of the diversity he experienced through his first twenty-three years of life.

"It could be the combination of being a little bit of a troublemaker growing up to becoming popular in school to becoming the best athlete," said Lydon. "And then to having a rude awakening when I got hurt and hitting a real low spot in my life. I've had high success, but I have also been in the outhouse and everywhere in between."

That swagger also enabled Lydon to excel in different arenas and broaden his personality.

"I can get up in front of a thousand kids and talk to them like it's nothing," said Lydon. "But I am also real reserved and chill. On my team, I will lead by example. But I will pull a kid aside and tell him what's up if I have to."

Some may have mistaken Lydon's swagger as being a bit cocky during his first week at TEST. He moved exceedingly well through each drill and did not hesitate to speak his mind. He asked questions, made comments and did not designate himself to one specific area. He roamed back and forth and occasionally conversed with whomever was next to him.

Morgan, Kenny and Frantz all had a front row view of Lydon's performance as all three of them were sidelined for that week. Swagger just wasn't enough to get any of them back into action. Kenny was still trying to heal his hamstrings after the Senior Bowl.

"I think it set me back a lot," said Kenny. "I also think if I cleared this hamstring up when it first happened, I wouldn't have these problems now. It messed me up a lot and it nagged me through the whole year. It nagged me when I came up here, but now I'm around people who are addressing the issue and we're getting it cleaned up."

Kevin was leading that charge as Kenny's daily workouts were now centered on getting his hamstrings right.

"We work a lot on his flexion in his big toe," said Kevin. "If we could get more flexion in that big toe, then he'll be able to push off that and it resolves the cause of the hamstring issue. He went into therapy for that. A lot of it was just working on mobility, taking the toe and pushing it back and getting mobility in the area. Deep tissue massage, some ultrasound, but mainly having somebody just crank down on that toe. It's very painful. He was also fitted for Orthotics. That helps correct his feet because if you can get a little heel lift, it's much easier for that joint to fall straight down. You have to actually get casted for Orthotics and we have a guy who we trust. A bunch of guys got them this year because we had a lot of guys with turf toe and flat feet. The foot is where all the force production starts. So if there's pain there, it will shut people right down."

While most of the other players went through their various drills, Kenny spent quite a bit of time with the physical therapists as well as Kevin. Quite often, when the other players were practicing their forty starts, Kenny was riding a stationary bike or getting some kind of treatment.

"It's been kind of good and kind of bad because I get a lot of one-on-one time and I can work on certain areas where I need work," said Kenny. "But I can't really work on everything else that everybody else is working on like your start and all the technique stuff. It's like I'm behind. But hopefully, everything will work out."

After spending two weeks at a pair of all-star games, Morgan was now spending a lot of his time getting treatment for a lower back problem. That week, he watched the other players run through drills while he was in street clothes.

"It's frustrating being hurt, but the people here are getting me right," said Morgan. "I should be straight for the Combine."

Frantz also joined Morgan and Kenny as a spectator, although he didn't have a specific injury. Frantz was simply resting his body after a taxing week in Texas. The three of them all appeared to be in good spirits, yet playing the part of a spectator did not sit well with any of them.

"I'm not going to lie, I'm getting tired of doing all the same drills," said Morgan. "It gets so repetitive. But now that my back is bothering me, I really wish I was out there doing those same drills."

Frantz also had the itch to get back to work. In fact, the staff had to order him to sit out and rest for a few days. But whenever Frantz found himself hurt, winded or dead tired, he was always able to summon the strength to push even harder.

"It's very easy to get distracted and say I don't want to do that extra rep," said Frantz. "The major thing is just staying focused and going hard on every drill, every rep. Every time I get tired or get off-track, I just think about my mother and things I've been through. Then, the motivation just kicks back up. If I don't do that extra rep, I'm setting myself up to go right back where I came from."

For Kenny, a similar factor enabled him to fight through fatigue, pain and adversity. Now, his success in the NFL would affect the quality of life for his newborn son. Being away from Keon also took its toll on Kenny. So, as sort of a welcomed diversion, Kenny's agent paid for one weekend trip during his training. Frantz and Morgan were also granted that same privilege. Instead of going home, Kenny opted to fly in his girlfriend and son so they could spend the weekend with him in New Jersey.

"We stayed in most of the time, but it was a great visit," said Kenny. "It eased everything up. It was a weekend where I could just chill and kick it with my little boy. It's important because going through this whole training, I don't really see anybody close to me. It kind of gets nerve-wracking. But when you take a weekend off and kind of relax, then you come back ready to work."

Morgan also welcomed Liz for the weekend and Brian even arranged for a car to take them into New York City where they enjoyed a night out.

"Other than going to New York, we just kind of chilled for most of the weekend but that's what we like to do," said Morgan. "It was great to see her though."

That same weekend, no one came out to New Jersey to pay Frantz a visit. That is because Frantz had already taken advantage of his weekend furlough a couple of weeks earlier. He won an award for his play on the field and wanted to be at a Florida Atlantic banquet to accept it in person.

"It was great honor and I wanted to be there to show my appreciation," said Frantz. "It was real nice. I miss home, but I got to get this work done. So if work is here in New Jersey, then I miss New Jersey."

It wouldn't be long before Frantz was back in Florida since his Pro Day was the earliest of any college in the nation. Just two days after the Combine, Florida Atlantic would hold its first ever Pro Day.

"I've had that day marked down for a long time," said Frantz. "If you're not working, then it will sneak up on you. I'm not really anxious, I'm just trying to take it one day at a time and stay focused. I might get a few butterflies because it is such a huge opportunity. But I can't rush it and try to get there too quick. Time flies. But when you're doing the things you need to do, it kind of slows down a little bit. Like when I used to be the last one in the weight room during those long summers and when I used to be the first one in there during those long winters. It really lets you think and see where you got to go and what you have to do in order to get there."

Very soon, Frantz's Pro Day would be upon him. Only days before that, Lydon, Morgan and Kenny would all get their chance to take center stage at the NFL Combine. Each of those four players all carried their own unique swagger through the draft season. Fueling that swagger was the determination of a man. But within them, there still lived the uncertainty of a boy. All of their futures were not yet written, yet all four were very curious, anxious and eager to see what the pages of tomorrow would read.

CHAPTER TWELVE

Training Winds Down

With less than a week to go until the NFL Combine, there was an upgrade in intensity throughout the TEST facility. Time had already seemed to expire on most of the laughter, smiles and light-heartedness that previously breathed life into the day-to-day training. It was almost as if there was a thick, stressful air of tension consuming the facility. Although there was no game to be played, players ran through their daily gauntlet of drills with lines of concentration chiseled into their faces. They had been training at TEST for six weeks now and the daily grind was starting to wear on them.

Towards the tail end of that training period, the players were tested in the various combine events. They had all shown great improvement, but it seemed like a few extra days might be able to shave a few more hundredths of a second off their times. That could ultimately mean the difference between playing professional football or going out to look for an entry level job that didn't pay anywhere near what the NFL doled out to its first-year employees.

Brian had announced to everyone in the TEST Football Academy that he would be introducing a new type of training during that final week. After one early morning session, he told the players to brace themselves for something they had probably never done before. With all of the players looking on with curious eyes, Brian walked out onto the middle of the turf carrying a large box. Wearing a sly grin, he opened up a box and let loose a pair of chickens.

"Now don't laugh, but you guys are going to have to chase these chickens," said Brian. "If you can catch these things, you can catch any little scat-back."

All the players immediately burst into a fit of laughter and the shrewd comments began to fly. However, Brian ignored those comments and pleaded his case.

"All right, who's going to be the first one to chase this thing?"

The players responded by spending the next few minutes laughing, joking and even ogling the chicken. Frantz then put on a pair of gloves and lined up behind the chicken. As he ran forward to grab it, the chicken barley moved. Frantz laughed as he picked it up and looked over at Brian.

"I guess he's not afraid of you," Brian joked.

Another couple of players did the same thing and the chickens did not seem too eager to exercise. Nevertheless, the players spent about twenty minutes on the turf laughing at such a humorous spectacle.

Afterwards, Brian said with a smile, "I just wanted to loosen these guys up a bit. I got the chickens from my dad's place. I think they're actually laying eggs so they probably don't feel much like running. I could have brought in some rabbits. Chasing them would have been quite a workout, but all I need is one of my players to get bitten and have to go get a Rabies shot. The real reason I did it was just to ease some of the guys' tension and have some fun."

Brian appeared to accomplish that goal as the players left the facility much looser than they were before being introduced to the sport of chicken chasing. However, that was not the only extracurricular activity on the agenda. A couple of days later, Brian arranged for the players to head into New York City to take in a Knicks game at Madison Square Garden.

Although TEST was only about an hour's drive into the city, the players hadn't really gotten a chance to experience the Big Apple. Since many of the players hailed from all over the country, a trip into the city was far from an everyday thing. Only days before the start of the NFL Combine, Kenny, Morgan and Frantz piled into a luxury bus that would take two-dozen NFL hopefuls and the TEST staff into the city.

Even though the Combine and subsequent Pro Days were only days away, the mood on the bus was very light. When Manhattan's towering skyline first came into sight, the players failed to resemble the same individuals who kept their composure on the gridiron. Some possessed the bodies of large men, yet they oohed and ahhed like little boys.

Flashes from cameras continued to shine as the volume on the bus increased.

Frantz took it all in with a laid back smile while Kenny bobbed his head to music throughout the entire bus ride. Morgan remained quiet on the back of the bus and wasn't too phased by all the glitz and glamour of the city. Lydon wasn't on the bus since he had to leave for the Combine in less than twenty-four hours. The offensive linemen were the first to perform, which meant that Lydon was scheduled to leave for Indianapolis on an early morning flight. As the busload of players rolled into the city, Lydon was one state away trying to thwart off his nervous anxiety.

"It still hasn't kicked in yet," said Lydon. "Brian just had us doing a visualization exercise. It's kind of like a blank right now. When you start visualizing things, it changes your perspective a bit. I think I've almost set the bar too high for myself, so I never feel accomplished. It's probably one of my problems. I never think I'm good enough to really be satisfied with myself. I don't know if that helps me or breaks me down, maybe both. It's kind of a big issue with me. With all my times and even if I make a good play, I'll think something was wrong with it."

While Lydon was busy worrying, Kenny strode off the bus seemingly free from any anxiety brought on by the NFL Combine.

"It really just snuck up on me," said Kenny. "I really haven't been doing too much for like three weeks. Rest is the best thing. I do want to put the cleats on and go out there right now. But I have to kind of control myself and just wait for my time."

Kenny walked with his familiar southern swagger and the casual observer would have no idea that a pair of questionable hamstrings carried him down that New York street. But unlike the Senior Bowl, Kenny claimed that his hamstrings presented no concerns.

"It's life and you have to deal with it," said Kenny. "But I'm not real worried, I'll just have to go out and perform. They know so much stuff at TEST and they have way better therapy than we had down in South Carolina. I wasn't expecting the physical therapy to be so great. In a million years, I never thought I was going to be around all this. It's a good experience and hopefully the results prove that it's a great experience. The goal is still to run a 4.3 and get drafted in the second round. I don't care if I'm injured or not. The goal is still the same."

Kevin stepped off the bus moments after Kenny and maintained the same confidence.

"We spent most of our time with Kenny just getting him pain-free and not really conditioning him," said Kevin. "We couldn't work on explosiveness and technique as much with him. It was mostly, let's get this kid pain-free so that he can run and rely on his natural ability to do what he does. I think he'll do well."

Frantz didn't seem too worried about his Pro Day as he looked at the bright city lights with a sense of wonder. He still had a little more than a week to prepare for the biggest day of his draft season.

"I think I've come a long way," said Frantz. "There's been a lot of improvements. But Pro Day is a lot different than playing a game."

Not far behind Frantz, Morgan beat the New York pavement with the same confidence he owned since he first arrived at TEST. Since then, his times, his strength and his body had undergone dramatic changes.

"I knew my forty start was getting better and I knew I was getting faster," said Morgan. "I could feel myself improving, but it's always great to be surprised. I was really only surprised on the bench. For a DB, if you get anywhere from 15 to 20, that's real good. To throw anything beyond that will be exceptional. It'll be exciting. I'm not going to say anything until I go and do it. It's going to be nice to see everyone's reaction. I don't know if anyone has any idea of how strong I am. I weighed 198 last week so I dropped down to like 193. If a team wanted me to, I could be 205 by next week. If they wanted me to play safety, whatever. I'll play wherever."

A couple of hours before tip-off, the players made their way into a restaurant across the street from Madison Square Garden. Morgan, Frantz and Kenny all handled themselves with the same respect they had shown the entire time they were in New Jersey. The same could not be said for all the players. A few of them surreptitiously ordered expensive alcoholic drinks and charged them to the master tab that would come out of Brian's pocket. One player even had a mysterious woman pop up and join him for dinner.

Some of the group started to shy away from the behavior of a disciplined athlete. The same ones who resembled fascinated boys on the bus ride were now starting to behave more like rebellious teenagers.

The rebellion continued after dinner when some of the players took their game tickets and disappeared. By the end of the first quarter, the section Brian had reserved for the players was not completely full. Apparently, some of the players had decided to take the streets of New York.

"Where's Kenny?" Brian asked.

"He said he wanted to go do some shopping," one of the players responded.

Brian then looked over at Frantz, who had made a quick stop in a store to purchase a couple pairs of sneakers. Frantz watched the game quietly with eyes that combined both interest and curiosity. Brian turned around and tried to do the same, but couldn't help himself from continually glancing around for any trace of the missing players.

Another thing to consider was that when wandering the streets of New York City, it really didn't matter how many touchdowns someone had scored during his college career. The education learned in the inner city was also very different from the education prescribed in college. That may have left some of the players at a distinct disadvantage on the concrete playing field of the big city. These players were grown men from a physical standpoint. But from many other angles, they still had quite a bit of growing to do.

More nervousness consumed Brian as the third quarter was set to begin. While he voiced his concern to his wife, Kenny came swaggering up the second level holding about eight shopping bags.

"Well, look at this," Brian said with a grin.

"I told you I had some shopping to do," Kenny announced.

Kenny then found his seat and attempted to squeeze in amongst the large contingent of shopping bags that crowded his area. By the end of the game, the rest of the missing players showed up, a couple not as sober as the others. Yet, every one of them found their way to the bus when it was time to leave; minus the mysterious woman who showed up at dinner.

All in all, the trip was a success even though Brian endured a bit of angst throughout the night. But these players would be subjected to much more temptation at the professional level. In the future, it would be up to them to make the wisest of decisions. There would be no Brian to advise them on what they should or shouldn't do. Unfortunately, as it has been popularly documented in the past, there are a good portion of professional athletes who don't think before they act. Perhaps the responsibility of being a NFL player comes while some of these boys are still transitioning into men. Perhaps it is their voice of youth that compels them to make such ill-advised decisions. Whatever the case, a new world was looming ever so closer. And with it came much more temptation than any of them had found during their few-hour jaunt through New York City.

Over the past six weeks, the training seemed both arduous and tedious. But now, many of the players wished for a few more days so they could improve their forty times or add a couple more reps to their bench press. However, making it to the NFL was more than just a six-week journey. These players had focused on a future in professional football for what seemed like a lifetime.

"It's always been my dream to make it in the NFL," said Morgan.

"This is all still very surreal to me. It's something I always thought I could do. I thought it was going to happen, but it happened so quick."

Regardless of how fast time unraveled, Brian and his staff had done everything possible to get these players ready for their time in front of the NFL scouts. Now, it was up to the players to go out and execute everything they had learned. The start of the NFL Combine was only hours away. It was easily the biggest event of the draft season and just a few moments in Indianapolis could determine a large part of each player's future.

CHAPTER THIRTEEN

On to Indy

Coaches, executives and scouts from every NFL team poured into the city of Indianapolis for the six-day extravaganza that has come to be known as the NFL Scouting Combine. Media outlets from all across the country also flooded the city along with hoards of renowned agents, up and coming agents and slick talkers who desperately wanted to be agents. Fans even gathered outside of Lucas Oil Stadium and the nearby Crown Hotel, anticipating the arrival of the top college prospects in the land. Their whitening knuckles were wrapped tightly around pens as they hoped to get a simple signature from a future NFL star. But the inclement February winds did not make anyone's time outdoors a very pleasant one. Arctic blasts seemed to rip right through the body and induce a chill that dug deep into the bone.

Many souls braved the conditions and turned Indianapolis into a budding metropolis. Some of the locals had dubbed the city 'nap town', but the city was far from sleepwalking through that week. Planes continued to touch down without an empty seat to spare. 'No Vacancy' was a common phrase uttered by many hotel receptionists throughout the city and taxicabs couldn't seem to kick people out fast enough. As soon as one passenger would set foot on the curb, there was another waiting to escape the icy backdrop that was Indianapolis.

On one of the 747's that was taxiing down a jetway at Indianapolis International Airport, there sat a man who had just endured a very uncomfortable flight. That was mainly due to the little room he had, thanks in part to the 6-foot-7, 310 pound Lydon Murtha who sat next to him. Coach seats were not built for someone of Lydon's size. Since Lydon had not yet signed a NFL contract, the extra space that comes with a first class seat was way out of his reach. The NFL did not feel the need to ante up and purchase a first class ticket for its Combine invitees. However, it wasn't the last time during that week when the NFL would impose quite a bit of discomfort on the players.

Having the luxury of more leg room was the furthest thing from Lydon's mind. Less than a month ago, Lydon could only hope for an invitation to the Combine. By some stroke of luck, that hope had turned into a reality. And now, Lydon finally had the opportunity to make his dream come true.

As Lydon collected his luggage and found the car that would take him directly to the players' hotel, he didn't entertain thoughts of playing in the NFL. All he could think about was doing well at the Combine. The more those thoughts raced through his head, the more nervous he grew. Inside the massive individual who exuded such mammoth strength was just a scared and nervous kid.

Shortly after Lydon checked into his room, the militant routine of the NFL Combine began. He immediately reported to orientation with the rest of the offensive linemen. Once that orientation was over, the players were shuttled to a variety of nearby hospitals. There, x-rays were administered to knees, shoulders, backs and feet. CAT Scans and MRI's served as sort of a welcome mat for these wide-eyed young men. That process took quite a while as players were forced to spend a good portion of the day in a place they so desperately tried to avoid.

It wasn't long after Lydon left the hospital that the interview process began. Teams were allowed to interview players for a fifteen-minute period and, in some cases, they would return for a follow-up interview the next day. But the interviews differed a bit from the ones at the all-star games. Now, it wasn't just scouts interviewing the players. Head coaches and GM's often sat in on many of the interview sessions.

"The interviews are always one of the most interesting parts of the Combine," said New England Patriots head coach Bill Belichick. "I never thought and I don't think you can analyze a player in a ten-minute interview. That's stretching it. But I find it interesting to see where some of these kids come from, what their background is, who's important to them in their life, what situations they've been through that kind of shape the way that they are; the way they approach the game and things like that. I find that very interesting."

Lydon had been through his share of interviews during the week he spent at the Texas vs. The Nation game, so he thought he knew what to expect. Knowing full well that the players would be adequately prepared, coaches purposely switched up some of the questioning.

New York Giants head coach Tom Coughlin noted, "Part of the challenge for us is we try not to ask the right down the middle questions. There aren't as many fastballs now as there are curves."

A curve immediately came Lydon's way during his first interview of the day. A coach showed him pictures of five offensive plays and five fronts that his team used. The coach spent about fifteen seconds going through each one.

When the coach was finished, he flipped the paper upside down and said, "Now draw up all those plays and the different fronts."

Lydon followed that directive and excelled as he remembered almost every play just as it was drawn up.

"It was kind of a curve ball, but I did really well," Lydon said. "They want to see how quick of a learner you are. Every person I talked to tested me like that. It wasn't just about my position, but about every position. They want to see if you know it across the board; what the center was doing, what the guards are doing and what kind of footwork do they have. They want to see if you're an overall smart football player."

Some NFL fans might turn on the television and view offensive linemen simply as gargantuan human beings whose primary skill is to push people around. But there is a lot more to playing the position than just size and strength. In fact, NFL teams look for a sound mind between the ears of those colossal kids.

"The first thing I want to see is how smart they are," said Cleveland Browns general manager George Kokinis. "They got to be smart. There's so much going on in those 3-4 schemes that people run in our division, they got to be able to think on their feet."

Lydon was sent from room to room and placed in front of coaches, scouts and GM's from all over the NFL. Each one threw a new curve ball his way and some of those questions even shied away from the realm of football.

"So we've heard that you have some handguns?" one scout asked.

"Heck yeah," Lydon shot back. "That's my right. It's amended in our constitution that we have the right to bear arms. I have an assault rifle, I have three handguns, I have shotguns, I have rifles. Me and my wife go shooting at the range all the time."

"Why do you have so many guns?" asked the scout.

"Because A, it's fun. B, I want to make sure I'm protected and C, it's also for hunting," said Lydon.

A few minutes later in a different interrogation room, another scout asked Lydon, "You got hurt during your sophomore year in a motorcycle accident. What the heck were you doing on a motorcycle?"

Lydon leaned closer to the scout and whispered, "It was actually a moped. I know I probably looked like a gorilla on the thing, but the only place I drove it was from my house to the stadium. It was great on gas and it was cheap. After practice one day, I came out of the garage and was going about twenty miles an hour. There was a car parked on the wrong side of the road. It flipped a u-turn on me and I t-boned him. That's how I tore my shoulder out."

That same scout then changed gears rather quickly.

"Have you ever done steroids?" he asked.

Lydon cracked a bit of a smile and said, "I'm just smiling because you're not the first person to ask me that. But no, I have never taken steroids."

"I just ask because there are not many guys that look like you who haven't taken steroids," said the scout.

"It's genetics, good nutrition and a lot of hard work," Lydon responded. "Don't get that wrong, it's a lot of sacrifice too. I don't go out and party at night. I eat right all day and I live at the gym."

"Well I only ask because last year's first overall pick, Jake Long, is 315 with hardly an ounce of fat on him. But you're leaner than he is."

That would not be the last time Lydon heard the steroid question that week. Other questions came at him and took him by a bit of surprise. Yet, in spite of all the curves that came his way, Lydon threw some curves of his own.

"I stopped and straight up asked the scouts right in the middle of the interview, how much they put into combine numbers? It was split like 50/50. Some teams said they don't care about any times and that they just want to see film. The other half said it's all about times because if you can show you're athletic, then they have something to work with."

The final pitch from the scouts came late in the evening. That meant that Lydon wasn't able to return to his room and practice lights out until just after the midnight hour. Shortly after four in the morning, the NFL came calling much like a drill sergeant. Lydon was given a wake-up call and his orders were to immediately take a drug test. After he passed that test, he was shipped over to a sort of 'mess hall' where he gobbled up an early morning breakfast. Weary and groggy-eyed, most of the linemen ate massive quantities of food in almost complete silence. Then, around 0700 hours, Lydon was commanded to take the Wonderlic.

The Wonderlic Test is taken by every player who attends the NFL Combine. It is a 50 question test measuring cognitive ability, and aims to gauge participants' ability to problem solve. The test was developed by Al Wonderlic in the 1930's. Today, companies all around the world use the Wonderlic to evaluate their personnel. It is distributed in fourteen languages and in 2008, more than 2.5 million people took the test. In the NFL, players have to think and react in fractions of a section and the ability to problem solve on the field is essential.

Players are given twelve minutes to answer as many of the questions as possible. Philadelphia Eagles wide receiver Kevin Curtis has recorded the highest score of any NFL player with a 48. However, a player's score is not directly correlated to how good of a football player he can be. Tennessee Titans quarterback Vince Young scored an 8 on the Wonderlic, yet he was still selected with the 3rd overall pick in the 2006 NFL Draft. Below are some sample questions from the Wonderlic test:

- Looking at the numbers below, which number should come next?

8, 4, 2, 1, 1/2, 1/4?

- When rope is selling at $.10 per foot, how many feet can you buy for 60 cents?

- ABSTAIN RETAIN. These words:

Have similar meanings

Have opposite meanings

Have neither similar or opposite meanings

- Fill in the blank:_____ is an appendage of the hand

Palm, Elbow, Shoulder, Finger, Wrist

- The hours of daylight and darkness in September are nearest equal to the hours of daylight and darkness in:

June, March, May, November

- A boy is 17 years old and his sister is twice as old. When the boy is 23 years old, what will be the age of his sister?

Lydon breezed through the test and was then subjected to another round of testing – this one psychological, filled with Rorschach tests and invasive questions. But that was nothing compared to what came next.

Lydon was led into a room where a balding doctor from a NFL team took out a piece of paper with an outline of the human body.

In a wheezy voice the doctor said, "I want you to tell me about your injury past and don't leave out anything. I want to know about every single injury you've ever had, even the littlest of injuries you've had throughout your entire life."

Lydon complied and proceeded to tell the balding man about his shoulder injury, his toe problems and his Staph infection among other things.

When he was finished, the balding man said, "Now go into the room over there and another doctor will come in and talk to you further."

Lydon did as he was told and went into an adjoining room where he was greeted by a gangly doctor with a very deep voice. The gangly doctor took a seat across from Lydon and dropped a very thick folder on the table that separated them. He started shuffling through some papers and began to ask about Lydon's shoulder injury. Then, he went into detail about Lydon's toe problems. From there, he asked Lydon to discuss his Staph infection.

"Right off the bat it's a test," Lydon pointed out. "They want to see if I told them everything. They already knew everything. They had detailed files dating back to my days in high school. They knew about a sprained ankle I had in high school. They even had the x-ray from when I broke my femur in the fifth grade."

The gangly doctor then asked, "Why didn't you tell us about the sprained ankle you had in high school or the AC joint sprain you had during your second year at Nebraska?"

"Honestly, I forgot about them," said Lydon.

Lydon professed that it was an honest mistake, unlike some players who blatantly lied about their past injuries.

"I completely forgot about those two injuries," Lydon acknowledged. "But there's kids who go in there and just lie like Michael Crabtree. He went in and said he never had any foot injuries."

Once that interrogation had finished, a small woman with beady eyes directed Lydon into yet another a small room. This particular room was set up for a physical examination as opposed to just an oral investigation.

"Strip down to your underwear and take a seat on that examining table" she ordered.

Lydon obliged and sat still with his feet dangling about a foot above the floor, wearing only his underwear. Unsure of what to expect, Lydon braced himself as the door opened and a bunch of doctors came hustling in. The woman with the beady eyes announced Lydon's name and began stating the various injuries he had suffered over the course of his life. The gang of doctors paused for a moment to size Lydon up and then moved quickly towards him. Without so much as a hello, one of the doctors grabbed Lydon's arm and immediately started bending it back and forth.

"Does this hurt?" he asked in a firm tone.

Lydon answered no and then diverted his attention to a female doctor who had just grabbed a hold of his wrist. She began to rotate it in every possible direction and didn't seem to care that it may have been causing him some discomfort.

Lydon shifted his eyes yet again when he noticed a pair of shorter doctors poking and prodding various parts of his legs.

"How's that feel?" asked the shorter doctor as he jammed his knubby little fingers into Lydon's calf.

"It's fine," Lydon said rather uneasily.

The other vertically-challenged doctor proceeded to bend Lydon's other leg in all sorts of directions. It almost looked as though he was trying to invoke an injury of his own. Lydon then turned and looked at another male doctor, who had a large mole on his forehead. As large and pronounced as that mole was, Lydon was distracted by the man talking into his voice recorder.

"Lydon Murtha, right shoulder," he said as he pushed an open palm into Lydon's shoulder.

Then, he muttered some medical jargon Lydon couldn't quite comprehend. This continued for a few minutes as all the doctors took turns pulling, prodding, bending and literally hanging on various parts of Lydon's body. Finally, the mole man commanded Lydon to lie down and the examination continued.

The littlest of all the doctors shuffled over to Lydon's head and began to bend his neck in all sorts of directions.

"How does this feel?" he asked in what seemed to be an excited tone of voice.

"Fine," Lydon replied even though that couldn't have been true from the way the little doctor yanked his head.

The little doctor continued to ask questions and also spoke into a small voice recorder the same way the mole man had done. Lydon responded just as he did to all their questions. He complained about nothing and told each of the doctors he felt no pain regardless of how deep they prodded or how hard they pulled. He just tried to relax as best as he could.

"It's like you're in a meat market," Lydon said. "They're poking and prodding you to see if anything's loose or hurting. You just have to sit there like a loose dummy. It's like they're examining something they're going to buy. When you go out to a car dealership to buy a car, it might look nice but you got to get in it. You got to drive it and see what the interior looks like."

Lydon had his share of injuries in the past and any team that might be considering adding him to its roster would undoubtedly look deeply into his medical evaluations.

"If we feel like a guy has a devastating injury or a tendency to never finish a year, that's something we look into," said Minnesota Vikings head coach Brad Childress. "Then, we can lean to the doctor's side of it, talk to those guys about it and whether or not this guy is going to be a chronic injury guy."

The mole man, the littlest of all the doctors and the woman with the beady eyes all represented different NFL teams. When they finished examining Lydon, another contingent of doctors barged in and repeated that process. Lydon had never been felt up in so many ways by so many strangers. And he had never been touched by so many people at the same time! The whole ordeal was nothing like he expected and was more than a little overwhelming. However, he understood why such measures were being taken.

"If a team is investing all this money in you, they have to know what they're getting," said Lydon. "It was nothing like I ever experienced in my life, but I know why they do it."

Needless to say, the medical evaluations were more than just a 'hi, how are you doing type of thing.' They were the most intensive and complex physical examinations any of these young men would ever experience.

"We do get tremendous medical information, which may very well be the number one reason for all of us collectively to be here," said New York Giants head coach Tom Coughlin.

After Lydon was finished being groped, he was sent over to continue with the interviewing process. Over the course of that day, players were also pulled aside so that they could address the large media contingent that gathered at Lucas Oil Stadium. Once that was done, the players were sent off to another extensive round of interviews.

As Lydon marched through that routine, Kenny's plane touched down and day one of his NFL Combine experience had begun. He rolled through the orientation which led to a hospital trip and then over to his first round of interviews. After the Senior Bowl and having so much media attention throughout his college career, day one wasn't too difficult for Kenny. However, that all changed on day two of his Combine experience.

With Kenny's injury history, he expected to be scrutinized rather intensely. Yet, as a small army of doctors poked and prodded his body the same way they had done to Lydon, he never expected it to be so intense.

"Man, that was crazy," Kenny said with surprise in his voice. "Every team had like three doctors pulling and poking at me at all times! I never went through anything like that."

At the conclusion of Kenny's medical evaluation, he was also summoned to a nearby hospital to undergo further tests, much to his chagrin. It was the second straight day he would have to go to the hospital and undergo more testing. On that second day, he traveled back to the hospital with fellow receivers Michael Crabtree, Percy Harvin and running back Chris 'Beanie' Wells. College rival James Davis of Clemson also joined Kenny and was equally as dumbfounded.

"One of the coaches from Baltimore wanted a MRI on my back," Kenny stated. "I never had a back problem in my life! I could have saved some time without that. Somebody ordered a back thing on James Davis too and he never had a back problem either. He said they ordered like five things on him. I think they might just make stuff up."

Kenny carried out the request, but never expected what came next. As he sat patiently in a waiting room, he looked up and saw a doctor walking towards him with a grim look on his face.

"Kenny McKinley?" the doctor asked.

"Yeah, that's me."

"I'm afraid I have some bad news."

"Bad news?" Kenny replied in a voice suddenly clouded with concern.

"We found something abnormal in your heart."

Although Kenny was sitting perfectly still, it seemed as if his heart instantly dropped down into the pit of stomach. Then, a sick feeling filled his belly. His heart had never given him problems in the past but, at that very moment, it started to hurt.

"We're going to need to take an EKG before we go any further," the doctor stated. "If you'll just follow me, we can get it done right now."

The doctor led Kenny into another room where an echocardiogram would attempt to tell his future. While they walked, the doctor offered no comforting words. He said nothing that might attempt to wipe the stunned look off Kenny's youthful face. Kenny's jaw drooped downward while harsh visions ran through his mind. For as long as he could remember, he had wanted to be a professional football player. It's all he wanted to do with his life and he had worked so hard to get to this particular point. The NFL was just within his reach and now that chance might be snatched away from him in the mere beat of a heart.

Before Kenny could imagine what kind of job would replace being a wide receiver, he started to think of his son. Now, Kenny might not be able to give Keon all the things he never had, but he also might not be able to see his son grow old. There was now a chance that Kenny wouldn't be around to congratulate Keon after he scored his first touchdown. A bad heart could also stop beating long before Kenny watched his little boy go out on his first date. And a faulty ticker could quickly wind down and keep Kenny from watching his son turn into a man. As much as Kenny wanted to make a living playing football, he wanted to see the third and fourth quarters of his life even more.

Worry continued to infiltrate Kenny's entire being as another doctor started to administer the EKG. Kenny asked a few nervous questions, but remained quiet most of the time. However, his look of duress spoke volumes. Once the test was finished, Kenny was asked to wait around for the results. During that idle time, he watched other players come and go, some carrying x-rays, some empty-handed. He secretly wished that all his trip to the hospital entailed was a few measly x-rays. If only things were so simple!

Throughout the entire draft season, Kenny's main worry was a pair of tight hamstrings. Now, that seemed frivolous in comparison to what was happening. More of Kenny's nerves tightened while he waited. His thoughts then shifted from his son to the unfortunate story of another player.

Just a day earlier, these same doctors discovered a problem in one of the heart valves of Northeastern University tight end Brian Mandeville. Following that discovery, the doctors advised that Mandeville never play football again. The end result for Mandeville was a quick exit from Indianapolis.

For Mandeville, there would be no forty-yard dash, no broad jump and no three-cone. A defective valve could even reduce the number of Super Bowls Mandeville might be able to watch from the comfort of his own couch. After that discovery, it pretty much guaranteed that football would now be a spectator sport for Mandeville. As Kenny waited for the results of his test, he prayed that he would not become a part of that same audience.

Painful seconds crawled by and turned into excruciating minutes. Those minutes lagged on and slowly mutated into an agonizing hour. Kenny had spent a great deal of time going through all the day's medical tests, yet he wasn't at all tired. Sitting on the edge of his chair, he also wasn't the least bit hungry. For even if he tried, it is doubtful that Kenny could get anything past the worry that clogged his throat. Kenny's eyes spied every doctor and nurse that passed by. He remained silent, but his eyes seemed to beg for an answer. Never before had time moved so slowly for Kenny. It was as if each second took an eternity to elapse.

Finally, a doctor walked into the room while looking down at a chart that rested in his hands.

Without even glancing up he asked, "Kenny McKinley?"

"Yes sir," Kenny anxiously replied.

"We have the results of your EKG."

"What are they?" Kenny implored.

"Nothing to worry about. We thought there might have been something wrong, but it turned out to be nothing. You're heart's just fine."

After hearing those words, that statement couldn't be any more true. Kenny broke out into a wide smile and thanked the doctor. It seemed ironic that Kenny would thank him since the doctor had just put Kenny through one of the worst hours of his life. Nevertheless, Kenny's future was not in danger nor was the chance to watch his son grow into a future image of himself. He stood up wearing his all too familiar smile and hurried out of the hospital with a newfound bounce in his step. Kenny's future was back within his reach and very soon, he would get the chance to make his future brighter than ever.

CHAPTER FOURTEEN

Time to Shine

Following Kenny's scary run-in at the hospital, he was rewarded with another round of interviews. By that point in time, Kenny was drained from riding such an emotional roller coaster.

"It's tough, but I have to go out and sell myself," said Kenny. "That's why I'm here."

Kenny didn't let the earlier events phase him and went through each interview exhibiting class and respect. After politely answering a barrage of questions, one scout finally said something to get under his skin.

"Why did you refuse to play special teams in college?" he asked.

"Why did who refuse to do what?" Kenny fired back.

"Why did you refuse to play special teams at South Carolina?"

"Man, I didn't refuse to play anything," Kenny said a little louder.

"That's not what your special teams coach said."

"Man, Coach Spurrier didn't want me to play special teams and he's the head coach."

"Well then, why would your special teams coach say that?"

Refusing to back down, Kenny responded, "I don't know, why don't you call Coach Spurrier and ask him? Man, I did everything I could for that program. I played hurt, I played sick. I did everything I could to help my team."

What Kenny didn't tell the scout was that the special teams coach only lasted one year at South Carolina. Another thought that Kenny didn't bother to share with the scout was that he had a good mind to call Coach Spurrier and tell him 'he better check the character of that special teams coach.' But Kenny refused to articulate those thoughts just as he refused to be bullied. When the scout attempted to push his buttons, he stood up for himself just as he had done at the Senior Bowl.

Throughout the entire interview process, some scouts and coaches were friendlier than others. Some would start off with simple questions and then quickly jump into more hard-hitting ones.

"The questions and interviews generally start out, tell us about yourself, tell us about your background, tell us about your family," said Tennessee Titans head coach Jeff Fisher. "Then, we ask is there anything we should be aware of, that we don't know, that we're going to find out? If the answer is yes, then we have a player that has had some sort of issue."

It went exactly that way for Kenny as he was hit with the general montage of introductory questions. Then, on more than one occasion, Kenny was questioned about the nightclub incident he was allegedly involved in a couple of years ago.

In a South Carolina nightclub, a fight had broken out involving some of the people who were with Kenny at the time. Although he did not partake in the incident, it was whispered that he had some sort of hand in the fray. Kenny had no problems answering any questions about that night and was only guilty by association. From his perspective, he had done an excellent job of sufficing every ounce of curiosity that was flung his way. But there was no way to determine exactly how the coaches and scouts graded Kenny's performance in the interrogation room.

"In the last three, four, five years, they've done a much better job preparing themselves for the interviews," Fisher added. "They have all the right answers."

Both Kenny and Lydon had quite enough of being questioned. By the time they were finished interviewing, both were eager to get out on the field and let their bodies do the talking.

On the preceding day, Lydon's body twitched with a bit of nervousness during the bench press portion of the Combine. He only managed to push the 225 pound bar up in the air 25 times before his arms gave out. That number wouldn't place him near the top ten, but not all the linemen had arms as long as Lydon's. His wing span did not make the bench press one of his most prolific exercises. That meant that he would have to perform much better in every other event.

Lydon knew that this would be his last opportunity to improve his draft status. With a good performance, he could shoot up draft boards and land somewhere in the middle rounds. Conversely, a poor showing would all but guarantee that he would not get drafted. It would also take him one step closer to the end of his football career.

Throughout the medicals, the interviews and even the bench press, Lydon could not help but fall victim to his own nerves. Now, Lydon also had to fight off the fatigue that threatened to consume him after three such long and strenuous days. He hadn't been able to sleep more than a dozen hours over that three-day span. However, Lydon was fully aware of why the NFL put him through such a hellacious seventy-two hours before he was called on to perform.

"Part of the game of football is how you react under pressure," said Lydon. "Being tired and being stressed is going to happen in a game of football. To wear us down to the max is important and it's all part of the process. I welcome it with open hands. It's only four days and it's something I've been working for my whole life."

The time had finally come for Lydon to step out on the turf at Lucas Oil Stadium and take center stage in front of the most influential group of people in the NFL. The stands were spattered with various members of the NFL brass, who casually looked on at the collection of players.

Seattle Seahawks head coach Jim Mora remarked, "These guys look up in the stands and there's about every head coach, administrator, general managers, presidents, scouts, ex-players, guys they've grown up watching on TV. There is some pressure."

That pressure seemed contagious among the burly group of linemen, although it didn't spread to Lydon. The moment he stepped out on that field, a complete calm settled over him.

"It was just like a game," said Lydon. "I completely forgot about my surroundings. When I play, I'm able to block out the crowd and just play football. As soon as I stepped on the field, the stands were basically empty. I just relaxed and I was ready to perform."

Lydon stretched out and pretty much kept to himself while the testing commenced. Other linemen began running the forty-yard dash and Lydon couldn't help but sneak a few glances their way. He kept a close eye on Baylor offensive tackle Jason Smith, who many believed could turn out to be the number one overall pick in the draft. Smith was staying loose by pacing back and forth and just so happened to walk past

Lydon. As Smith neared, Lydon seized the opportunity to share some words with one of the top-ranked players in the nation.

"So what do you think you're going to run?" Lydon haphazardly asked.

Smith turned to Lydon with a cocky look and said, "Faster than you motherfucker!"

The inevitable first-round pick then turned and strutted away. Lydon shook off the comment and began to pace back and forth, trying to stay as loose as he possibly could.

Some of the more portly linemen began registering times far from what Lydon expected to run. But there was no scoreboard posting the results. Only hand held watches revealed those times. The hands that held those watches belonged to scouts from every NFL team. Each team used their own scout's time as their official mark for each player. And almost every scout seemed to think his own watch could dictate the ebb and flow of time itself. Some players tried to peer over and ask the scouts about their times after they ran while others just turned and walked away.

After about a dozen linemen ran the forty, Lydon finally heard his name called over the loudspeaker. His time to shine had finally arrived! Now was his chance, a monumental chance to prove that he deserved to be recognized as one of the best athletes at the NFL Combine. He inhaled a deep breath of air and took his time lining up. Lydon bent down and made sure to perfect his stance. He positioned himself right on the starting line, then cocked his arm. He held it for a couple of seconds and took off.

Lydon exploded down the field covering leaps and bounds with every one of his long strides. It seemed like it only took a few blinks of the eye before Lydon had blown through the finish line. All the scouts depressed the buttons on their stopwatches as he sped by and quite a few brows immediately vaulted upwards. A few scouts turned and kept their eyes glued on Lydon while others scrambled to check that their times coincided with everyone else's. Although mere hundredths of a second separated most of those times, many of the scouts had clocked Lydon somewhere in the high 4.7's. Never before in the history of the NFL Combine had an offensive tackle ever run that fast! A few of the scouts even looked up and made eye contact with the coaches and GM's who sat in the stands. They stared at them with a look that seemed to say 'did you

125

see that?'

One of the scouts lipped Lydon's time to him as he walked by the impressed group. Lydon had no trouble making out the 4.77 on the man's lips. The official television time used by the NFL Network would later be announced at 4.89 even though teams generally use the time recorded by their own scouts. That television time was taken with a laser and was always very unforgiving. Those times were always bumped up regardless of who ran. For all intensive purposes, that time was simply something for the television audience to chew on.

Nevertheless, the laser time of 4.89 was the second fastest time ever registered by an offensive tackle in the history of the NFL Combine. When all the forty-yard dashes were completed, the next best television time by an offensive lineman that day was a 5.03. Lydon had registered a time that was .14 seconds better than any other lineman at the Combine. He was, by far, the fastest of the big men.

The day was far from over for Lydon. Once he was finished turning heads in the forty, he made his way over to the three-cone, also known as the L-Drill. As much emphasis as there is on the forty-yard dash, the three-cone is an equally important event.

Lydon did not waste any time showing that he had more than just linear speed. He weaved his way in and out of the cones and forced scouts to double check their times once again. Lydon's official three-cone time was announced at 7.06. The next best time registered by an offensive linemen at the Combine was a 7.35. In all the years of the NFL Combine, only one offensive tackle has ever posted a better time. Indianapolis Colts starting offensive tackle Ryan Diem registered a whopping 7.00 back in 2001. Other than Diem and Lydon, the next closest time in the three-cone for an offensive tackle was a 7.30 recorded by New England Patriots tackle Matt Light also back in 2001. Light turned out to be a second-round pick while Diem was drafted in the fourth-round and both were still playing in the NFL. In a matter of seconds, Lydon quickly found himself in some very good company.

As Lydon continued to stay loose, word of his incredible times started to reach the stands. If some of the people who looked on were not too familiar with Lydon Murtha, they were quickly learning how to pronounce his name. And the Seattle Seahawks contingent had an even better view.

"Five members of our staff are actually conducting position drills," Coach Mora explained. "I think that is another thing that's helpful in that they get to get up close and personal with those young men as they work on the field. They're with them behind the scenes a little bit. That's just a little added insight into the kids and how they compete, if they get nervous, and how they handle the pressure."

Lydon may have been nervous on the preceding days, but he handled the pressure with flying colors on the last and most important day. He continued to fly through his next drill, where he moved more like a tight end in the twenty-yard shuttle run. Many eyes continued to follow him over to the vertical jump where he rose up and leapt 35 inches off the ground. Only one other lineman was able to beat that mark by soaring a half-inch higher. Lydon's jump was also the third highest mark ever recorded by an offensive tackle at the NFL Combine.

The NFL Scouting Combine was created to get an in-depth look at some of the top prospects in the land. Record times often led to fruitful careers in the NFL. The first official NFL Scouting Combine took place in 1982, but it wasn't until four years later that the most memorable moment took place. At the 1986 NFL Combine inside the New Orleans Superdome, Bo Jackson was rumored to have recorded a 4.12 in the forty-yard dash. A few years later, Deion Sanders supposedly posted a time just below a 4.2. However, the technology and record-keeping may have not been as thorough back then. There was also no laser to record the times, yet they were still eye-popping numbers. While Lydon's time may have been a bit higher than Jackson's and Sanders', it was still astounding for someone of his stature.

"That's why we're here," said Green Bay Packers head coach Mike McCarthy. "We're here looking at all the college prospects. Our scouts have done a great job grading those players and fitting them in to the positions we think they could play."

Ironically, not all teams shared McCarthy's sentiment. At the start of the following season, nine NFL teams would begin play with a new head coach. Of those nine teams, not every coaching staff appeared to have the firmest grip on the future.

"At this point for the coaches, we spend a lot of time digging through schemes, systems, what we're going to be and what we're going to do," said first year St. Louis Rams head coach Steve Spagnuolo while at the Combine. "So we haven't made a lot of hard decisions on our roster right now, but that's forthcoming. And we all know free agency is right around the corner. We haven't made a lot of concrete decisions. Those will come later on. But we have done a lot of digging into the draft right now and hope when it's all said and done, we got a pretty good beat on it."

As loose of a grip as the Rams seemed to have on their future, Kenny had a firm grasp on the present. It was now his time to shine! Kenny stepped onto the turf inside Lucas Oil Stadium knowing just how important it was that he run well.

"Now, it's just business," Kenny said before he ran. "I'm hoping for that 4.3, that's what I've been pushing for. All my drills are good and my body feels good. That's all I've been thinking about and now I'm ready to go."

Watching Kenny warm up inside Lucas Oil Stadium, there was not the slightest indication that he had any injury whatsoever. However, if Kenny erred in some portion of an event, he was determined not to let that affect the rest of his performance.

"The Combine is here so I am going to take advantage of it and do everything I can," said Kenny. "If something don't go right, I gotta keep my head so I can do the next drill."

While Kenny loosened up his muscles, Brian scoured the audience for his newfound nemesis from the Jacksonville Jaguars. He was prepared to make good on his promise to call Terry McDonough just after Kenny showed the world his speed. Brian could not locate McDonough, but had seen him in passing on the preceding day. As Brian walked by, he noticed McDonough offer him a brief but peculiar look. Brian didn't antagonize the situation and simply went out about his business. Now, Brian's phone was fully charged and his fingers were waiting to tap dance on the buttons seconds after Kenny blazed up the turf.

Some players talked and laughed while they waited to run the forty, but not Kenny. He paced back and forth with his face sculpted into an impenetrable fortress of concentration. Kenny had that rare and unique quality that turned him into a player who transcended most others the moment he took the field.

Kenny waited while track stars like Darrius Heyward-Bey and known speedsters like Percy Harvin posted forty times in the low 4.3's. Finally, Kenny was announced and the spotlight now shined on the small, yet tough receiver from the University of South Carolina. He followed every bit of instruction he received at TEST as he took his time getting set for one of the most important moments of the draft season. Brian looked on with his heart racing probably much quicker than Kenny's. Kenny raised his arm and then took off out of his stance. As Kenny coasted across the field, there didn't seem to be much difference in his forty-yard dash and the other speedsters' who had gone before him. He crossed the finish line and Brian jumped up in the air knowing full well that Kenny had accomplished what he had set out to do.

Both Kenny and Brian immediately turned to search for someone who could verify a time. Kenny looked over at the collection of scouts who were whispering to each other. One of the scouts saw Kenny's curious eyes and told him '4.33'. Kenny immediately reacted and made no attempt to hide his joy.

"I knew I could do it," he rejoiced. "I knew I had it in me. It felt great to run that time. I was so excited!"

A few moments later, Brian received word of Kenny's time and also made no attempt to hide his emotion. Then, with hands shaking from excitement, Brian pulled out his phone and dialed the number of Jacksonville Jaguars director of player personnel, Terry McDonough. After one ring, the call went right to his voice mail. Once Brian heard the beep, he spoke in a very calm voice.

"Hello, this is Brian Martin from TEST Sports. I promised to call you after Kenny McKinley ran a 4.3 at the Combine. Well, I'm here in Indianapolis and that just happened. So if you would be so kind as to call me back, I'd love to talk to you about it."

Brian left his number and hung up the phone wearing a wide smile. However, it wasn't just because he was able to shove Kenny's time in the smug face of McDonough.

"People that know me well know that I'm not doing this for money," said Brian. "I love to help kids, I love to be around football and help kids get as far as they can go."

Brian's smile widened as Kenny continued to excel in each of the ensuing combine events. When the time came around for the positional drills, Kenny caught every pass that came his way. He ran smooth, crisp routes and showed why he had become South Carolina's all-time leading wide receiver. It was just another day at the office for Kenny. And much to his delight, his office was a football field.

By the end of the positional drills, Kenny's hamstrings started to tighten up. However, he gutted it out and finished each drill without showing the slightest wince, cringe or look of discomfort. Even though the Combine was very different from a football game, Kenny was still a gamer. That meant that he would not let up until the very end of the fourth quarter. And once the fourth quarter of Kenny's Combine experience had come to a close, the score was just where he hoped it would be.

CHAPTER FIFTEEN

Owning the Moment

Over the course of a lifetime, millions of moments come and go. More often than not, moments continue to have their way with people over and over again. But there are some extraordinary instances when someone is able to take control and own a moment. It is almost as if time stands still and it is that person who suddenly dictates exactly how a certain chain of events plays out.

Morgan Trent began training at TEST before the Christmas holidays. While other players were busy preparing for bowl games, Morgan was preparing for his future. And while other kids his age were partying through the holiday season, Morgan was starting to get himself in the best shape of his young life. He set out to do everything he could in order to make a solid showing at the NFL Combine. Everything he had done over the last few months was building towards this one moment in time.

The NFL had a specific regimen that players were forced to undergo at the Combine. It was designed to break the players down as much as possible before they would perform on such a grand stage. However, Morgan seemed to go through each moment on his own terms.

Upon arriving in Indianapolis, Morgan breezed through the orientation and his initial trip to the hospital. Then came the first round of interviews. After being at both the East-West Shrine Game and the Senior Bowl, Morgan knew what to expect. Still, he didn't feel as though that experience was preparation enough.

"My agent gave me a booklet with all the names of the people you want to know on all the teams," said Morgan. "The defensive coach, the secondary coach, the GM, the head coach and all that stuff. I studied that and learned all their names so I wasn't going in there blind and I knew who I was dealing with."

Morgan walked into each interview calm, cool and composed. Although there were many young players at the Combine, it was quite obvious that Morgan was no kid.

"Some of them can walk out and you're like this kid's got no idea what it's gonna take," said New York Jets head coach Rex Ryan. "But some of them, you just know that's your kind of person. Everyone at this level has ability. They really do. But I try to separate the guys that have the will, the will to prepare, to win, to do the little things."

From the time Morgan had played his last down of college football, he had done every little thing he could to prepare for this moment. He was hopeful that it would pay off, but it was difficult to figure out what was going through the mind of each scout, coach and general manager.

"You get a different vibe from each one," said Morgan. "A lot of guys are straight business like. Some want to talk a little and laugh a bit. I met with so many teams, you have no idea who likes you and who doesn't. There's no way to tell."

Coaches' personalities differ from one person to the next. There were some who were very impressive, some who seemed like they were in need of a pill, and a few who seemed to have a rather large chip on their shoulder. There were also a few whose good nature seemed to shine through every time they spoke. Cincinnati Bengals head coach Marvin Lewis was among those good-natured individuals. He had an ease about him that seemed to extend to his audience. Even the simple questions he asked the players had a soothing effect to them.

"I like to ask them to tell me about their typical Tuesday," said Lewis. "Through your college career, what did you do on a Tuesday or Wednesday?"

Through the first day of interviews, Morgan didn't waste any energy worrying about who liked him and who did not. On day two of his Combine experience, Morgan's swagger carried him into the intense medical portion of the Combine. As hoards of doctors played touchy feely with him, he tried to handle it as smoothly as possible.

"The medicals are outrageous," said Morgan. "You're on this table in front of everybody and they're all tugging at you. You got five or six people at a time tugging at you, going over x-rays. Does this hurt, does that hurt? You want to hide as much as you can from them. I think I did a good job with that. Overall, it went pretty smooth, but nobody would really understand it unless you see it. They're all talking in their little microphones, talking about you and stuff. It's like you're a piece of meat up there. That's what I felt like."

Morgan realized long before the Combine just how important the medical aspect was to professional football. As a freshman at Michigan, he was forced to undergo minor surgery on his thumb. The procedure went off without a hitch and Morgan had no troubles afterwards. About a year later, the University of Michigan Hospital phoned his home and left a message saying that he should call them immediately. It turned out that the hospital was just notified that Morgan was already a NFL prospect. In response to that, the doctors wanted to go back inside his thumb, take out the pin they had originally inserted and reinsert titanium.

Morgan refused, citing that such a procedure would be 'ridiculous'. One refusal was not enough to stop the doctors from calling. Morgan had to refuse on more than a few occasions. The persistent doctors kept pestering him. It was as if they had previously done enough to get an unproven freshman back out on the field. But now that the doctors knew the NFL was looking at Morgan, all of the sudden, they wanted to give him the absolute best medical attention money could buy.

At the Combine, the combination of medical evaluations, unending interviews and repetitive tests couldn't prevent Morgan from sleeping soundly once his head finally hit the pillow. But that didn't mean he enjoyed the 4:30 wake up calls.

"They make it so you really can't get a good sleep," said Morgan. "They want you to be tired without rest. It's the hardest job interview you'll ever go through. I don't know any other place or any other company that's going to give you four days of no sleeping, drug testing and all this stuff. But no other jobs are going to pay you $310,000 right out of college. You can't complain about it because you don't have to be here. It's a privilege."

By day three of Morgan's Combine experience, much of the city had emptied out. Media was no longer granted any access and a lot of the fanfare had died down. There were still autograph seekers trying to get Morgan to sign various items every time he left the players' hotel. Morgan never turned down a kid seeking an autograph regardless of how cold it may have been outside. However, these signature hounds were a different animal altogether.

They weren't fans simply looking for the John Hancock of one of their favorite players. They did not want a souvenir to take home and put in their scrapbook. They were two-bit hustlers looking to cash in on those signatures. Many of the people mulling around would ask players to sign a glossy white piece of paper. What the charlatans would then do is take that glossy paper and photocopy it onto hundreds of pictures of that player so that it looked like each one was individually signed. Then, they would attempt to sell the paraphernalia as an authentic item for an inflated price.

"I just ignore those jokers," said Morgan. "But I'll never walk away from a kid."

It was also no coincidence that Morgan had already perfected his signature. While he was at Michigan, trading card deals gave him plenty of practice. Yet, he had started perfecting the art of his signature years before his time in Ann Arbor.

"I signed my first autograph in high school, but I started practicing my autograph in the third grade," said Morgan. "I remember sitting in class and I would practice in my binder. It has to be pretty, but ugly at the same time. You want to have something sweet about it, but you don't want people to really know exactly what it says. It's just an art I guess."

Morgan left those scoundrels out in the cold and headed inside Lucas Oil Stadium where he began prepping for the bench press portion of the Combine. Typically, the cornerbacks did not put on a stunning display of strength at the Combine. The record for most reps by a cornerback was set in 2007 by Arkansas' Chris Houston who pushed 225 lbs off his chest 27 times. In the entire history of the Combine, four other cornerbacks were second to that mark, all of them registering 23 reps on the bench press. Morgan was hoping to leave them all in the dust.

Morgan was classified as a big corner, but it wasn't because of his strength. At 6-foot-1, he was considered very tall for a cornerback. At the Combine, most people expected him to be among the tallest of the cornerbacks. However, it isn't likely that many people expected to see such a physically developed Morgan Trent.

Wearing the number 54 on his blue Under Armour uniform, Morgan didn't look like an average cornerback. At a solid 193 pounds,

Morgan looked more like a powerful safety. He also didn't resemble the skinnier version of himself who produced only 11 reps on the bench press just three months ago. Hard work and dedication combined with top-notch training had enabled Morgan to get into phenomenal shape.

A lot of eyes followed Morgan as he warmed up and prepared to take his turn on the bench. With the same swagger that had carried him this far in life, Morgan finally got his chance to show off just how strong he had become.

The strength coach who was in charge of overseeing the bench press portion informed Morgan that it was his turn. Morgan laid down on the bench, took a couple of deep breaths and gripped the bar tightly. He then began pumping the weight up in the air. He heard the strength coach count 'one, two, three, four, five, six, seven.' Then, Morgan stopped and held the bar in the air when he felt the strength coach grab hold of his knee and scream for Morgan to 'stop and lock out.' What he had meant was that he didn't think Morgan was lifting the bar high enough in the air. Locking out meant extending his arms as high as he possibly could.

"I was going well," Morgan later acknowledged. "I thought I was doing it just like the other guys were. I was going at a real fast paced like I normally do. It's hard to lock out when you got long arms like I do, but I did what I could. The guy thought I had to get it a little more up there, so I did."

After holding the bar in the air for a few more seconds, the strength coach screamed for Morgan to continue. Morgan followed the instruction and, on each following rep, he made sure to push the bar up as high as he could. In fact, he locked out much higher than any player had done before him. All the while, the strength coach refused to remove his hand from Morgan's knee.

The distraction of the man holding Morgan's knee, the elongated pause after the seventh rep, and the insistence that Morgan lock out higher than everyone else caused Morgan's arms to shake when he reached number seventeen. But Morgan dug deep and summoned more strength. He let out an audible breath as he pressed his eighteenth rep up in the air and then looked as though he might be finished.

The other cornerbacks who looked on yelled out words of encouragement. Morgan reached deeper inside of himself and conjured up even more fight. Still holding Morgan's knee, the obnoxious strength coach counted out 'nineteen, twenty, twenty-one, twenty-two.' The bar got heavier with each rep and seemed to gain more weight as Morgan dropped it to his chest and tried to push up number twenty-three. His heart pounded, his muscles flexed and his eyes glared with determination. By now, all the other players were shouting loud exclamations urging Morgan to go on. The bar slowly moved upward and the strength coach hollered out, 'twenty-three.'

That would be the final time Morgan was able to push the weight in the air. And it was only after Morgan put the bar back on the rack did the strength coach finally remove his hand from Morgan's knee.

When Morgan stood up off the bench he smiled at the group of on-lookers who were now offering loud words of congratulations. He stepped away from the bench and didn't even bother to give the strength coach a look of scrutiny, although it may have been rightfully deserved. Had it not been for that distraction, Morgan might have still been pressing the weight. Yet, at the beginning of the draft season, there were not many people who would have predicted that Morgan Trent would be able to bench press 225 pounds 23 times.

"I'm proud of that," said Morgan. "I think I could have done a little better but, considering the circumstances, it wasn't too bad. I told all the scouts in the interviews I was going to do twenty-plus. I backed up what I said."

More important than staying true to his word, Morgan was able to own the moment. No matter how much the strength coach tried to take that moment away from Morgan, he couldn't. Morgan fought through the adversity and managed to shine brightly on one of the biggest stages of his life. And it wasn't just strength that enabled Morgan to accomplish such a feat. His heart, desire and confidence helped push that heavy weight up in the air. Morgan was already managing to stand out from the rest of the cornerbacks the same way he stood out from most other people in everyday life.

That afternoon, three other cornerbacks would go on to beat Morgan's mark of 23. Two players pressed the weight 24 times while Illinois' Vontae Davis posted a high of 25 reps. Still, Morgan ranked fifth among every cornerback who ever participated in the bench press at the NFL Scouting Combine. Of all the cornerbacks who ever came through the Combine, only four showed more strength than Morgan. And it is doubtful that any of them did so with a dramatic pause after their seventh rep and a hand gripping their knee throughout the entire ordeal.

Following the bench press, Morgan was allowed a bit of free time. He opted to spend that time in the suite Brian had rented out for the week inside the Indianapolis Convention Center. To keep all their players in the best possible condition, the TEST staff was available twenty-four hours a day. Former pros were on hand to help with any last minute preparations while massage therapists were available to help ease any of the players' tension. Brian personally helped make some last minute adjustments to each player's techniques. However, Morgan wasn't in need of any adjustments. He was ready.

Regardless of how the final day of Morgan's Combine experience would pan out, he'd be able to live the rest of his life without a shred of regret. So many people look back on their lives and long for the chance to relive days of the past. Morgan would not fall into such an unfortunate category.

"I'm going to sleep well tonight," Morgan said with a smile. "I've been dreaming about this for so long. I'm going to go out there and do what I can. My fiancée put it in her words. She said it's like taking a test. She knew when she was ready for a test in school. When you've studied and you're ready, there's nothing to worry about. I'm ready and I'm going to go out and do what I do. For three months, I've been preparing for this one day, for these few moments. I just want to go and do it. I can't imagine what it's going to feel like to reach my goal."

The next morning, nervousness did not accompany Morgan into Lucas Oil Stadium. The same thing could not be said at the Trent household back in Brighton, Michigan. The whole family gathered to watch live television coverage of the Combine while nervousness engulfed the room. Since Liz did not have the NFL Network at her place in California, she listened the whole time on the telephone as the family updated her on Morgan's every move. Her nervousness became audible every time she shouted a question through the phone. But nervousness was not uncommon among families of college football players.

Tina stated, "Braylon Edwards' dad told us during Morgan's redshirt year, 'Just enjoy this year. It's the last year it's going to be fun.' He was right. It's not enjoyable, you got fans criticizing, you're worrying about him and his injuries. It's just a lot of pressure as a parent."

Out in Indianapolis, the defensive backs were the last group scheduled to perform. Once that group had finished, so was the Combine. There was definitely a different feel now that the Combine was winding down. Some of the life seemed to be siphoned out of the city as the downtown area lost a bit of its hustle and bustle.

Morgan's final day in Indianapolis would begin with the forty-yard dash. He had practiced it so much over the last couple of months that it had become almost second nature. Other players nervously practiced their starts as their tension became quite apparent. That was not the case with Morgan. When his name was called, he walked up to the starting line with a confident swagger that signified he was both ready and able to own the next few moments of his life.

With great precision, Morgan set himself up to run some of the most telling strides of his life. Back in Brighton, none of the Trents were as calm.

"It was painful," said Tina. "We know all about Morgan's capabilities, but it just came down to this moment, this one day, this one opportunity."

All that worry quickly vanished as Morgan exploded and showed the entire world just how fast he actually was. He blew by the scouts and heard them utter his times as he came back around. One scout clocked Morgan at a 4.35 while he checked in on another stopwatch at a 4.38. But once again, the television times somehow differed from all the stopwatches down on the field. Notwithstanding the network's suspicious calculations, Morgan and the rest of the defensive backs sensed something different about the brand new turf at Lucas Oil Stadium.

"Because we were the last group running, the surface was really mushy," said Morgan. "You could tell it was run on a lot. It wasn't what I was running on in New Jersey. This is the first time anyone has ever ran there. It's a new place. The surface is brand new so you can't really compare times from this year to last year. It's a whole different field. The scouts know what the deal is, so that's what's important."

When the official times were posted on television, three players tied for first place with a 4.46 and Morgan was just behind them with a 4.47. He had proven not only that he was strong, but that he was also one of the fastest defensive backs at the Combine.

Morgan's brilliance did not end with the forty-yard dash. He went on to finish first in the sixty-yard shuttle, third in the twenty-yard shuttle, sixth in the broad jump and seventh in the vertical jump. All the while, his family tried to steal as many glimpses of him as they could in between commercial breaks. And Tina continued to worry that NFL Network analyst Deion Sanders might say something unfavorable about her son.

"Deion was trying to get Morgan to come and train with him at his place instead of TEST," said Tina. "Because Morgan didn't go there, I was afraid he might use that against Morgan and say something negative. But he had only very nice things to say about Morgan."

Perhaps even more impressive than Morgan's performance in the various Combine events was his performance in the positional drills. He impressed scouts with his fluidity and seemed to tackle every single drill with tremendous ease. And when Morgan finally stepped off the turf at Lucas Oil Stadium, he left nothing out on the field. Morgan was ready to leave Indianapolis.

A few hours later, Morgan boarded a plane that would take him back to New Jersey. He was looking forward to another plane ride on the following day, which would take him to Los Angeles to see the future Mrs. Trent. In the cramped confines of that coach section, Morgan was very much at ease.

"I was relieved," said Morgan. "It was the first time in a while that I could really relax. I sat back and played it all over in my head. I just enjoyed the moment. I sat there feeling real happy about what happened and how things went. I knew I did everything I could. And to know I did really well and helped myself, it was just a great feeling."

CHAPTER SIXTEEN

Frantz's Pro Day

For sixteen NFL scouts, the tepid Florida air was a pleasant change from the frigid Indianapolis chill that nipped at their flesh only a few days ago. On a sunny Thursday morning in Boca Raton, Florida, scouts from across the league assembled for Florida Atlantic's first ever Pro Day. Although there were more than a dozen players participating in the day's events, there was really only one player that the scouts came to see. It wasn't difficult to decipher who that player was. All anyone had to do to figure that out was keep an eye on the five-man crew from ESPN.

For the third straight day, that crew followed every step Frantz had taken. As Frantz readied himself for his biggest day of the draft season, that crew was no more than a couple steps behind him at all times. Even though it was essentially game time for Frantz, he didn't have a look of intensity etched across his face. Instead, Frantz wore a smile.

"This is one of the biggest days of my life," said Frantz. "So I'm just taking it all in and enjoying every single minute of it."

The day began with Frantz testing his strength on the bench press. The scouts crowded into the Florida Atlantic weight room as agents and spectators were ushered out by campus security. Those scouts huddled around the bench where Frantz had just warmed up, eager to see how many times he could push 225 pounds up into the air.

Still wearing that same vibrant smile, Frantz grabbed hold of the bar and quickly dropped it down to his chest. He began firing the weight up in the air, but started to fizzle out as he neared the twenty mark. Following his nineteenth rep, Frantz couldn't get the bar off his chest again.

There was a noticeable difference from the twenty-three reps Frantz had produced a little less than a week ago in New Jersey. But there were no camera crews following his every move at TEST. When he had repped out twenty-three times, there was also no semblance of a light-hearted smile on his face.

Next, the players moved outside to a small concrete area behind the gym. It was here that the players would be tested in the vertical jump. Brian immediately took one look at the setup and clamored, "This isn't even close to an official setup. The ground is slanted and the entire setup is wrong!"

It was a far cry from the meticulous way the vertical jumps were conducted at the NFL Combine. Nevertheless, Frantz showed no uneasiness and continued to walk around with that same smile pasted on his face. When his turn came around, he only cleansed his face of that smile for a few brief moments. He then leapt up in the air and reached as high as he could. After three similar attempts, Brian hustled over to see that the scouts had written down 27.5 inches. Embers of crimson immediately ignited on Brian's face.

"They're not even measuring it right," he fumed. "There's no way that can be official."

That measurement of 27.5 inches was also down from the 31 inches Frantz had jumped a week before right in front of Brian at TEST. Yet, as the players left that sloped area and headed over to the practice field, Frantz's smile remained intact. The camera crew inched closer to Frantz and filmed every pace he took. The scouts walked that same path in the midst of conditions that were a stark contrast from those inside Lucas Oil Stadium.

Trade winds whipped in from the east and forced quite a few palms to depart from the surrounding trees. As the players began to stretch out and prepare to run the most crucial forty yards of their lives, they would have to do so amidst some unfavorable conditions. However, that was nothing new for Frantz. Winds of adversity had gusted through his life since the time he was born.

With only a few subtle memories of a father to cling to, Frantz was forced to walk through life with forceful gales of misfortune constantly pushing him around. Even as he stepped onto the Florida Atlantic practice field, he still had no father looking on. There was no one of the same lineage to provide him with an encouraging word. There was no mentor basking in the glow that was Frantz Joseph. There was only a 20 mph breeze attempting to hinder the most telling five seconds of his life.

Leading up to this moment, it seemed as though the winds of change were finally starting to blow in Frantz's direction. A once in a lifetime opportunity had finally breezed into his world. That opportunity could mean a new way of life for both Frantz and his mother. All the poverty, struggle, and utter despair they were forced to endure could become a distant memory with a strong showing in front of this band of NFL scouts. But staying true to the course that his life had taken, Frantz would have to overcome one more blast of adversity.

Just a few days before, these same scouts watched other top college athletes put their skills on display in the comfort of a peaceful dome in Indianapolis. Frantz was uninvited to such peaceful conditions. Instead, he now faced a swirling wind that seemed to be trying to push him back to the crime-infested streets where he had spent most of his life.

Frantz began to stretch out, yet he was gracious enough to answer a few questions from the ESPN crew. He even took a moment to joke with a few of the scouts. While he took his time prepping for his forty, an interested bystander took notice of his demeanor.

Cornerback Derrick Roberson had just recently signed a contract with the Minnesota Vikings and was hoping to finally make an active roster after spending two years on a couple of different NFL practice squads. Roberson, a Broward county native, previously trained at TEST and made it to the NFL on the laurels of his impressive Pro Day numbers.

Roberson knew the importance of these next few moments and said with grave concern, "Frantz looks too relaxed. NFL scouts don't want to see you smiling. At my Pro Day, I had to psyche myself up and get even more intense. Scouts don't want to see all those smiles."

Perhaps the swirling winds were not powerful enough to carry those sage words into Frantz's ear. He knelt down and loaded up for his forty, still sporting a carefree grin. Frantz took his time setting himself up in that tight position and then raised his arm. Then, in an instant, he popped out of his stance and was off. As he sprinted towards the finish line, the wind maintained its pace. He pushed himself through that oppressive air and let out a deep grunt as he passed the finish line.

Standing alongside the row of scouts, Brian frowned when he

looked down and saw a 4.83 on one of their stopwatches. Frantz walked away from that first attempt without even inquiring about his time. Even as he caught his breath, he maintained a firm hold on his smile.

Frantz had one more opportunity to better that time, but his next attempt played out in the exact same fashion. While the bulk of his competition in the upcoming draft registered higher times at the NFL Combine, Frantz had to settle for a 4.83 while battling through the unforgiving Floridian wind. He followed up that performance with mediocre times in both the three-cone and the shuttle run. All the while, ESPN had numerous shots of a smiling Frantz Joseph.

There were a few moments during that day when Frantz did wipe away his smile. One of those moments came when he heard a familiar question that was uttered by more than one scout.

"Have you ever had any off-the-field problems we should know about?"

"I failed a drug test for marijuana the year I sat out because of my transfer," said Frantz.

"When was that?" asked the scout.

"That was in 05," said Frantz. "But I've been tested numerous times since then and I've never failed another drug test."

Frantz was also asked about the incident that happened a year later in which he was arrested and charged with misdemeanor possession of marijuana.

"I was young and I made a mistake," Frantz confessed. "I know it was wrong, but that's all part of the past now."

Once Florida Atlantic's Pro Day concluded, Frantz received some congratulations from those in attendance. He heard some encouraging words from the scouts, but he didn't post the kind of numbers that would've silenced the critics who questioned his linear speed. Fortunately for Frantz, not everyone in the NFL places that much stock in combine numbers.

While at the NFL Combine a few days earlier, Minnesota Vikings head coach Brad Childress referred to the Combine as 'underwear football'. Childress then went on to downplay the significance of the Combine.

"We know that the résumé is really what the players put on tape," Childress stated.

Such thinking would truly benefit Frantz since his game film was far more impressive than his Pro Day numbers.

Following the Pro Day, the ESPN crew finally gave Frantz a few hours of peace. They did, however, plant themselves in his mother's apartment later that night for an extensive interview with her and Frantz. Upon entering his mother's cramped apartment, Frantz immediately felt the glare of the bright lights that were set up all over the room. Frantz wore his familiar smile into the living room and tip-toed past the hoards of extension cords that now slithered across the floor.

The room, which was more or less a small shrine devoted to Frantz, now looked more like a makeshift studio. Behind all the bright lights, Frantz's high school jersey still hung from the wall alongside framed newspaper articles and plenty of pictures that captured his journey from boy to man. Frantz ordered all of his family on hand, which now totaled eight, into the bedroom so he could begin the interview. His sister, mother, cousins and aunt all disappeared so that Frantz could have some one-on-one time with the entire nation.

Under the bright lights which bred beads of perspiration across Frantz's brow, a man in a suit started to ask questions which became more personal by the moment. He asked Frantz about all of the adversity he faced growing up. He didn't leave out Frantz's absentee father, the nights Frantz spent without electricity, the mornings he awoke without running water or the countless times he tried to fall asleep on an empty stomach. Frantz answered each question sincerely and without hesitation.

It was almost as if the man in the suit was trying to strike a soft spot within Frantz. But what the man didn't seem to understand was that Frantz had lived through all that adversity and experienced the harsh realities that came with each answer. Compared to living through that adversity, talking about it was not a difficult task.

"I have no problem talking about my past," Frantz stated. "I'm not embarrassed of what I went through nor am I ashamed of who I am. Everything I went through made me who I am. So why should I have a problem talking about it?"

Then came the question Frantz had already heard far too many times.

"When do you think you'll be drafted?"

Frantz grinned and went on to say, "I have been hearing everything from the third round on."

Frantz did an excellent job of answering question after question and finally ushered his mother out of the bedroom so that she could join him for the final part of the interview. She sat down with a bit of hesitance and offered a few words of broken English to her son. Frantz answered her back in their native Haitian tongue and tried to make her feel more at ease. He sat down next to her, placed his arm around her and kissed her on the cheek. He remained seated next to her with a gentle demeanor that obviously eased a bit of her apprehension. Moments later, the questions resumed.

The man in the suit began firing questions at Marie, questions that were very similar to the ones he asked Frantz. Marie's answers were rather concise and Frantz frequently intervened to better explain the

146

questions in their own dialect. She really didn't understand the exact details of Pro Day or how important it was for Frantz to run a good forty. And when asked how it would make her feel if Frantz got drafted, she simply replied, "I would feel good."

As much as the man in the suit wanted to make it seem as though a future in the NFL should have meant everything to Frantz and his mother, he couldn't. No matter what questions he asked, she retained the same look in her eyes. And no matter how much he tried to bring drops of moisture to those eyes, he couldn't. That is because her eyes were full of pride. In her eyes, Frantz was already a champion. He had already gone above and beyond the duties of a son. The possibility of cashing a lucrative NFL paycheck really wasn't of the utmost importance to either of them. The family had made it to this point wearing smiles that were not bought by financial security. It may sound a bit cliché, but there are some things money cannot buy. One of those things was the look of pride that swept across Marie's face every time she spoke about her son.

When asked what Frantz meant to her, she proudly stated, "He is everything to me. He is my friend, he is my son, he is my husband. There is nothing we can't share with each other."

Part of the reason why Frantz smiled throughout that entire day was because he was already a success. Life with or without football would go on for Frantz Joseph. If football did not work out, Frantz was confident that he could tackle the business world with not one, but two college degrees. Yet, football was still close to his heart and he believed he had the ability to make it in the NFL.

"All I want is a chance to get into somebody's camp," Frantz said in a very calm voice. "I don't even care if I get drafted. I know if I get a chance, I'll make it. All I want is a chance."

Frantz was grateful for the opportunity to share his story with the entire country on national television. He was also thankful that the cameras were finally turned off after three straight days of shooting. Now, he could take a break from the draft season and return to being a normal twenty-two year old. Following the interview, he tapped away on his Blackberry sending text messages en route to meet up with some friends he hadn't seen since he left for New Jersey. Frantz would go on to spend the rest of that night free from the worry of forty times, draft status and NFL scouts.

147

CHAPTER SEVENTEEN

Getting in Touch

Following the Combine, teams didn't waste any time getting in touch with Kenny. No sooner than he was back in South Carolina, he received calls from the New England Patriots and the Denver Broncos requesting private workouts. They had already seen Kenny at the Senior Bowl and the NFL Combine, but now they wanted to take a closer look.

"I got those calls and I was like man it's so early," said Kenny. "I wasn't expecting to get any workouts until after my Pro Day. But that shows they like me and they're interested."

Kenny's Pro Day wouldn't take place until a full month after the NFL Combine, however it looked as though he was going to be busy until that time. The New England Patriots were the first team to come through Columbia and see Kenny in person. The Patriots sent brand new wide receivers coach Chad O'Shea down to Gamecock country. When he spoke with Kenny, his interest seemed very high.

"He said they really liked how well I did at the Combine," said Kenny. "They didn't know I could run that good and things like that. He asked if I was running the forty and stuff at Pro Day. I told him no and he said I didn't need to because I did real good at the Combine. We watched film for about an hour and then I went out and gave him a show. I know it will just keep getting my status higher and higher."

The show Kenny spoke of consisted of some positional drills, route running and pass catching. O'Shea left Kenny with a feeling of enthusiasm, but Kenny would have to shake off that feeling and do the whole thing over again. The Denver Broncos were next up to visit.

The Broncos also had a brand new wide receivers coach in Adam Gase. The Broncos had done a bit of an overhaul in the coaching department, recently hiring former New England Patriots offensive coordinator Josh McDaniels as the team's new head coach. Ironically, those two teams visited Kenny one right after the other. Gase came down to Columbia with the presumable intention of running Kenny through a gamut of workouts. But their first interaction did not take place on the football field.

"It was different," said Kenny. "We watched film for a few hours. Then, he went and talked to my coach for about an hour. After that, we went and worked out on the field for about forty-five minutes."

Once that workout was over, Gase was gone and Kenny was left with another impression of where he might spend his future. Yet, the luster of playing for New England seemed to fascinate him. The Patriots had won three Super Bowls since 2001 and narrowly missed out on a fourth in 2007, which would have capped off an undefeated season. Not many people would dispute the notion that the Patriots were the team of the decade.

"They're looking for a receiver just like me," Kenny said in an excited tone. "They already got Randy Moss and they got Wes Welker, so they need another receiver that can bring speed on offense and can also play the slot position. I think that's why I'm really high on their board."

Kenny also knew about Denver's coaching ties with New England and did not hesitate to mention that when he spoke about the Broncos.

"The head coach from Denver just came from New England so he's been on me for more than a minute. I think Denver likes me also because they run the same offense as New England. But they already have a lot of receivers on the depth chart so I don't know why they have so much of an interest in me. But they seem to really like me. I'm just going to perform for whoever picks me up."

Meanwhile, down in Florida, Frantz's phone seemed to be ringing off the hook. But it wasn't any NFL teams on the other end. Many times, it was people Frantz barely even knew. His ESPN special had not yet aired, but word of its filming had spread throughout his hometown. Despite the fact that the NFL Draft was still more than six weeks away, people were already starting to treat Frantz like he was a professional football player.

"All of the sudden, everybody wants my number," said Frantz. "I'm wondering why everyone didn't want my number when I was in college? I guess people change when you're doing things. I even had a guy and a girl come up to me and tell me they were my cousins. People are just trying to get into my life like they knew me forever."

It seemed no matter where Frantz went, someone pretended to know him.

"Even in the grocery store, people are coming up and telling me that they know I'm going to get drafted," said Frantz. "Guys I have never seen before in my life know my first and last name. They're asking me where are their tickets?"

Members of the opposite sex also took more notice of Frantz in what is perhaps one of the best and worst aspects of being famous.

"Now, every girl wants to be my girlfriend," said Frantz. "Every girl wants to get next to me and spend every minute of the day with me. They weren't nearly as aggressive before."

Even when Frantz turned off his phone and locked himself inside his apartment, he still could not get a moment of peace.

"Every time I log on to my Facebook, I get instant messages from people I've never seen in my life," said Frantz. "And they're talking to me like we've known each other for years. I'm getting friend requests from people I might have seen around school, but have never said a word to me. All of the sudden, they want to be my friend."

Frantz would have to keep himself available in the event that a NFL team wanted to bring him in for a private workout. Each team had the same contact number that now seemed to be in the hands of quite a few strangers. But once the draft season was over, Frantz promised to keep those strangers at a distance.

"After the draft, they're not going to be able to find me," said Frantz. "I'm going to keep myself away from those people. I don't need to be around the bad influences, the distractions and things of that nature. I'm just going to stay close to my family. I changed my number after college and it looks like I'm going to have to do it again. And I might just have to log off Facebook for good and call it quits."

At night, while Frantz would wait for NFL teams to call, he usually kicked back and watched a rundown of the day in sports. With March Madness coming up, Frantz was particularly excited for the final month of college basketball. A former standout basketball player in high school,

Frantz still had a tremendous love for the game.

Intertwined with coverage of college basketball would be random updates on the NFL Draft. Supposed draft experts chimed in with their thoughts on who would be the most sought-after picks on Draft Day. When it came time to talk about the linebackers, Frantz's name was rarely mentioned. However, Frantz was oblivious to that reality.

"When I watch Sports Center, I don't even turn the volume up," said Frantz. "I just watch it for the highlights."

Far away from Fort Lauderdale, football was always a permanent fixture on television for the people of Nebraska. Similar to South Carolina, there is no professional football team in the Cornhusker state. That only brightens the spotlight that shines on college football in the city of Lincoln.

During this particular time of year, each college team is allowed fifteen practice sessions in what has become known as Spring Practice. While most colleges have a few media outlets covering each practice, the local press takes it to a whole new level in Lincoln.

"The first day of spring practice, there were twenty-two cameras shooting the pre-practice," said Sean Callahan, beat writer and publisher of HuskersIllustrated.com of the Yahoo Sports network. "That's how many different media outlets were there. You probably don't get that many for NFL teams. Every day, there's thirty to forty reporters at practice. It's a very competitive, intense football culture. Every little thing around Nebraska football is a big thing. It's like covering a pro team."

That also meant there would be plenty of press coverage for Nebraska's Pro Day. Nevertheless, Lydon wasn't too concerned with the publicity or even the actual Pro Day itself. After performing so well at the NFL Combine, Lydon was simply going to go through a round of positional drills in what he believed was going to make for an easy afternoon.

"Everyone's always told me that Pro Day isn't that bad," said Lydon. "They just run you through some stuff and they're not going to kill you. It's supposed to be like a quick fifteen minutes. The scouts work out all the players and usually just run them through the same drills that they did at the Combine."

Scouts from twenty-eight different NFL teams were in attendance, but only two coaches made the trip up for Nebraska's Pro Day. Coincidentally, both of those men were offensive line coaches. First year Miami Dolphins offensive line coach Dave DeGuglielmo and Carolina Panthers offensive line coach David Magazu were sent to Lincoln with an ostensible purpose in mind. Yet, there was not a large group of offensive linemen to evaluate. There were only two; Lydon and fellow Cornhusker Matt Slauson. Since both of them had participated in the NFL Combine, there wasn't much too see other than a quick run-through of some positional drills.

Whether it was by design or request, Lydon and Matt were the first positional group to perform. Those drills went as expected. When they were finished, the scouts moved on to the next positional group. Lydon and Matt started to walk off the field, but stopped when they heard the voice of Magazu.

"All right guys, come on down the other end of the field. We got some more stuff for you to do."

Lydon's afternoon was about to get a lot longer.

"I thought we were done, but that's when the workout really began," said Lydon. "They had us doing everything. We were blocking, pulling, doing wave drills and running through bags. It was just non-stop. After about ten minutes went by, we were pretty tired and we didn't have one break. There was only two linemen so if I'm not going, I'm holding the bag for Matt. They worked us to the bone. We started first and by the time we were done, everyone was already off the field. They went through every single position by the time we were done. We were working straight for like forty minutes. Those workouts are supposed to only last fifteen minutes."

By the time Lydon was finished, he was exhausted. He was also the last Nebraska player to leave the field.

"It was one of the harder experiences I've had in terms of straight endurance," said Lydon. "We probably had about four breaks for about twenty seconds each. It was just enough to swig a water bottle and get back. It was very, very intense. The other players are not even breaking a sweat and we can barely even stand. My legs burned more than they ever did after a game. Matt said the same thing. It was a very tough experience. It was also kind of a shock. Towards the end, we were both really tired and we were stumbling a bit on some foot drills. Otherwise, I think I did really,

really well."

It seemed as though the coaches had a purpose for putting Lydon and Matt through such a strenuous workout. However, there was no way to tell.

"After the workout, the coaches just left," said Lydon. "They had planes to catch. They just said 'good job and we look forward to talking to you.' And the scouts that were there don't really talk to you that much."

By the time Lydon left the facilities, there was no sign of the large media contingent that usually swarmed the Nebraska players on a daily basis. But Lydon never objected to an interview. In return, the media was always glad to exchange a few pleasantries with him.

"Lydon's a fun guy," said Callahan. "He's always had one of the best personalities and was always one of the team jokesters. When Bill Callahan was the coach, he could do a great Callahan impersonation. It was scary how good it was. He was always the guy that would get up in front of the team and pretend he was the coach giving a speech, just goofing around."

Keeping consistent with his unique personality, Lydon walked over to his car, which he had dubbed 'Black Beauty'. It was a 1989 Oldsmobile that he had spray painted black. Across the back window was a bumper sticker that read, 'Guns don't kill people, people kill people.' Driving home in that car, which he had only paid a few hundred dollars for, Lydon hardly looked like a guy who was on the verge of making hundreds of thousands of dollars, perhaps even millions.

He pulled up outside his small apartment which was not located in one of Lincoln's most affluent neighborhoods. He parked next to the new fully-loaded red pickup truck which his wife, Tasha, used on a daily basis. Even though none of his neighbors addressed him as he walked up to his apartment, almost everyone in Lincoln knew who he was.

"From a player's standpoint, everybody knows who you are," said Callahan. "When they go around town, people pretty much know who these guys are. It's a good thing and it could be a bad thing because a lot of times, these guys may not have that much of a private life."

Less than a year before the Combine, Lydon saw the unfortunate side of being so recognizable. Only two days after he and Tasha had purchased their new truck, his private life was invaded.

"I got called down to the stadium because some guys from the NCAA wanted to have a sit-down with me," Lydon explained.

Upon Lydon's arrival, representatives from the NCAA did not greet him in the most welcoming tone. Instead, they immediately started grilling him in voices that were both condescending and accusatory.

As soon as Lydon took a seat, one of the men barked out, "I want to know your income and how much you have saved up in the bank!"

A bit taken back, Lydon replied, "Whoa, what are you talking about?"

"We need to know all the details of your current financial situation."

"I don't need to tell you any of that," Lydon returned.

"Whose truck is that?"

"The red truck?" Lydon asked.

"Yeah."

"It belongs to me and my girlfriend."

"Is it registered in your name?"

"No, it's in my girlfriend's name."

"Well did you just meet this girl?"

"No."

"Is she just doing this as a benefit for you?"

"She's my fiancée," Lydon said with a bit of a chuckle. "I've been with her for seven years. And how did you even know I got a new truck?"

"Do you honestly want to know?"

"Well, yeah," Lydon answered.

"A parking enforcement person saw you get out of the truck so they called the NCAA. But that's not important. What's important is that you can't afford that truck. So you need to bring us in the title, a copy of your payment and any receipts you have involving that truck."

"I don't have to bring you anything," Lydon responded. "I already told you, it's not my truck, it's my girlfriend's."

Apparently, the NCAA swooped into Lincoln with hopes of finding some unscrupulous evidence linking the university to the purchase of Lydon's truck. But Lydon wouldn't even entreat them with more than a few moments of conversation. He simply got up and walked out of the room.

"They couldn't do anything to me," said Lydon. "So I just got up and left. I mean who does that anyway? We're in like a fish pool here in Nebraska. We're the pro team, but we can't get away with anything."

The incident also darkened Lydon's already unfavorable opinion of the NCAA.

"They say they are out to protect the athlete, but it's almost like they're out to get you," said Lydon. "For some reason, it feels like that. They could have sat me down and said, 'listen, we know you have a nice truck. We just want to make sure it's legal and it's not going to hurt you or your team in the future. Just tell us how you got it and everything like that.' But the way they did everything pissed me off. Tasha and I did everything legit. We took out a loan for it, we traded in her car and we're making a hefty payment. For them to even accuse me, it's just pathetic."

Such an incident came with the territory of being a Nebraska football player. From the time a high school athlete commits to the university, he is instantly thrust into the spotlight.

"When there is a recruit that commits to Nebraska, every radio show is interviewing the recruit," said Callahan. "It's on the local news that night. It's pretty unique in that every little aspect is balled up into a big deal. Nebraska football is 365 days a year around here."

For many teenagers, the initial experience of becoming a Nebraska football player is often a bit overwhelming.

"We're treated like kings here," said Lydon. "For our meals, we can eat whatever we want. If we want steak and lobster every day of the week, it's available. And we can eat as much of it as we want! We have player lounges all over the facilities. There are 65-inch televisions on the wall, video games, pool tables, everything you could imagine. But some kids still get spoiled. Suddenly, the TV's could be bigger and the facilities could be better. It's crazy because we have the best of the best here."

Despite all those amenities, the players were still expected to comply with certain team regulations. For example, no player was permitted in any bar on O Street. O Street is the main drag that runs through the center of Lincoln. O Street is also littered with numerous bars, which are usually packed with college students. According to team policy, any player caught inside one of those bars is automatically suspended for two games. Lydon rarely ever drank alcohol, but he could attest to the trouble that exists on O

Street.

"There always seems to be a fight in one of those bars," said Lydon. "One time I was in one and some little shit comes up to me and tells me I suck and so does our team. He stood right in front of me like he wanted to fight. Now, if I had hit the kid, there's a good chance I would have put him in the hospital. So I just turned around and walked away. When any of the players go out to a bar, it's always a small place far away from O Street. But I really don't go out and party. I don't put myself in that position. I'm always with my wife so we pretty much just hang out."

Very soon, Lydon was hoping to find himself far away from O Street and far away from Lincoln altogether. After a record-setting day at the NFL Combine, he was hopeful that he and Tasha would soon find a new home somewhere across the country.

"I'm anxious," said Lydon. "Before I know it, I'll be in rookie mini-camp. I'm anxious to see where I'm going. It's kind of like a huge lottery. That's the biggest part of this next month and a half. But I don't dislike any team. No team is going to draft me if they don't see me fitting into their offense. So whatever team drafts me will be the right one. It will be a good match. I think about the city and not just in terms of football. There's big decisions to make all around. Am I going to go rent an apartment, a condo, or am I going to buy a place? All kinds of stuff flows into my head."

Lydon would have plenty of time to ponder the future now that the NFL Combine and his Pro Day were behind him. Now, he was forced to play a new game. For Lydon, the waiting game had begun. All he could do now was sit back and wait; wait for teams to contact him, wait for the possibility of a private workout, and wait for someone else to decide exactly where he would call home in just a few short months.

CHAPTER EIGHTEEN

Back to Michigan

Following the NFL Combine, the ringer on Morgan's phone was receiving quite a workout. Morgan always showed traces of a smile when answering congratulatory calls from family and friends. But he would distort that look into one of disdain when some unfamiliar voices crept into his ear.

"Morgan, great job at the Combine," a stranger squawked in the early hours of one March morning.

"Who's this?" Morgan replied after being shaken from a deep slumber.

"I'm your cousin from Detroit. I just found out we were related and I wanted to call and catch up with you."

Morgan didn't give the caller a chance to elaborate. He simply hung up the phone and refused to hear any more preposterous details. Morgan also responded in the same fashion to the slew of reporters who continued to ring his phone.

"These are the same reporters who talked all kinds of trash on me all through the season," Morgan stated. "Now, after the Combine, they all want to be my best friend. But I don't need to see my name in the newspapers. Some guys love it, but that's not important to me. I don't even read the stuff they write. I'm just not someone whose hungry for fame."

That same morning, Morgan made another startling discovery when he turned on his computer. Apparently, someone usurped his identity and created an entire myspace page pawning himself off as Morgan Trent. The imposter downloaded pictures of Morgan off the internet and pretended to be him. When Morgan came to the entry under personal interests, he chuckled as he read 'FOOTBALL BABY'. Before Morgan could read more about his bogus personality, his phone rang again. This time, it was the balding man who first bothered Morgan on the sidelines during the East-West Shrine practice. The balding man, who claimed to be a financial planner, repeated his similar sales pitch.

"Morgan, I got a great financial plan that would be just right for you."

As soon as Morgan realized who the man was, he swiftly hung up the phone and professed, "That's it. As soon as the draft is over, I'm changing my number!"

Morgan could not change his phone number just yet because his agent told him to expect calls from various teams requesting private workouts. Morgan had already spoken with every team at the Shrine game, the Senior Bowl and the NFL Combine. After taking part in so many conversations, it was tough to make an accurate guess on where he might wind up.

"For some reason, I keep thinking Oakland," said Morgan. "Their coaches said they really like big corners and can't stand little guys in the secondary. I got a good vibe from them."

To give further credence to Morgan's hunch, he inadvertently bumped into a person while purchasing some take-out on the previous day. As Morgan excused himself, he glanced over and noticed the man was wearing an Oakland Raiders jacket.

For now, Morgan envisioned the possibilities of playing for the Oakland Raiders. He could seem himself decked out in black and silver. He could also envision finding a nice, quiet home on the coast. Being from California, Morgan grinned at the thought of returning to his home state. He pictured himself and Liz sitting out by their pool in the backyard of a home topped with a terracotta roof. Before Morgan's daydream could go on any longer, his phone rang once more. He looked down and sighed when he saw that the call came from an unknown number. Reluctantly, he said hello in an unenthusiastic voice.

"Morgan, this is Coach Lopez from the St. Louis Rams."

Morgan immediately perked up and said, "Good afternoon, sir. How are you?"

"Great, I wanted to come down and meet with you."

"Sure thing, Coach. My Pro Day is tomorrow," Morgan informed him.

"I don't care about the Pro Day. I don't need to see you do anything there. I've seen all I need and I know you can play. I want to come down there, watch some film and spend some time with you. I'll call you later and we can work out the details."

When Morgan hung up the phone, he had a tentative meeting scheduled with St. Louis Rams defensive backs coach Clayton Lopez. The meeting would take place the next morning at the University of Michigan sometime before Morgan was scheduled to begin his Pro Day.

Morgan now began to imagine the possibilities of making a new life in St. Louis. He had never been to St. Louis, but it wasn't that far from Michigan. However, it couldn't be nearly as cold there as it was in Michigan. It wasn't quite California, but Morgan began to picture what it would be like wearing a Rams uniform. He thought about the large arch that made the city famous. He remembered watching the Rams win Super Bowl XXXIV, but also recalled how poorly they had fared during the previous season.

Thoughts of St. Louis would continue to fill Morgan's head for the remainder of the day. Even as he used his credit card to buy lunch, he thought how he could help a struggling team rise out of the basement in the NFC Western Conference. Morgan then took his receipt and jammed it into his pocket next to a bunch of other similar slips. Being as though he was currently unemployed, that was his only means of paying for just about everything. But, one day very soon, Morgan was hoping to open a new bank account and fill it with more money than he had ever seen. Nevertheless, Morgan didn't plan to buy any particular item once those funds were transferred to his name. Some players had already picked out which cars, houses and other play toys they would buy before they made a single dollar. Morgan, on the other hand, didn't fancy all those flashy items. He had other ideas of how he would spend some of his first paycheck.

"I want to help out Liz's family," Morgan said with conviction. "There's five of them living in a one bedroom apartment in LA. It doesn't have to be anything extravagant, but I just want to get them somewhere so they have more room to live. I also want my brother and his family to come with me wherever I go. Aside from paying off my wedding, there's no one particular thing I really want."

The future was right around the corner for Morgan, but there was still some idle time before that future would be revealed. For now, Morgan was stuck half a country away from Liz. And even though Liz was many miles away, her thoughts were with Morgan. She had stayed up almost the entire night before his Pro Day so that she would be able to sleep through the morning and not have to worry about how Morgan was faring.

"I get so nervous," Liz admitted. "I don't know too much, but I know what happens in the end. I never dated anyone like this. So for me, I don't enjoy the game. I feel so nervous and anxious at every one of Morgan's games. It's the same thing with his Pro Day. I just want it to be over because there is so much at stake."

That morning, Morgan awoke early and still had not received a call from Coach Lopez to finalize their meeting. So instead of waiting for that call, Morgan took the initiative and dialed Coach Lopez's number. The coach seemed a little flustered when he answered Morgan's call.

Lopez finally collected himself and told Morgan, "I still want to meet with you and we still like you, it's just that a mandatory meeting came up and I can't be there today."

Suddenly, Morgan's thoughts of building a home in St. Louis halted their construction. Maybe playing for a last place team wasn't such a good idea. Perhaps Missouri got a little too cold in the winter. And there was a chance that another uniform might fit him even better. In the blink of an eye, St. Louis suddenly seemed that much farther away.

Morgan offered Coach Lopez a few pleasantries before he hung up and then sighed as he told himself, "You can't stress over what you can't control."

Morgan quickly shifted his focus from living in St. Louis to having an excellent Pro Day. In a few short hours, Morgan would be on display in front of plenty of NFL scouts and he could see himself wearing a wide variety of NFL jerseys in the future.

That morning, frigid winds chilled the Michigan air. To combat those wintry blasts, bundles of clothes layered the bodies of those who traversed the Michigan campus. Most of those layers were colored with blue and maize as many showed their support for the fabled university.

In the midst of that quiet March day, Michigan Stadium stood tall without a single soul sitting in the stands. To the casual observer, it was just another football stadium. But to anyone with even a shred of football knowledge, 'The Big House' was one of the most storied places in the history of college football. Even on such a tranquil March day, the stadium screamed tradition.

The Big House opened in 1927 and, since that time, history has been built year after year. Some of the greatest players in the history of the game did battle on that very field. It was almost as if the energy from those ghosts engulfed the campus. There are a few select places in this country where a sports fan can stand in awe and feel their jaw drop from the mere sight of a structure. The Big House is among those illustrious structures for there may not be a more revered place to play a game of college football in the entire country. But Michigan's Pro Day would not take place on the same field where so many great athletes once played. The day's events would take place indoors.

Michigan's field house was a lot newer than the Big House and it was impressive for different reasons. The facilities were among the nation's best with a grandiose weight room and an indoor field that was flawless. It was here that Michigan's top seniors would perform in front of a host of NFL scouts. Having performed so well at the NFL Combine, Morgan would only join those players toward the latter part of the Pro Day.

While the other players warmed up, Morgan strode out onto the field and offered some hellos to those in attendance. He had a noticeable swagger that caught the eye of almost every spectator. But Morgan's gait was interrupted when he heard a voice that was very new to him.

"Morgan, I'm Ron Milus, secondary coach from the Carolina Panthers," the man said as he extended his hand.

Morgan turned and introduced himself with a firm shake of the hand before Milus continued, "That's our GM over there."

Morgan shifted his eyes over to Carolina Panthers general manager Marty Hurney, who already had his sights aimed at Morgan. As Morgan nodded, Milus spoke in a firm voice.

"We're only here today for one reason, Morgan."

Little did Morgan know, less than twenty-four hours ago, the Panthers had cut one of their starting cornerbacks. Morgan was also unaware of the fact that each of Carolina's cornerbacks measured in at 6-foot or taller. Evidently, the Panthers were a team that preferred taller corners. There weren't many corners in the draft who were taller than Morgan. With Carolina owning the 27th pick in the second round, a strong performance by Morgan could significantly help his chances of hearing his name called on the first day of the NFL Draft.

Pro Day commenced with the other Michigan players going through a gauntlet of various drills. All the while, Milus remained right next to Morgan. The two talked about everything from life as a Wolverine to various cover schemes in the NFL.

Morgan enjoyed being in his company and would later say, "I'd really like to play for him. I like his coaching philosophy and how much he was into it. He's a very impressive guy."

Meanwhile, many of the other scouts stole peeks in Morgan's direction. Since it was a bit of a down year for Michigan players in the draft, there were really only a couple of players the scouts came to see. And it was no secret to anyone inside the field house that Morgan was one of them.

The time finally came for Morgan to take the field and do some positional work. As he stretched out, Milus approached him and stated, "We're having you go last because some of these scouts might have left if you went first. That wouldn't have been too nice for these other guys."

Morgan grinned and then finished his warm-ups with a bit more swagger. Morgan was the first of his group to begin the positional drills and he did not disappoint. He moved through every drill with excellent quickness and fluidity. The players who went after him had a stiff task before them. Even on their very best day, none of them came close to playing up to Morgan's level. Each of them gave it his all, but not everyone is destined to make a living playing alongside the most elite athletes in the world.

Milus came up and congratulated Morgan when the positional drills had concluded.

"You did good," Milus said. "We got you as a second-round grade. Maybe we'll see each other again soon."

Each scout in attendance walked off the field and just about every one of them offered Morgan one last glimpse on their way out. While they did this, Morgan walked over to his brother who had watched the day's events unfold.

"You did good," Jarrad told him. "I'm proud of you."

Standing next to Jarrad, Brian was also brimming with pride. He had traveled all the way from New Jersey to make sure Morgan had everything he needed before his Pro Day. Morgan's close friend Mike Hart of the Indianapolis Colts was also on hand to show his support. Morgan would go on to spend the next few minutes joking and laughing. But on the inside, he was relieved that his Pro Day was behind him.

On his way home from the legendary campus, Morgan now entertained thoughts of a new future.

"What's Charlotte like?" he asked his brother.

"It's a lot better than it is here," Jarrad said. "I could get used to Charlotte."

"Me too," Morgan said as he thought of what life would be like in North Carolina. He imagined himself wearing a black Carolina uniform tinged with teal. He then thought of Liz and how the two of them might find a nice little starter home somewhere in Charlotte. He wondered how far it was to the ocean and if it was a reasonable drive for him to take a weekly fishing trip. Those thoughts continued to play through his mind while Liz remained far away in California.

Now that Pro Day was finished, the main thing on Morgan's itinerary was to sit around and wait for NFL teams to call and request a private workout. Yet, he probably wouldn't hear from any teams that weekend. And the one place he wanted to be was far away from the quiet confines of Ann Arbor. As that thought bounced through Morgan's mind, a burst of spontaneity surged through him.

Later that night, Liz was just about drift off to sleep when her phone rang. Morgan spoke to her briefly and told her that he was very tired from such a long day.

"How did it go with the Rams?" she asked.

"It went well, we just watched a lot of film and talked for a while," Morgan lied. "That's why I couldn't call you all day. But I'm really beat so I'll just talk to you tomorrow."

Liz was a bit surprised at just how short-lived their conversation turned out to be. Nonetheless, she said good night and was ready to fall victim to a night of slumber.

No more than a few seconds later, Liz's brother came barreling in the apartment and coerced her to go for a quick ride to get some take-out. It took a few minutes of coercing before she finally agreed and walked out to her brother's car. She immediately noticed someone sitting in the front seat of the car, but a hood concealed that person's identity. Liz casually climbed in the backseat and said hello. The person in the front seat did not even attempt to respond. In her mind, Liz thought, 'how rude.'

Then, in an unrelenting tongue, she asked, "And just who is this?"

That is when Morgan removed his hood and turned around wearing a sly grin. Liz's eyes widened in unison with the ascension of her voice.

"Oh my Gosh, I thought you were in Michigan!"

She then sprung forward and wrapped her arms around him as a watery joy began to fill her eyes. Morgan held her tightly after spending the last few hours on a flight that he booked earlier that afternoon. The two would go on to spend the next hour sharing burgers, french fries and a couple of cokes. Later that night, they would return to Liz's one bedroom apartment where the rest of her family had already drifted off into a temporary dreamland. It was in that crowded apartment where Morgan and Liz fell asleep in the comfort of one another's arms. There was no king size bed for them to sleep in nor was there a lavish down comforter to fight off the nocturnal chill. There were only two hearts beating to the exact same rhythm. Their future was uncertain, and the road ahead remained unpaved. Yet, regardless of where Morgan got drafted, it seemed as though he was already home.

CHAPTER NINETEEN

The Waiting Game

The last of all the college Pro Days were now wrapping up. Scouts were finishing up their nationwide tours as a full month had elapsed since the NFL Combine. One of the final stops on the scouting itinerary was Columbia, South Carolina where Kenny was looking forward to the arrival of his Pro Day.

"I wish it was earlier," said Kenny. "I just want to get it over with. I'm still working out every day, but it's going to be nice to get it out of the way. To me, Pro Day isn't that big of a deal because I did so well at the Combine. But it's still in the back of my mind. After Pro Day, I won't have to worry about too much of anything. I'm just going to sit and wait for the draft."

Kenny figured that Pro Day would be a rather easy one which would consist mostly of brief positional drills. And he wasn't at all worried about his hamstrings giving him any kind of problems.

"My hammies are one-hundred percent now," said Kenny. "They both feel good, I'm one-hundred percent all around."

Kevin had made the trip down to South Carolina for Kenny's Pro Day and still has some concern regarding his hamstrings.

"If he stays healthy and has a good support team around him, I think he'll do really well in the NFL," said Kevin. "But he has to stay on top of his recent injuries. I'm a little concerned he's not doing everything he could be doing to keep his hamstrings right."

Incidentally, it was another part of Kenny's anatomy that troubled him before his Pro Day. Just before the Pro Day was set to begin, stomach pains forced Kenny to rush into the bathroom. However, he vowed that it wasn't nerves that upset his stomach.

"I don't know what it was," said Kenny. "I took one of those little five-hour energy drinks and then I had to go throw up and take a couple of dumps. After I did that, I felt better. It knocked everything out."

It would take more than a little stomach discomfort to keep Kenny from going out and making a good impression on scouts from thirty different NFL teams. His stomach problems were merely a subtle afterthought once he finished excelling in those various drills.

"Pro Day went really well," said Kenny. "I didn't really do anything other than my positional drills. I ran good routes, caught the ball and did everything the scouts wanted me to do."

Perhaps the most beneficial part of the day came when Kenny had stepped off the field. Once Pro Day had concluded, the scouts gathered behind closed doors to have a few words with the South Carolina coaching staff. This was a common practice at all Pro Days. Scouts relied quite a bit on the coaches' opinions regarding each player.

Behind closed doors, Kenny would not be hurt by the words of South Carolina head coach Steve Spurrier. A scout who was present in that room leaked word that Spurrier had said that Kenny was a great kid who was always on time. Spurrier also went on to say that Kenny is a smart football player with an incredible football acumen and the best receiver that he has ever coached.

Meanwhile, Morgan's Pro Day was already a two-week memory. He had returned from California and was passing the time with strenuous daily workouts followed by a lot of idle waiting. Not one team requested to see him in person, although that didn't stop them from ringing his phone.

"Arizona just called me and wanted to talk," said Morgan. "Other than that, it's been slow. I talked to my agent and asked him if I should be worried."

Morgan's agent told him, "Not at all. You've been at the Shrine, you've been at the Senior Bowl and you've been at the Combine. Everybody knows about you and a lot of teams aren't working as many people out this year."

Morgan tried to take it all in stride, but each day seemed to drag on a bit longer than the last.

"It is what it is, there's no point in worrying about it," said Morgan. "I did what I could do. I'm not really worried because teams have been

calling, so I know they're interested. I just want the whole thing to hurry up. A lot of the stuff is so political, working guys out and not working guys out. Some teams try to be quiet about guys they like. I'm not really looking that deep into it."

Simply because a team requested a private workout from a player did not necessarily mean they were extremely high on drafting him.

"The interesting thing is different teams have certain philosophies," said NFL Network draft analyst Mike Mayock. "Some teams will bring no players in because they don't want to tip their hand. A lot of teams bring in players they really like and players they really don't like for the same reason, they don't want to tip their hand. Some teams just bring in players they're interested in. It's almost like playing poker."

Some coaches even brought in players that they had no interest in drafting at all.

"I've been in some meetings trying to figure out what do we put out as a smokescreen?" said former Detroit Lions head coach Steve Mariucci. "And say we're really interested in these couple of guys, knowing full well that we may not be,"

Like many other college players, there was nothing more Morgan could do. He simply had to sit by and play the waiting game. While he waited, decision makers across the NFL were quietly adjusting their respective draft boards.

"When you do all this research and put all these man hours in, you try to put a fence around all this information," Mariucci added. "You have meetings with your scouts and coaches and you stress confidentiality. It's very imperative that you have your people not visiting with other friends on other teams. It's a time where you got to keep some secrets."

Down in South Florida, Frantz was forced to play the same game. Frantz also received no requests for a private workout. Simply waiting around for something to happen quickly became too much to bear. So instead of sitting around and playing the waiting game, Frantz opted to take action. He returned to TEST and began training for rookie camp, which would take place a week after the draft.

"Coming back to New Jersey, I was happy," said Frantz. "Everywhere I went in Florida, someone's trying to hype my head up talking about draft this and draft that. I have people that care about me in Jersey and they keep me grounded. I'm back here for a reason and that's to get better than everybody else. I also wanted to get away from distractions back home. I'm isolated in Jersey. I'm away from the garbage, the distractions, the people talking in my ear. I don't need things like that leading up to the draft. I need to be clear minded, focused and grounded. Plus, every time I step foot in my hometown, that is one of my biggest motivations. I see the lack of opportunity and the lack of resources around there. Then, I go to a better city and I see so much more. It really makes me understand the situation I'm in. But it was wonderful to have a break. I was going hard since the Motor City Bowl. I came right out here to TEST and just kept grinding all the way through Pro Day. It was cool to relax, spend some time with my family and just unwind. But I'm a hard worker so I never want to sleep. I even felt bad about the couple days I took off when I went back home."

The training had suddenly changed for Frantz. No longer did Frantz have to work on his forty-yard dash, his three-cone or his short shuttle. It was back to football, back to basics.

"I'm glad all that combine training is over," said Frantz. "Football isn't played in shorts. And I don't necessarily do well on test days. That doesn't mean I don't know how to test. I didn't think I lived up to my expectations on Pro Day. But I'm not someone who dwells on what I did in the past. There's no time to think about the past. It's all about tomorrow."

While Frantz continued with his training, Kenny was taking a more leisurely approach to his free time. The Seattle Seahawks had invited him out for a visit but never made good on that offer. That enabled Kenny to enjoy himself down in South Carolina. He was invited to take part in a celebrity golf tournament even though he hardly ever swung a club.

"I didn't play any golf in the tournament," said Kenny. "I basically just rode around in a golf cart all day and drank some beers. Everybody else golfed all day, but I don't do the golf thing."

Meanwhile, Lydon was also enjoying the comfortable southern air. He and his wife took a trip down to Florida a few days prior to his private meeting with the Miami Dolphins. The Murthas spent some time relaxing in the Florida Keys and then made the trip up to the Dolphins' facility where Lydon had some one-on-one time with Miami Dolphins executive vice president Bill Parcells.

"He talked to me about how the team has changed over the past couple of years," said Lydon. "He even went back to talk about the Osborne and Devaney era and how he used to follow Nebraska football during that time. He's just a really nice guy, really down to earth. He said he hoped I enjoyed my visit and maybe he'll see me there in a few months. I took a tour of all the facilities, the fields, the weight room. It's awesome. The palm trees and sun are awesome. I would do anything to play down there."

The Dolphins were not the only Florida team showing an interest in Lydon. While he was in the Sunshine State, another nearby team was also expressing their interest.

"The Tampa Bay Buccaneers called me and said that their staff just got done watching my film," said Lydon. "They were watching me at my all-star game and then at the Combine. They were just overly impressed. They said that I would be a perfect fit for their program and they're going to keep in close contact with me over the next couple of weeks."

Up in a much chillier part of the country, the waiting game continued for Morgan.

"Everything's been really uneventful over the last few weeks," said Morgan. "They've been very repetitive. All I really been doing is working out. That's it, no private workouts. I'm ready to get out of here and go get married. I just want to know if I have a workout. If not, then just let me know. If not, I'd like to go spend some time with my fiancée."

The highlight of Morgan's day usually consisted of a grueling workout at the University of Michigan where he trained alongside current pros LaMarr Woodley and Larry Foote.

"My workouts are really intense," said Morgan. "I thought I was done with this when I left school. But these cats are running us so hard, it's ridiculous. It's not even mandatory, we're just doing it to do it. It's rough times. We bench a lot and go with a lot of heavier weights. Right now on the bench, I'm doing three sets of eight at 285. I'm still strong, it's definitely the strongest I've ever been. That's from being out at TEST with Brian and them. I've also been doing a lot of sprints and some long-distance running. It's really hard."

While in the company of his former teammates, who now made their living in the NFL, Morgan admitted that very little of their conversation revolved around the game of football.

"We don't really talk about football. We talk about everything else and joke around a lot. For me, football is just what I do. That's it. When I come home, I'm not really trying to talk about football. I don't dwell on it like some cats do."

Morgan did learn from Woodley that his Super Bowl Champion Pittsburgh Steelers had their eye on him.

"Wood was telling me that the Steelers like me a lot. He said, 'don't be surprised if they pick you, we need corners out there'."

Pittsburgh was now just one more city to throw into the jumbled collection of places that might soon serve as Morgan's home. For now, the University of Michigan was his home away from home. He spent countless hours there, training for his future. Mostly everyone he encountered at his alma mater was very welcoming, but not everyone.

One afternoon, on his way out of the field house, head coach Rich Rodriguez walked by Morgan and did not even offer him a hello. Apparently, Rodriguez had not really taken to many of the seniors as none of them were players that he recruited. He also had another reason for ignoring Morgan, however inane it may have been.

Just days before Michigan's Pro Day, Morgan was finishing up a workout when the team's strength coach approached him.

"Morgan, you should really go up and apologize to Coach Rod," said the strength coach.

"Apologize for what?" asked Morgan.

"He's been getting a lot of calls about your helmet at the East-West Shrine Game. A lot of people are calling and complaining about the way you covered your helmet with all those stickers. It was disrespectful."

Evidently, a lot of Michigan fans saw Morgan's helmet as an insult. Most of them felt that the Michigan helmet was a proud and reverent symbol that Morgan desecrated with emblems from rival colleges.

"Apologize?" Morgan said in a stunned voice. "I don't have anything that I need to apologize to that man for."

Instead of getting into a back and forth debate with the strength coach, Morgan took the high road and left. He walked out of the facilities even though the strength coach seemed like he wanted to prolong their disagreement. But Morgan wasn't concerned with the trivial details of how some overzealous fans overreacted to something that was completely innocent and entirely unimportant.

Far away in New Jersey, TEST was unusually quiet. Frantz did not have much company as he trained on the indoor turf. That lack of activity was a definite concern in Brian's mind.

"The average agent believes that a guy should train for six weeks to get ready for the Combine," said Brian. "But the players have a ten to twelve week window to get ready for mini-camp. A lot of good work goes bad during this time. Ninety percent of athletes also need a coach to guide you, to push you, to motivate you."

Brian helped motivate Frantz, but Frantz was not in need of much more motivation. He attacked his workouts with the same hunger, desire and determination that was a steadfast part of his everyday routine.

"This is when the hungry dogs like me just keep on working," said Frantz. "Other guys may be a first or second-round pick. But when they sleep, I'm going to keep on working. It's the same old turtle story. When you sleep, I'm going to keep on working and one day I'm going to catch you."

Although Frantz's workouts ate up a nice chunk of time, he was still left with quite a few free hours over the course of a day. Sitting around and waiting was significantly more difficult than any of the exhausting workouts Frantz put himself through.

"Days still go by slow," said Frantz. "These are probably the longest days of my life. I try to do things just to kill time. Sometimes, I take naps during the day just so it will go by a little faster. I've never done that before."

Frantz ate up his idle time in different ways each day. Yet, those long days couldn't affect his appetite for the NFL. And even if Frantz made it to the professional level, he vowed that his hunger would never be sufficed.

"Even when I get there, there's still so much work to do," said Frantz. "When you sit back and think that you made it, that's when other people are going to sneak up and catch you. Until you retire and hang up the cleats, there's always going to be another obstacle in front of you. That's life in general. A wise man once told me, you can look at your awards and accomplishments when you retire. I'm nowhere near retirement so it's just a waste of time being mesmerized with myself."

Frantz still had plenty of time to wonder what the future would bring. Nevertheless, he tried to ignore the endless myriad of possibilities that could turn into his reality.

"It's human nature to think about what's going to happen or where I'm going to end up," said Frantz. "It runs through my mind every day. I don't even know if I'm going to get a shot for the most part. I hear good things and bad things, but I try not to go by what other people say. You never know what's going to happen. I'm just hoping and wishing."

CHAPTER TWENTY

Get Money

Winning a Super Bowl is something every football player dreams about. Scoring a winning touchdown as time expires on Monday Night Football is another thrilling vision that runs through the mind of anyone who has ever carried a pigskin. But in the NFL, there is one ultimate goal. That goal is to make money.

The window of opportunity for players to make money in the NFL does not stay open forever. The NFL is commonly referred to as 'Not For Long' given the harsh brutality of the game. Careers can end with one swift hit and, in a matter of seconds, a player's life on the gridiron can quickly expire. NFL player contracts are not guaranteed like the ones in Major League Baseball or the National Basketball Association. Therefore, injuries can affect more than just a player's body. Injuries can also do some serious damage to a player's bank account.

To compensate for that, players receive signing bonuses when negotiating their contracts and rookies are not exempt from those bonuses. Those bonuses fluctuate according to where a player is drafted as do their salaries. In the previous NFL Draft, 2008 number one overall pick Jake Long received a $30 million signing bonus as part of his five-year $57.5 million dollar deal. Long gave the Miami Dolphins their money's worth by going out and making the Pro Bowl during his first NFL season.

However, success can be had through each round of the draft. For instance, in the same draft, third-round and 89th overall pick Steve Slaton signed a four-year deal worth a total of $2.37 million. That deal included a signing bonus of $664,000. Slaton went on to rush for 1,282 yards for the Houston Texans, which ranked sixth among NFL running backs in

2008.

The New York Jets drafted San Jose State cornerback Dwight Lowery in the fourth round and gave him a $464,500 signing bonus as part of his four-year $2.17 million deal. Lowery would start the first ten games before getting benched for the final six contests. But even if the Jets were to cut Lowery and he would never play another down of football again, he would still be $759,000 richer after just one season in the NFL.

Contracts were structured to pay players more money each season. After receiving a signing bonus of $120,000, Arizona Cardinals fifth-round pick Tim Hightower made another $295,000 in salary. Hightower was scheduled to see a pay increase of $385,000 in 2009 and another bump up to $470,000 in 2010. Hightower was considered a bargain for the Cardinals after he rushed for 10 touchdowns during the regular season. He even scored the winning touchdown in the NFC championship game, which led Arizona to Super Bowl XLIII.

Sixth-round pick Josh Morgan wasn't far behind Hightower as he received a $106,000 signing bonus as part of his $1.86 million four-year deal. Josh Morgan was the 174th player chosen in the draft and fought off some early season injuries before finishing the season with 20 receptions. That total might not seem like much, however it surpassed the total of many of the wide receivers taken in the second round of the 2008 NFL Draft. A total of ten receivers were selected in the second round, although six of them combined to catch just 34 passes during their rookie season. Josh Morgan's case is just one more example of the talent that can be found up and down the draft.

Despite all of those six and seven-figure signing bonuses, there is usually a significant drop-off in the money tossed out to players drafted in the seventh round. The seventh round is kind of like 'no man's land'. The signing bonuses are significantly lower and there is not a whole lot of job security. Signing bonuses for players drafted in the seventh round typically range from $40,000 to $60,000. Those lower payouts make teams less likely to hold on to their seventh-round selections.

In recent years, undrafted rookie free agents are starting to become more successful than players drafted in the seventh round. Fourteen players on the 2009 Pro Bowl roster were all passed over in the NFL Draft and had to make their way into the league via free agency. In 2008,

Brian had a firsthand experience with a player who fell into that free agent fold.

On the second day of the 2008 NFL Draft, Brian attended a draft party in honor of Rutgers defensive lineman Eric Foster. Eric did not receive a NFL Combine invitation, but he did dominate in the Texas vs. The Nation game. Yet, as each round passed, Eric did not hear his name called. Throughout the draft, seconds ticked off the clock at a rate that seemed to get slower and more insufferable by the moment. Finally, the time came for the last pick of the draft. For the 252nd time that day, a name other than Eric Foster's was called out.

"That was one of the longest days of my life," said Brian. "After that day, I'll never watch the draft with another player again. It's horrible waiting there all day long. And I feel so bad for them and their family when they don't get picked."

Before that day was over, Eric wound up signing a rookie free agent contract with the Indianapolis Colts. He received a signing bonus of $5,000 and would have to make the team in order to collect the $295,000 that was part of his three-year $1.15 million deal. Consequently, Eric did more than just make the team. He went on to start eleven games for the Colts as a rookie.

"Not only did I make the team but I was able to get on the field and contribute," said Eric. "It's kind of crazy and it stinks that they didn't invite me to the Combine, but I think I've grown a lot from that and it's been fuel to my fire through training camp and into the season. I think too much emphasis is placed on the Combine. You go back to a guy like me who didn't even get a shot. It's all based off numbers and whatever politics that have to do with what school you went to."

With a year's pay now secured in the back, Eric wasn't content to just go through the motions. He returned to TEST and continued to train while many other NFL players were enjoying the off-season in more social environments.

"I'm able to go back there and work out whenever I want and get professional training," said Eric. "It's huge. I want to keep that up throughout my career. I know I have a home there. It helped me big time and having a family there, it just took my game to another level."

During Eric's intermittent trips back to New Jersey, he was able to sit down with Frantz and lend him some words of advice. Unlike

Morgan, Kenny and Lydon, Frantz never played on a team with anyone who went on to the NFL. He didn't have a person whom he could call and ask questions. So whenever he got the chance to speak with Eric, he listened intently to every word.

"I feel like Eric went down the same kind of path as I'm going," said Frantz. "It was great to talk to him and hear what he's been through. I really took what he said to heart."

Frantz was hoping to mirror Eric's early success. If that were to come to fruition, Frantz would be able to do a bit of shopping in the future. Yet, he wasn't thinking beyond the bare necessities.

"I'll definitely get health insurance, good dental care and a good vehicle to get me from point A to point B," said Frantz. "My whole life I've been relying on other people to get around. It's frustrating when I have to get to a workout or run some errands. It's tough without a vehicle."

But Frantz's own transportation was not atop his future shopping list.

"The first thing I want to buy is a new minivan for my mother's church group," said Frantz. "Right now, they have this old beat up van that barely runs. I want to get them a new one so that they can go to church or go get groceries and stuff when they need to. They're all older and none of them have a car. That's really the first thing I want to buy."

While training at TEST, Frantz took one more step towards getting that ever-elusive first paycheck. He finally got a call from the Miami Dolphins requesting a private workout down at their facilities.

"I was very excited when I got the call," said Frantz. "Having a chance to play for the Dolphins would be a dream come true. I try so hard not to even think about it. I always try not to think about things I can't control. But I can't help it because growing up around the area, I've wanted to play for the Dolphins all my life. I think about being in that uniform all the time."

The workout was set to take place two weeks before the draft. Meanwhile, Kenny was just finishing up another private workout in his hometown of Atlanta. However, Kenny wasn't as keen on playing in his hometown.

"I've always been a Falcons fan, but I don't think it would be the best fit for me to play there," said Kenny. "During my first couple of years, I think it'd be good for me to get away from all the distractions. Being back at home, there's a lot of trouble I can get into. It could be good and it could be bad. But I think getting away would be a good thing."

The Falcons seemed to have a genuine interest in Kenny, but they brought him in to get a look at more than just his ability to play the wide receiver position.

"I did a lot of positional drills and then I spent some time in the classroom with the coaches," said Kenny. "They also wanted me to take a physical on my toe. Then, I had to go to the hospital and get a MRI."

Injuries were one of the foremost concerns of any NFL team looking at a prospective employee. Similar to any asset that is a part of a company, the big wigs wanted to make sure everything was in proper working order.

Kenny did not remain in Atlanta after the workout, but returned to South Carolina where he eagerly awaited the arrival of the Gamecocks' annual spring game. It was there that Kenny's number 11 was supposed to be retired. In the week leading up to that game, Kenny purchased some space in a local newspaper and posted the following letter:

To The University of South Carolina and loyal Gamecock Nation:

I would like to personally thank you for your faithful support throughout my career as a Gamecock. I will never forget while in high school during my recruitment, I attended a spring game and the Gamecock Nation made me feel as though I was already a part of the team. This was well before I made my first reception or scored my first touchdown. Because of your support I was able to exceed my expectations and achieve record-breaking numbers!

As I prepare for playing at the next level I will forever be grateful and appreciative of your continued support. I will always be a USC Gamecock.

Go Cocks!

Kenny McKinley

"I just wanted to let them know that I appreciate everything they've done for me," said Kenny. "Carolina fans are the best fans in the nation so I just wanted to let them know how much I appreciate them."

Unfortunately, when Kenny and his family arrived at the spring game, he wouldn't get the ovation he anticipated. Because of a new stipulation enacted by the university, Kenny's number couldn't officially be retired for another four years.

"They didn't retire it," said Kenny. "They'll put my name up there though next to Sterling Sharpe's as the all-time leading receiver. Coach Spurrier said he's going to do that sometime next season. They didn't even really do anything for me. I was just hanging out. I understood the policy and that they're going to retire it. But they can't do it for like four years."

Kenny's college career had done more than earn him the right to have his number retired. It also put him in a position to make quite a bit of money in the NFL. Making money was now the name of the game. Kenny even advertised that on his body. On his upper left arm, he had a tattoo that read, 'Get Money.'

"I got the tattoo in college when I knew I had the chance to make it to the NFL," said Kenny. "It's about living a dream. Playing football and getting paid for it would be living a dream."

While making money might be the primary fuel that drives many players to pursue a career in professional football, it wasn't the only blaze of ambition lit within Morgan.

"It's more than the money," said Morgan. "I want to be in a position to take care of my parents. They've done everything for me. They put me through private school my whole life and, in one instant, to be able to care of them is probably something that won't hit me until it happens. I'd like to be financially blessed enough to bless others. I really want to be in a position to bless others."

Regardless of how much money an individual takes in over a fiscal year, there is no better way to make a living than by doing something you love. Morgan was living proof of that theory.

"I enjoy everything I'm doing," said Morgan. "I've been waiting for this for so long. I'm truly blessed to be in this position. I want to enjoy it. It is a business, no question about it, but I still want to have fun."

For Morgan, some fun in the sun would be a pleasant diversion from the grind of the draft season. With his wedding rapidly approaching, a few wrinkles were thrown into his upcoming plans. Yet, Morgan ironed out those wrinkles with the poise and maturity of someone far beyond his years. When the hotel where Morgan was planning to hold the wedding started to give him problems, he simply adjusted. Instead of bickering back and forth and quibbling over details, Morgan went out and found another location. The new location was actually a step up as Morgan found a gorgeous villa on the beach. During a time when most people stress over the most minute details, Morgan ran through his wedding preparations with his all too familiar confident swagger.

"I don't raise my voice and I try not to stress," said Morgan. "I'm just a relaxed kind of guy."

A few states away in Nebraska, Lydon was eager to land a job that would help him knock off a few of his bills. But when it came down to it, Lydon really didn't care where that job would relocate him.

"It's not all about being somewhere nice," said Lydon. "It's about playing and being on a good team and getting some money. Finally, I won't have to struggle with paying the bills. We're not really struggling, but it sucks living paycheck to paycheck."

Ironically, the word paycheck was a bit foreign to Lydon. He was able to make his way through college on his scholarship money but he really never had a job to speak of. At twenty-three years of age, his only experience in the working world came when he was an employee at the Domino's Pizza shop his father owned in Minnesota.

"I worked for my dad now and again, but I'd usually wind up eating more than I would make," said Lydon. "It wasn't like a full-time job. I could work whenever I wanted; twice a week, one hour or ten hours. That's about it. I only did it for about a half a year."

Not only did rent, electricity and gas all cost money, but Lydon also spent a pretty penny on food. His cupboards were stocked with items, which included some rather unique ones. Organic fat-free peanut butter was something that wasn't on everyone's shelf nor was the certain type of Chef Boyardee that Lydon mixed with dry cottage cheese for one of his many daily meals. It wasn't so much the individual cost of everything that caused Lydon's grocery bill to soar, but rather the massive quantity that he ate. He ate every two hours and, over the course of a day, it seemed like he was always hungry.

Lydon's wife was not so lucky. Tasha was currently training for a body building competition and her diet was painfully strict.

"Food is all calculated and measured down to the gram," said Lydon. "She has to keep muscle mass and lose fat, so she has to have the perfect amount of protein and carbs and fats ratio. She calculates it all out and measures it out."

Needless to say, dinner at the Murtha household wasn't a run of the mill experience. While Tasha gobbled up some brown rice followed by a rice cake, Lydon would shovel mounds of more appetizing food into his mouth. Nevertheless, more food wouldn't be the first thing Lydon planned to buy when he received his first NFL paycheck.

"I really want to get a new gun," said Lydon. "But the first thing I am going to buy is a bed where my legs don't hang off the end. I've never slept in a bed that's been big enough for me. My feet are always hanging off the end no matter where I sleep."

The more popular trend of purchasing a new car was also not on Lydon's shopping list.

"Wherever I wind up going, I'm taking Black Beauty with me," Lydon proclaimed. "And when I go to training camp and all those other guys are driving up in their fancy cars, I'm going to be pulling up in Black Beauty."

Even though Lydon adopted such a light-hearted approach, he realized that with money also came fame. That combination caused temptation to lurk around every corner.

"It could blindside me from any direction," said Lydon. "I have quite a few friends in the NFL and every one of them told me that when you get there, there's going to be a lot more pressure to do stupid things. Women don't care if you're married and even though you're an athlete, drugs come at you harder. The only way to stay positive and remain on the right path is through faith."

CHAPTER TWENTY-ONE

Who Will Take Thee?

Throughout the entire draft season, NFL teams are continually adjusting their draft boards. Players rise and fall according to All-Star, Combine and Pro Day performances. Interviews and medical tests also play a critical part in where a player is ranked. A player's individual workout may also help or hurt his cause. This jockeying of positions continues all the way through the actual draft itself.

"Things are being tweaked until the end, but we have preliminary grades on all our guys and we want to stay as close to that as possible," said New York Jets general manager Mike Tannenbaum. "The Combine and spring workouts obviously affect that, but we don't want any one part of the process to sway the scales too far."

In a similar fashion, draft experts also have their own draft boards as they try to predict where a player will be selected. They too will move players to coincide with the constant influx of information, which is more readily available than ever.

"It's like any industry you look at right now," said former Baltimore Ravens Super Bowl champion head coach Brian Billick. "The explosion of technology is the biggest difference. There was a time when you didn't have the resources, the access or the man power. There were some teams that did, but most did not. That's when you found those gems from small schools because you committed resources to them. Today, everybody knows about everybody."

Today's top draft experts are privy to a lot of the information made available to NFL teams, but they don't know everything. Still, some experts are very reputed for their opinions. Just weeks before the draft would take place, draft expert Scott Wright had Frantz pegged for the sixth to seventh round range.

"I think he has a chance to be drafted," said Wright. "I think he's a draftable prospect. This isn't necessarily a great crop of linebackers. I think after you get past the first six or seven of them, Joseph is right in there with the rest."

In addition to Frantz's questionable speed, the reports of his past involvement with marijuana may have also thrown up a red flag for some teams. However, NFL coaches may be a bit more understanding than some people tend to believe.

"We look at that very seriously and obviously the NFL looks at that extremely seriously," said former Super Bowl champion head coach Jon Gruden. "We don't overlook that. We do a lot of research with our scouts, with our general manager and we do that. You talk to the head coach, you talk to the support people at the university. And at the same time, you realize that a lot of these players come from some very difficult backgrounds where they've made some mistakes. Some of these guys deserve an opportunity to live their life like you know they can live it. They need some guidance and they need some structure around them. And when you have that environment, it's conducive for a guy to come in and explode onto the scene. You don't hesitate if you trust the kid."

That meant that NFL organizations were spending a lot more time poking around in the private lives of these prospective employees.

"These teams are doing more in-house research," said former San Francisco 49ers head coach Steve Mariucci. "They're not only going to sit down with these kids, their agents and their coaches, but the secretaries and the trainers and the weight room guys and teammates and all kinds of opposing coaches and high school coaches to dig for information on these kids."

So where did all of that digging leave Frantz? He wasn't quite certain.

"I'm still hearing everything from the third round to the seventh round," said Frantz. "If I get drafted, that would be a blessing. That's my main goal. But if not, it is what it is. That's life. You can't down yourself for that. You just have to go from that point, which is undrafted, and just try to get into training camp."

Frantz may not have performed as well in shorts as some other linebackers, but he always made plays when he put on the pads. He also had a tremendous passion for the game, which had to account for something.

"I think you're wrong if all you do is look for the so-called super talented guys without having the passion," said New York Jets head coach Rex Ryan. "Are they the team players that we're looking for? Those are guys that sometimes might not be rated as high as other guys, but those are the kind of winners that you try to surround yourself with."

Ryan had his share of experience coaching outstanding linebackers. As the former defensive coordinator for the Baltimore Ravens, he had the opportunity to coach Frantz's boyhood idol Ray Lewis. Yet, Ryan admitted that there is no handbook to follow when drafting a player.

"It's interesting, there's no magic formula for this," said Ryan. "I just want guys that I think can represent our football team, that plays like a Jet. And that's going to mean something. That's going to mean they're physical, tough, passionate people and that's what we're looking for. In the past, we've always tried to build our defense that way in Baltimore. We're going to try and build our team that way with the Jets. And I know that's a formula for success that we had in Baltimore and we're going to look for those same type of players moving forward with the Jets."

If that was indeed the criteria for drafting a linebacker, Frantz wouldn't have much to worry about. He didn't receive a Combine invite, but made the most out of his time at the Texas vs. The Nation game. He also performed well at the Dolphins' private workout, which turned out to be a private session for a few other players as well. But once again, it was still a workout in shorts.

"When you put the pads on, that's when you separate the men from the boys," said Frantz. "That's what I live for."

Following his workout with the Dolphins, Frantz was enjoying some quiet time back in Florida with his family.

"If I get the opportunity to go to camp, I won't see my family for a while," said Frantz. "As far as being back down here otherwise, I'm not too high on it just for the simple fact that there are so many distractions. People all of the sudden want to be around me and things are starting to appear that weren't there before. I'm genuine and authentic and if something is not genuine or authentic, I don't want to be around it. If it's not real, then hit the road."

Coincidentally, Kenny decided to hit the road as the draft was nearing. He flew out and spent some time in Las Vegas for the first time in his young life.

"I'm staying cool and just kicking it," said Kenny. "I'll probably get a little more excited right before the draft, but I'm just coolin' right now. I came out here with my manager just to get away from everything. I'm just trying to take a lil' vacation before everything goes down. It's fun out here. I've never seen anything like this. It's pretty amazing."

Back in New Jersey, there was some concern over how Kenny was spending his time.

"I'm worried about Kenny," said Brian. "I don't know what he's doing. I think he's a top-100 guy for sure, but he needs someone on top of him to push him and guide him through. I think he can stick for a long time, but I'm a little worried about him getting caught up in the NFL lifestyle."

Coming into the draft, Kenny was determined to be a second-round pick. Now, according to most draft experts, the second round was a bit of a stretch.

"I think he's going to have to be a mid-round pick," said Wright. "The thing that he's going to have to fight is the Steve Spurrier wide receiver stigma. Spurrier has taken that with him from Florida to South Carolina. For the most part, the Gator wide receivers who came out of that program had real trouble adjusting to the NFL game whether it be Reidel Anthony or Jacquez Green. We could go on and on with those guys. So that's a stigma Kenny's going to be battling."

Draft expert Rob Rang agreed with the notion that the Spurrier offense may have hamstringed Kenny.

"There are some teams out there who are not going to be willing to consider any receiver who comes from a Spurrier offense because of the struggles they've had acclimating to the NFL," said Rang. "Kenny's been a standout his whole career at South Carolina, breaking Sterling Sharpe's record will do that for you. But when I watch him on film, I don't see him being as fast as he ran at the Combine. We had Kenny McKinley entering the year as a second to third-round pick. We have him now in the third round."

Kenny seemed to think that the three teams who worked him out showed the most interest, even though many other teams continued to check in on him.

"I've been hearing from a lot of teams, but I like New England," said Kenny. "It just seems like I would fit better in their system. Atlanta's already got like four or five receivers. Denver has a lot of receivers also. New England has Randy Moss and Wes Welker, but they don't have anybody after that. The coaches said they have a great need for receivers and they also have six picks in the first three rounds. Hopefully, they'll get me in the first three rounds."

Lydon was also hearing from quite a few teams and his name was being mentioned more often by draft experts across the country.

"I think of Murtha as a fourth or fifth-round prospect," said Rang. "He's athletic enough to possibly squeeze into that fourth-round area. But because of the talent at offensive tackle this year, I think it pushes him down a little more. But he has such athleticism. I think someone's going to be willing to bite as we get into that mid-second day."

Coming into the draft season, Lydon was not even on most draft boards. Rang had no doubt that Lydon's Combine performance changed that.

"I think what he did at the Combine was that he got teams to look at him on film," said Rang. "Before, with all his durability question marks, a lot of people were just casting him off. Once he put up the numbers he put up, every team in the league had to take a pause and see what this guy is all about because his numbers were just eye popping. I think that certainly does help him. But it doesn't matter how impressive you are in shorts if you can't stay on the field. And he's had his struggles in doing that."

Teams still had a lot of questions regarding Lydon and they continued to ask them as the draft inched closer. A scout from the Seattle Seahawks spent about a half-hour on the telephone with Brian, relentlessly assaulting him with questions.

"He wanted to know how Murtha got those numbers and if they were consistent with what he was doing here," said Brian. "I assured him they were, but the guy just couldn't get over Lydon's numbers. He also kept asking me if he was on anything."

Following the Combine, teams seemed a lot more interested in Lydon as calls were coming in far more frequently.

"I think Miami is showing the most interest, but my agent says the Chiefs talk the most interest," said Lydon. "There's also other teams that haven't called my agent. But they'll call me and tell me that they're really interested. They always tell me to make sure my phone is on."

Still, after all the phone calls, Lydon truly had no gauge on when he was going to be drafted. He simply hoped for the best and expected the worst.

"Getting picked late is my biggest fear," said Lydon. "If I'm going to go play football, I want to play. I don't want to be bouncing around and having to prove myself all over again. I want to go in there already being known and ready to roll. I don't want to have to work my way up just to make a team. I want to go in there and play. When you're picked late like that, they don't look at you the same. I don't know much about it, but I know being a seventh rounder, you kind of go into camp as meat and not a priority. At that point, you kind of want to be a free agent because that way you can go to a team that really wants you as opposed to just going to a team that picks you for whatever reason."

Lydon had made tremendous strides during the draft season given the fact that he wasn't on many draft boards after his bowl game. Things were a little different for Morgan. The general consensus at the start of the draft season was that Morgan would likely fall somewhere in the fifth or sixth round. Throughout the draft season, Morgan had done everything he possibly could to up his status.

"Right now we have Morgan Trent as a mid-second day kind of a guy in the fourth to fifth round," said Rang. "He did help himself out at the Combine. He has good speed and he shows that. But on film, there are times he is a little inconsistent. I was a little hesitant to put him up as high as the third round, but we had him there at one point."

For Morgan, the end of the draft season would include more than one monumental event in his life. A little more than a week before the draft, Morgan stepped off a plane and felt the warm Mexican air welcome him to Cabo. He and Liz seemed to push all their worries aside and were determined to enjoy the few days leading up to their wedding.

"If I get a call from some team when I'm down here, they better fly down to Cabo and work me out on the beach or something," Morgan said with a grin.

The wedding was on the minds of all the family and friends who had journeyed south of the border, but so was the draft. Everyone also picked out a destination where they hoped Morgan would land.

"I still love the idea of Carolina but whoever takes me, I'll love it there," said Morgan. "When you're in the top of the first round, you have more of a say in where you want to go. But when you're just trying to get drafted, I'd just love to go anywhere. Of course, I would love to go somewhere warm. My brother wants me to go to Arizona. My parents want me to go to Detroit so I'll be close, but they're probably the only ones that want me to go there."

It was a relaxing few days leading up to the wedding as Morgan continued to ignore the stress that overwhelms so many people during what is usually a hectic time. One day before he and Liz would exchange vows, Morgan, Phil, Jarrad and Brian all set out on a deep-sea fishing trip. Many miles off the coast of Mexico, Morgan made a heartfelt revelation.

"I just want to get drafted," he said. "I don't care where it is, I just want to get drafted. My biggest worry is not getting drafted at all. I got my mind set for Sunday, late Sunday. Anything before that is great. It's been a long season, but I would do it all again. It's a lot of hard work, but there really is no other job like it."

The fish weren't biting that afternoon, but Morgan would make his biggest catch the next day. It was on that Saturday afternoon, one week before the draft, that he took Liz's hand in front of a gorgeous backdrop. The calm sea and feathery sky served as a picturesque scene for the moment when Morgan and Liz pledged to spend the rest of their lives together. And just as it was throughout his entire life, Morgan's family was right there looking on with pride.

Tears of happiness leaked from the eyes of some of the spectators, but it wasn't because those eyes were watching a football player take one of the biggest steps of his life. Those eyes focused on someone who epitomized what it meant to be a noble and upstanding young man. Once those nuptials had been exchanged, a round of applause came from the group of forty or so people who had gathered for the ceremony. That applause wouldn't be nearly as loud as the NFL crowds that Morgan hoped to hear in the future. However, those people applauded a young man who wasn't wearing a football uniform. Their cheers were for someone who had already succeeded on the playing field of life.

CHAPTER TWENTY-TWO

The NFL Draft

The NFL Draft is anything but a new phenomenon. It began back in 1936 when the league consisted of only nine teams. Future commissioner Bert Bell devised a system where the weakest teams would get first crack at the top college prospects. That system remains intact, although the modern-day draft hardly resembles what it looked like during that inaugural day in a cramped Philadelphia hotel.

In the first ever NFL Draft, 81 players were selected through nine rounds. Ironically, the first ever number one pick did not even pursue a career in professional football. Heisman trophy winner Jay Berwanger from the University of Chicago was the first ever NFL Draft pick selected by the Philadelphia Eagles, who later traded his rights to the Chicago Bears. Berwanger would never play a down in the NFL, citing that it was not a very lucrative career. How times have changed.

Radio City Music Hall in New York City now plays host to the annual extravaganza that has become known as the NFL Draft. The two-day event moved to Radio City Music Hall in 2006 after being held at other popular New York venues such as Madison Square Garden. Year after year, fans flock to the Big Apple to watch the day's proceedings. Much has changed over the course of time, particularly over the last few decades.

"My first draft was 1978," said Charley Casserly, a former general manager of the Washington Redskins and Houston Texans. "In preparation for that draft, we didn't even have our own copy of the Senior Bowl. Our first pick wasn't until the sixth round so the Redskins wouldn't even buy the tape of the Senior Bowl. They would share it with some other teams. We didn't have films of college games in our office.

We had to order it and hope that they send it."

Video tapes eventually evolved into DVD's which will likely be replaced by the next innovative and more compact technological creation. However, Casserly remembers a time when just having a video tape of a player was a novelty.

"1986 was the year the NFL went to video tape," said Casserly, who was a major player in the Texans' decision to select Mario Williams over Reggie Bush with the first pick in the 2006 NFL Draft. "And then, as that tape became clearer, you had the NFL center form a tape library. So now, when you'd sit down and talk about a prospect, you've got six to seven games of his senior year there. In the old days, when you would have a discussion about a player, it would be one scout's word against another."

Times have indeed changed, yet the NFL has one policy that remains even amidst the explosion of technology. The NFL generally invites nine or ten of the top prospects to attend the actual NFL Draft. The rest of the players in the country are left to spend the weekend however they see fit.

Morgan and his family would be spending the weekend in Las Vegas and would arrive just a few days after Kenny had left Sin City for his hometown of Atlanta. Lydon and his wife packed a few hearty lunches for their six-hour drive back to his hometown of Hutchinson, Minnesota. Frantz decided to take it easy at his mother's place down in South Florida where he was hoping to become the first ever Florida Atlantic player to be drafted. If that was to be, it would not only help Frantz's family and his school, but it would also help out the Sun Belt Conference.

The Sun Belt didn't have a very celebrated history in the draft, especially compared to much bigger conferences. Since the inception of the Sun Belt in 2001, fifteen of its players have been drafted in the NFL. Of the teams that make up the Sun Belt conference, a grand total of twenty-seven players have been selected in the entire history of the NFL Draft. But Frantz warned about underestimating players from that conference.

"I think the Sun Belt doesn't get as much credit as a conference because the linemen are probably not as legit as a SEC conference," said Frantz. "They're not as big, strong, fast and athletic. But as far as the skill positions and the linebacker and quarterback play, it's not a big drop-off. It's a lot faster than people think. You're isolated in the open field a lot. Just that offense alone forces you to play in open space."

Frantz had played against a few SEC schools and could attest to their size and speed. Coincidentally, the SEC had the most players drafted of any conference since 1990 with a whopping 696 selections. Kenny's South Carolina Gamecocks were part of that conference, which continually produced top-notch players every year. Right behind the SEC was the Big Ten, home to Morgan's Michigan Wolverines. The Big Ten managed to put 612 players in the NFL Draft since 1990. Morgan was hopeful that he would personally increase that number by one.

During the week of the draft, phone calls started to come in from teams all over the NFL. Morgan even received a personalized letter fed-exed by general manager George Kokinis of the Cleveland Browns.

"They basically said we just want to congratulate you on a great college career and how far you've come," said Morgan. "They just wanted to let me know that I'd be a great asset to their team and that their coaches and scouts would be talking to me."

Perhaps it wasn't as personal as Morgan believed since Frantz received the exact same piece of mail. The Cleveland Browns were just one of thirty-two NFL teams that took to the phones on the day before the draft.

"I've been getting calls from a lot of teams," said Frantz. "They mostly wanted to make sure they had the right phone number where they could reach me. Cleveland and Jacksonville talked to me for a good while and acted like they were really interested. I really think Jacksonville might draft me. They seemed to come at me the hardest."

Teams wanted to make sure they had the right contact numbers because that's how a player would know when he was drafted. Before the selection would be announced at Radio City Music Hall, the team would place a phone call to the player informing him of their decision. So while the players eagerly watched the draft on television, they were watching their phones even closer.

That day, Morgan's phone only stopped ringing for a couple of hours. That was because he spent part of the afternoon on a plane bound for Las Vegas. Even when Morgan was in the air, calls continued to fill up his voice mail.

"I've gotten calls from twenty-eight teams," said Morgan. "They have just been calling and making sure they have my right phone number. They all asked how much I weighed and stuff like that. I wasn't expecting that many calls. It's been almost every single team. Only four teams didn't call."

One of the most compelling calls came while Morgan was more than 30,000 feet off the ground.

"I got a call from the Dallas Cowboys secondary coach Dave Campo," said Morgan. "He left me a really nice voice mail while I was on the plane. He said that he watched my film and that he's really impressed. He would love for me to be a Cowboy and he thinks that I could help them out right now. If he could recruit me, he'd be out there recruiting me. And he hopes that they have a chance to draft me before someone else does. That really made an impression on me. The way he spoke, it really struck me. I didn't want to read much into it, but when a coach tells you he wants you to play for his team, it's like wow."

Another particular phone call was able to carve out a place in the back of Morgan's mind as well.

"The Cincinnati DB coach called me and talked to me for a bit," said Morgan. "He coached me at the Senior Bowl and my friend Leon Hall plays up there and he's doing well. Coach told me that I remind him of Leon and I would look great in the NFL and hopefully he would get the chance to coach me."

Morgan also spoke to Leon earlier that week.

"Leon told me the owner asked about me," said Morgan. "He also told me the lot next to his house was available. We just kind of joked around for a bit. I didn't want to read too much into it."

Plenty of calls were also made to Atlanta and Minnesota where Lydon and Kenny both formed early opinions of where their futures might lie. Kenny seemed to still be holding on to the idea of playing for New England while Lydon entertained thoughts of playing for one of the three Florida teams.

Kenny and Lydon also shared a similar belief that they had an outside shot of getting drafted on the first day. It was pretty much a given that a good number of wide receivers and offensive tackles would be selected on day one of the NFL Draft.

"There's probably eight offensive tackles that will go in the first

The NFL Draft

two rounds," said draft expert Mike Mayock. "Last year we had eight go in the first round. The problem with this year is that after those eight, there's a drop-off. So I think there's going to be a run again on offensive tackles. I think they're going to go earlier than they should and then other guys will get artificially pushed up."

That theory boded well for Lydon. Yet, as more so-called 'gurus' dispensed numerous draft predictions, he didn't pay attention to any of them.

"I try not to look too much into it just because there's a lot of analysts out there," said Lydon. "Mr. John Doe and his friend Joe Blow think they're the next ESPN analysts. But who knows? I know that soon I'll be working out with a team and they'll still be where they are now."

The first day of the draft had finally arrived and very soon, Morgan, Frantz, Kenny and Lydon would all know their fates. The long draft season was coming to a close, but not before a little more waiting.

On a balmy Saturday afternoon in New York City, fans arrived early for the chance to jam into Radio City Music Hall and be firsthand witnesses to the 2009 NFL Draft. Many grown men painted their faces and donned jerseys of their favorite players while waiting to gain entrance. Some of those men jawed back and forth with other adults who wore opposing colors. They attempted to outdo one another with loud shouts that usually contained obscenities and sometimes barely made any sense at all.

The event in New York City is basically for the benefit of the fans. Most of the coaches and team executives spend the weekend in what they referred to as 'the war room'. Inside these war rooms, phones continued to ring, scenarios were presented and decisions were made. War rooms were usually located at the team's facility in their respective cities.

Every year, the number of people who watched the NFL Draft from the comfort of their living rooms continued to climb. In 2008, an estimated 34.8 million people tuned in for the NFL Draft. This year, Frantz, Lydon and Kenny would add to that growing number, but not Morgan. He planned to spend a good part of that Saturday playing golf with his brother. It was also somewhat fitting that Morgan was spending this weekend in the same place where his football career began.

"It's funny that I'm here in Vegas because this is where I first started playing football," said Morgan. "The first game I ever played was

193

out here in Vegas when I was in the sixth grade. And now I'm back."

Morgan planned to enjoy the day and really wasn't expecting to be drafted in the first two rounds. In his mind, he was going to be a day-two selection.

"I'm really not expecting to get a call on Saturday," said Morgan. "My agent told me the worst case scenario is the fifth round. He said 'I can't see you going any later than the fifth round.' We're honestly thinking anywhere from the third through the fifth."

Frantz was also resolved to the fact that he probably wouldn't slide into the first two rounds. Much like Lydon, he also paid no attention to what was being said by any of the draft analysts.

"You can't listen to any draft experts or read any publications because they don't know what they're talking about," said Frantz.

So after four months of hype, anticipation and speculation, the 2009 NFL Draft was set to begin. Only two rounds would take place on that first day with a ten-minute time limit between each first-round selection. Through the second round, teams would have seven minutes to finalize their pick.

The first overall pick was made known a couple of days prior to the draft. The Detroit Lions owned the first pick and had already signed Georgia quarterback Matthew Stafford to a six-year $72 million deal one day before the draft. Stafford was guaranteed to see at least $41.7 million of that deal and that was before he threw a single pass in the NFL. That announcement was made official when the draft kicked off and then the St. Louis Rams quickly snatched up Baylor's Jason Smith with the second pick. Lydon snickered when that pick was announced and remembered what a jerk Smith had been at the Combine.

Three of the first eight picks turned out to be offensive tackles and, as the first round wore on, wide receivers were being drafted at an alarming rate. Kenny Britt of Rutgers became the sixth wide receiver taken in the first round with the 30th overall selection by the Tennessee Titans. Britt was one of four first-round receivers to gain more than 1,000 yards during the previous season. All the while, Kenny McKinley knew that his senior year numbers were one of the reasons he was still waiting for a phone call.

"Not having a quarterback was a problem all year long," said Kenny. "If the quarterback can't get you the ball, then it's going to be a big problem. That was probably the main reason my numbers were a little down. And I also wasn't one-hundred percent with my hamstrings hurting."

Still, the high number of receivers already selected was a good sign for Kenny. The more receivers that came off the board, the better his chances were of being drafted.

The time came for round two to begin and Frantz haphazardly checked in on the draft. Out in Las Vegas, Morgan was oblivious to everything that was going on inside Radio City Music Hall. He and his brother were enjoying an afternoon of golf. Even if Morgan did get drafted, he wouldn't have known about it.

"We went out early and we were on the course for a while," said Morgan. "Then, about halfway through the course, I realized that I left my phone in the car. When I realized I left it in there, I was just like 'oh well.' The draft really wasn't on my mind at all."

Through the first part of the second round, the players who were expected to be drafted at that time were announced in front of a somewhat raucous crowd. But just about every spectator let out a collective gasp when the 47th overall pick was announced. The Oakland Raiders selected safety Michael Mitchell from Ohio University. Mitchell was without a Combine invitation, he played in no all-star games and did not appear on the draft board of any major expert. Television announcers, spectators and even players were stunned.

"Who?" Frantz said in a tone of disbelief.

Mitchell was a virtual unknown who was not projected to be drafted at all, let alone in the second round. But Raiders' owner and general manager Al Davis had his own way of doing things.

"The neat thing about the Raiders is that they have a group of scouts that have been there forever," said former Raiders head coach Jon Gruden. "Those guys have worked with Al Davis in concert with who they pick. And they've given the coaches their opportunity throughout the previous weeks and months to give their input. But ultimately, Al makes the call. The great thing about working for Al Davis, an owner that makes the calls, is that this guy isn't afraid to take chances. I always admired that about him."

If a little-known player like Michael Mitchell could sneak into the second round, there was no reason why Lydon, Kenny, Frantz or Morgan could not duplicate that feat. Seeing an under-the-radar player like Mitchell get drafted so early inspired all the players with hope, save for Morgan. Morgan had other things on his mind. He was busy sizing up a chip shot after just barely clearing a sand trap.

Eleven picks later, another relatively unknown was announced with the 58th overall pick. University of Houston offensive tackle Sebastian Vollmer was selected by the New England Patriots.

"Are you kidding me?" Lydon shouted at the television. "He was at the Texas vs. The Nation game with me. I was way better than him. How the heck did he get drafted before I did!"

Vollmer's stint at the Texas vs. The Nation game was his only postseason invitation. He wasn't among the players invited to the NFL Combine. Unlike Lydon, Vollmer didn't even have the chance to break records. Yet, he became the seventh tackle chosen in the 2009 NFL Draft.

"It just doesn't make sense," Lydon rang out.

Before Lydon could continue any more of his rant, Tasha nudged his arm and told him to look at the screen. Lydon's name now appeared as the sixth best offensive tackle available according to ESPN draft analyst Mel Kiper Jr. With offensive tackles being one of the most sought-after positions in the NFL Draft, it seemed as though it was only a matter of time before Lydon received a phone call.

The early selections of Mitchell and Vollmer also shed some hope for Frantz. Similar to Frantz, neither Mitchell nor Vollmer were invited to the Combine. One year ago in 2008, there was a total of thirty-six players drafted who were without Combine invitations. This year, that number was expected to grow. There were also plenty of rumors swirling about Frantz creeping up in the draft.

"The Saints liked him early on," said Brian. "They were very impressed with what he did at the Texas vs. The Nation. I talked to their director of scouting and he said they have him at a third-round grade. They even sent two scouts to his Pro Day."

The waiting game would continue while the final six picks of the second round were announced. Lydon was up on the edge of his seat as his name now taunted him from the television screen. If he was truly among the top six available tackles, there was a good chance he might be drafted before the day was over. He reacted a little less emphatically when another offensive tackle was taken with the 60th pick of the draft. But that would be the last of the tackles to be selected on day one. After more than five hours, sixty-four players were drafted and Lydon, Frantz, Kenny and Morgan were not among them.

Lydon, Frantz and Kenny all turned off their televisions and would have to wait another day to know their future. Meanwhile, the sun was just beginning to dip below the Las Vegas horizon. Yet, Morgan had no idea that day one of the draft had ended.

"After playing golf, we all went out to eat and then we went to the mall," said Morgan. "I kind of just chilled all day. All in all, it was a very relaxing day."

There was a good chance Morgan wouldn't utter those same words the next time the sun left the desert in darkness. Now, only one more day remained in the draft season. For most players, it was a time of uncertainty, angst and dread. However, Morgan had no trouble falling asleep that night.

"There's nothing I can do about it," said Morgan. "Whatever is going to be is going to be. No point in me losing sleep about it."

On the following day, an entire season of wondering would finally come to an end. Morgan, Frantz, Kenny and Lydon all hoped that day would turn out to be the glorious culmination of a lifelong journey filled with hard work, dedication and sacrifice.

CHAPTER TWENTY-THREE

A Long Day

After a long, anticipated wait through a lengthy draft season, day two of the 2009 NFL Draft had finally arrived. Kenny, Frantz and Lydon all rolled out of bed well before the third round began. Kenny's family welcomed a long list of guests to their house while one of Lydon's friends treated him to a Draft Day party in his honor. Those packed houses wiped away any chance of oversleeping for Lydon or Kenny.

Frantz had no choice but to wake up early as a camera crew from ESPN rang his mother's doorbell more than an hour before round three got underway. That crew would remain with Frantz throughout the day, or at least until he got drafted. More than halfway across the country, Morgan took his time introducing himself to another day. While other players anxiously awaited the start of round three, Morgan slept peacefully next to his wife.

Frantz appeared very relaxed in his mother's living room as a producer from ESPN riddled him with questions. He sat calmly on the couch and casually answered those queries. He briefly explained how he had watched a little bit of the draft during the preceding day. He also reiterated that it would be a blessing to just get drafted and he once again talked about the first purchase he would make with his newfound NFL income. The producer let out a heartfelt sigh when Frantz informed her that he wanted to buy a minivan for his mother's church group. For a kid who never had the luxury of having his own car, that selfless purchase was just one more example of Frantz's caring and thoughtful nature.

A handful of friends also gathered with Frantz to watch the day's events. Just as the draft was set to begin, those friends were abuzz wondering exactly when Frantz would be drafted and where he would spend his future. Early predictions ranged from the third to fifth round, but Frantz refused to make his own projections. He just sat quietly next to his mother, wearing a look that always seemed to be on the verge of a smile.

Things were a bit different in Minnesota where Lydon was up on the edge of his seat anxiously awaiting the start of day two. Offensive tackles were a valuable commodity in the draft. But as the third round began, teams started to shy away from that position. The first ten picks passed without any offensive tackles being selected. Teams were now only allotted five minutes between selections, but those minutes seemed a lot longer to Lydon.

"I live a stress free life," said Lydon. "I've only been stressed a couple of times in my life; my college transition from high school and the biggest job interview of my life, the NFL Combine. But this draft is taking my stress to a whole other level."

From his parents' home in Atlanta, the hands of time seemed to have a bit of arthritis as far as Kenny was concerned. More than an hour into round three, Kenny watched the ninth wide receiver selected with the eighteenth pick of the third round. But his anticipation heightened as the New England Patriots were now on the clock. The Patriots were rumored to be in the market for a receiver and were also the first team to request a private workout with Kenny.

Kenny looked down at his phone and anticipated a ring while seconds ticked off the clock. He then looked over at his son and thought of his future. Kenny suddenly became less eager for those seconds to speed up.

"I want him to have the best life possible," said Kenny. "And for him to have the best life possible, it takes money. The second round money make things a lot more easier than seventh-round money. I always think about that."

The second round had already passed, but third-round picks still warranted lucrative signing bonuses along with contracts that crept into the millions. The clock continued to tick down, yet Kenny's phone remained silent. Those seconds trickled until New England made its decision with some time left to spare. Kenny frowned as he heard the Patriots select North Carolina wide receiver Brandon Tate with the 83rd overall pick.

Tate was almost the exact same type of receiver as Kenny. They were both about the same size and Tate also had his share of injury problems. The former Tar Heel missed half of his senior season after suffering a tear in his ACL as well as his MCL. Kenny's hamstrings were fully healed, yet he was forced to sit and watch as Tate became the tenth wide receiver taken in the draft. For Kenny, the wait would go on.

Back at Frantz's mother's apartment, the living room began filling up.

"I didn't expect all those people to be here," said Frantz. "I expected about ten people at the most. But I guess people called their friends and another called their friends and all of the sudden there was a lot of people in the house. I was originally going to have something at Dave and Buster's, but I cancelled it. Can you imagine if we got a private room there and I didn't get drafted?"

The end of the third round was approaching and Frantz didn't appear bothered by the fact that he hadn't been drafted. He smiled for the ESPN camera crew and joked with his friends as they ate platefuls of food. The mood was light, but Frantz continued to look down at his phone more frequently.

The dawn of a new day had finally come for Morgan. He joined the conscious world after a refreshing night of slumber in which he neither tossed nor turned very much at all. His family joined him for a morning meal, which wasn't quite a typical breakfast. With the effervescent glow of youth, Morgan munched on an In-N-Out Burger along with some fries and a soda for his first meal of the day.

To compensate for the full load of people, Morgan drove a minivan around Las Vegas. It may have not been his first choice of vehicles, but it was the only one that would hold Morgan, his brother, his sister-in-law, Liz and his parents. Morgan drove the minivan while Jarrad threw in an occasional joke from the passenger seat.

"We drove around and I showed Liz my old neighborhood, my old house, where I played football for the first time," said Morgan. "I also showed her my junior high school and basically the whole area. I really didn't know what round it was throughout the day. But I knew a phone call was coming sooner or later."

Everyone in the minivan anticipated that phone call. The draft was on everyone's mind, although it was never a topic of conversation.

"No one was really saying anything about it," said Morgan. "There was kind of a tension in the air. Everybody just wanted it to be over with. We were trying to have a good time, but that was obviously the overlying factor of what was going on."

At that time, no one in the minivan knew that Carolina had just made its third-round selection. The Panthers had remained true to their word and selected a tall cornerback in 6-foot-1 Sherrod Martin out of Troy. This was the same team that told Morgan they had him at a second-round grade at his Pro Day. But when the end of the third round came around, they were reluctant to make him a Panther. Morgan's family was oblivious to that reality, but an anxious feeling started to speak up even though a word about the draft was not even whispered.

That same feeling permeated through Frantz's mother's apartment as more and more people crammed into her living room. The fourth round had just gotten underway and an inside linebacker was taken for the first time on day two of the draft. The Cleveland Browns selected USC's Kaluka Maiava. Apparently, the Browns' personalized letter to Frantz may not have been as genuine as it originally seemed. With that selection, Maiava became only the third inside linebacker selected in the entire draft. Nevertheless, that was not an uncommon trend.

"If you look at the history of drafts, inside linebackers don't go very high," said Baltimore Ravens general manager and hall of fame tight end Ozzie Newsome. "It's the same reason why centers don't go high. Unless you're a special tight end, you don't go high. We put the premium on quarterbacks, corners, left tackles and pass rushers. Those are the guys for the most part who are going to come off the board early."

The picks continued and more offensive tackles, cornerbacks and wide receivers found new homes. Yet, none of those players happened to be Lydon, Morgan or Kenny. Thirteen more picks passed and the New Orleans Saints were suddenly on the clock. The Saints were one of the teams that expressed quite a bit of interest in Frantz.

Frantz checked his phone while nearly half of the crowded room looked over at him with anxious eyes. It was almost as if they held their breath and were waiting for something to happen. Then, with the eighteenth pick of the fourth round, something did happen. The Saints selected Wake Forest inside linebacker Stanley Arnoux. Frantz's brother immediately looked at him with a facial expression that seemed to say 'huh?'

Stanley was no stranger to Frantz. He attended a nearby high school and the two developed a friendship over the years.

"We kind of grew up together," said Frantz. "I was happy for him but, at the same time, I was wondering why I wasn't getting picked. But it is what it is."

Instead of lamenting over why the Saints did not draft him, Frantz sent Stanley a congratulatory text message.

"I just wished him the best and told him I really hoped everything works out for him," said Frantz.

Unfortunately for Stanley, that wouldn't happen. One week after the draft, he would go on to rupture his Achilles' tendon during the first practice of the Saints' rookie camp. After that injury, his future in the NFL would be questionable at best.

Following Stanley's selection, eighteen more picks remained in the fourth round. During that span, another two offensive tackles were taken which further enhanced Lydon's angst. Two more wide receivers were selected forcing Kenny to continually ask, 'why not me?' And another pair of cornerbacks were taken off the board, one of which wasn't even invited to the Combine. The other cornerback turned out to be one that Morgan beat handily in almost every single event at the Combine.

Round four finally came to an end and Morgan, Frantz, Lydon and Kenny all remained undrafted. Each of them also knew full well that the money flowing through the fifth round would be a bit less. The longer they waited, the less they would get paid.

As the fifth round commenced, a lot of the talk in Frantz's living room died down as conversations were becoming more infrequent and more inaudible. It was almost as if there was a silent, collective wish for Frantz's name to appear on the television screen. Moments after Frantz glanced down at his silent phone one more time, he looked up and noticed Kenny McKinley's name pop up on the screen.

The Denver Broncos had traded up to get Kenny and drafted him with the fifth pick in the fifth round, making him the 141st overall selection. But unlike the eruption of excitement in Kenny's living room, there was very little sound at Frantz's. No one leapt off the couch and screamed with excitement. No parents wrapped their arms around Frantz while saying heartfelt words of congratulations. No tears of joy were shed as a boyhood's dream was realized. And there was no infant image of Frantz to provide inspiration as a future in the NFL awaited. Unlike Kenny, Frantz had no reason to jump up and celebrate. Unlike Kenny, Frantz still did not have a home in the NFL.

Lydon was also completely ignorant of the jubilance that sweltered through Kenny's home. The people at his party had no reason to exhale the anxiety that seemed to suffocate the room. His friends didn't have the opportunity to cheer with delight and christen the Denver Broncos their new favorite team. What was even more dissuading was that Lydon's name continued to taunt him from the television screen. The ESPN experts had him as one of the top ten players still available. Yet, Lydon's phone did not make a sound.

"When you know you're a first-rounder, it's not a huge stressful deal," said Lydon. "But when it comes down to not knowing whether or not you'll be drafted, it's really nerve-wracking. No one knows. While I was waiting, I felt like I was going out of my mind."

Two picks after Kenny had learned where he would spend his future, the Dallas Cowboys found themselves on the clock. Dallas had already made five selections, but had not yet taken a cornerback. After receiving what seemed like such a sincere message from the Cowboys, Morgan could be next in line to receive a phone call. Nevertheless, his tour through Las Vegas would continue as the Cowboys selected cornerback DeAngelo Smith out of Cincinnati. Smith was another player Morgan smoked at the Combine. Smith came nowhere near Morgan in any statistical category, but his wait had come to an end.

Frantz continued to glance down at his phone more often as the number of people in his living room expanded. All eyes were either fixed on the television or they were busy studying Frantz. Seconds seemed to slow down to a crawl and the minutes between draft picks seemed more like hours. Frantz watched three more inside linebackers get drafted before he got up and walked out of the living room. He disappeared inside one of the bedrooms, leaving his slew of guests to watch the draft without his company.

The fifth round lagged on, although Morgan and his family had no idea what was going on inside Radio City Music Hall. Suddenly, all of their attention shifted to the draft as Morgan's phone rang. Everyone fell quiet and, except for a couple of nervous gulps, complete silence inundated the minivan. But Morgan quickly broke that silence.

"Hello," Morgan said in a clear, firm voice.

"Morgan, this is Coach Lopez from the St. Louis Rams."

"Hi, how are you, sir?"

"Good, listen Morgan, we have a pick coming up in the next round."

"Oh yeah?" said Morgan.

"We're thinking about drafting you next round. But if we don't, maybe we'll pick you up in free agency."

"Excuse me?" said Morgan.

"We got a pick coming up and we want to pick you, but you might be gone. We also might not pick you, but we have another pick in the seventh round. And if we don't pick you then, maybe we'll still call you back."

Morgan offered him a calm 'sure thing', but was very confused by the ordeal. He had waited all day for a phone call, a call that was supposed to let him know where he would spend his future. When his phone rang, he immediately thought it was the call he had been waiting for his whole life. But it wasn't. It was a coach telling him there was a chance he might get drafted later on, or, not at all!

The move seemed both unprofessional and inappropriate. On one of the longest days of Morgan's life, Coach Lopez only pretended to end the excruciating wait. No thanks to the St. Louis Rams, Morgan's waiting game would continue to play on.

The fifth round came to an end and draft picks started coming at a much quicker pace. It was then, during the later rounds, when war rooms started to get a little messy.

"Later in the draft, when the board is kind of falling apart and the top tiers are gone, my experience is there is still a lot of lobbying going on between coaches and scouts," said former Baltimore Ravens head coach Brian Billick. "It's a lot more subjective in the later rounds."

Inside those war rooms, Morgan's name must have been tossed around quite a bit as he was one of the top players that remained undrafted. Shortly after Coach Lopez had phoned Morgan with his version of a prank call, Morgan's phone rang out again. His family all perked up as Morgan swiftly answered the call.

"Morgan, this is Coach Lewis from Cincinnati. How are you?"

"I'm hanging in there," said Morgan.

"I know it's been a long day and you're probably not too happy to hang around this long," said Lewis. "But we have a pick coming up and we're going to pick you. I just wanted to welcome you to Cincinnati."

Morgan shook his head to notify his family this was indeed the call they had been waiting for. Everyone in the minivan immediately started to scream with excitement. The wait was finally over! Liz and Tina started to cry while Jarrad and Phil donned proud smiles. They were all so loud that Morgan could barely hear Cincinnati Bengals head coach Marvin Lewis. Morgan's family had no idea who was on the phone or where Morgan was going to play. Still, elation overwhelmed the entire minivan as Morgan's dream of being a NFL player was coming true right before their very eyes.

Coach Lewis then put Morgan on the phone with his new positional coach, Kevin Coyle, and the two talked for a few minutes. Coach Coyle said he was very excited to have Morgan and looked forward to his future in Cincinnati. After all was said and done, Morgan wound up being the 179th player selected in the 2009 NFL Draft.

The congratulatory calls and texts starting coming in just after Morgan was officially announced as the sixth selection of the sixth round. Friends, family and former teammates all wished Morgan the best for the future. Even former Michigan head coach Lloyd Carr called to congratulate Morgan.

"Congratulations and when you get back to Michigan, come over and see me," Coach Carr told Morgan. "We have to talk."

Morgan obliged and was able to share the smiles that quickly spread through the inside of the minivan. No such smiles appeared in Minnesota or Fort Lauderdale as the sixth round dragged on. One name after the other was announced, but neither of those names belonged to Lydon or Frantz. Lydon's name had been staring at him for what seemed like forever. The television experts felt as though he was one of the best players available, so why didn't any NFL teams share the same sentiment?

By the end of the sixth round, there was still no sign of Frantz. He remained tucked away in one of the bedrooms, hidden from the television, the ESPN cameras and the multitude of people who clogged up the living room.

Now that the seventh round had begun, Lydon's biggest fear was realized. He couldn't believe he was still undrafted. But it wasn't long before Lydon's phone started to ring as calls began coming in at a swift pace. He answered each call with tremendous haste, hoping, praying and begging that his wait would be over. The San Diego Chargers, the Jacksonville Jaguars and the Tampa Bay Buccaneers all told him slightly different versions of the same story. They were going to draft him with their next selection, so he should be ready.

Lydon was frantically answering the phone, trying to juggle calls from different teams as well as his agent. Then, as he was hanging up with one team, his phone beeped. He tried to answer the call, but accidentally hung up the phone.

"Shoot," he yelled out when he made that realization.

Lydon scrambled to redial the number of whoever it was that just called him. His heart picked up its pace as he waited for someone to answer. The phone rang once and nothing happened. It rang again while Lydon made a silent plea for someone to answer.

Then, a recording picked up and a voice said, "Hello, you have reached the office of the Detroit Lions."

"Shoot!" Lydon yelled out again.

He quickly hung up and tried to dial the number again as he rushed from the kitchen back into the living room where the television was showing the draft. Once again, he reached the same recording. With his heart pounding against his chest, Lydon looked over at the screen and saw his name pop up as the Detroit Lions selected him with the 229th overall pick. Even though he had hung up on his future team, Lydon had finally found a home in the NFL!

A few minutes later, following the eruption at his draft party, Lydon successfully answered a phone call from the Detroit Lions.

He quickly explained the mix-up and listened to a Lions' coach tell him, "That's okay. You're a steal in the seventh round. We couldn't believe you lasted that long, but we're happy to have you. We think you have a bright future in Detroit."

Despite the record-setting numbers Lydon put up at the Combine, eighteen other offensive tackles were drafted ahead of him. But there was a dramatic lull in the run on tackles in the later rounds. Lydon became only the second offensive tackle chosen since the 162nd overall pick,

A Long Day

which came just after the midway point of the fifth round. Nevertheless, relief ensued for Lydon just as it did for Kenny and Morgan. Down in Fort Lauderdale, it was a different story altogether.

As the last part of the seventh round began to wind down, it seemed imminent that Frantz would not be drafted. His living room was still filled with people, but it was quieter than it had been all day. Blank stares of disbelief filled the room. Not much time elapsed between picks and it seemed as though teams were in a hurry to finish up the draft. The time finally came for the last pick, which had come to be known as Mr. Irrelevant. On that day, Frantz would not even be irrelevant. Two-hundred and fifty six picks had come and gone without even a mention of Frantz Joseph.

Moments after the draft had ended, Frantz's brother, Jimmy, emerged from the bedroom and called for everyone's attention. His face was painted with disappointment and his watery eyes seemed to be on the verge of a flood.

In a voice that nearly cracked, he said, "I want to thank all of you for coming out and supporting Frantz. Unfortunately, he didn't get drafted. But this isn't the end for Frantz. He thanks you all for coming out, but he doesn't want to see anyone right now."

After hearing those words, the crowd started to disperse and the ESPN producer came running up to Jimmy.

"Can we just interview him for a couple of minutes?" asked the producer.

"I'm sorry but Frantz does not want to talk to anyone right now," said Jimmy.

The television cameras were turned on but they just couldn't capture the heavy weight of disappointment that filled the apartment. It was almost as if that disappointment placed a sick feeling inside everyone's stomach. Frantz had fought through the draft season and done everything he could to find a home in the NFL. Just as he had done throughout his entire life, Frantz put forth every bit of effort in order to succeed. That effort just didn't seem to be enough. After nine grueling hours of watching the draft, Frantz was still just as unemployed as he was when the draft season began.

CHAPTER TWENTY-FOUR
The Aftermath

Following the draft, it was easy to see that everyone in Frantz's living room was extremely disappointed. Frantz would have loved to hear his name called out, but he wasn't too broken up over how things had turned out.

"To be honest, I didn't go in expecting to be drafted just because of all the circumstances that came into play," said Frantz. "My school never produced a guy that got drafted or even a guy that played in the NFL. It's kind of hard to convince a scout that our guys know how to play football professionally. In life, I'll look at the worse case scenarios so that I'll be prepared for it when it happens. If I went in there thinking I was going to get drafted fourth, fifth round or whatever, I would have just been setting myself up for a huge failure."

When Frantz withdrew from the living room early in the fifth round, he did something not many players would be able to do on Draft Day.

"I actually went inside and took a nap because there was a lot of things running through my mind," said Frantz. "I had to just cool down a little bit. It definitely felt like one of the longest days of my life, not knowing what was going to happen. I was thinking of a backup plan and stuff like that. I saw these guys going ahead of me and just wasn't really understanding why. Maybe these teams used a different type of scouting than I would."

Frantz's phone did ring by the end of the fifth round, but it was not a call from a NFL team. It was his agent.

"The agents don't know themselves if you're going to get drafted or not," said Frantz. "He was doing his work as far as marketing and being there for me. He kept telling me to hang in there and try not to worry about it. He gave me some words of encouragement so I wouldn't lose my mind."

Then, toward the end of the sixth round, Frantz finally received a call from the Washington Redskins.

"When they called me, I thought I was going to get chosen," said Frantz. "But they told me right away they didn't have any more picks left. They were calling to tell me that they were interested in me as a free agent. They offered me a three-year deal right there on the phone. When they call you and offer you as a priority free agent, that means they really want you. Then, you still have to go to mini-camp and prove yourself."

When Frantz received that call, he suddenly envisioned himself wearing a Redskins uniform and playing in the nation's capital. He didn't have too much time to fantasize since the Oakland Raiders contacted him shortly thereafter. They too approached Frantz with an offer.

"Those guys came at me in a way that sounded like they were very interested," said Frantz. "It was like 'we need you. We don't have depth at this position and we need you. There's a huge opportunity. If you just show what you can do, you're going to make the team.' It wasn't like a desperate situation. It was more like getting drafted in the fifth, sixth or seventh round."

Frantz's phone kept on ringing. The Baltimore Ravens called with the proposition of a one-year deal and the Denver Broncos quickly followed up with a three-year offer. The Jacksonville Jaguars and Miami Dolphins called later, but seemed to be procrastinating with their offers.

"Jacksonville and Miami were talking, but they didn't go as far to offer me a contract," said Frantz. "They were on the phone with my agent mostly."

Even though the draft had just ended, it was suddenly a very busy and exciting time for Frantz.

"I talked to my family and there was numerous calls back and forth," said Frantz. "They kept calling, they all kept calling and showing a lot of interest. I was going back and forth with my agent. But if I waited too long, they might go after somebody else."

Each team was eager to sign Frantz and did not hesitate to apply some pressure. Finally, Frantz came to the decision that he would sign a two-year contract and officially become an Oakland Raider.

"Looking at their depth and the opportunity I would have there, I'm already used to their scheme," said Frantz. "All the inroads just said go for me. It wasn't even about the money. The Broncos and the Redskins offered me more money. But the opportunity was the best with the Raiders."

About an hour after the last pick of NFL Draft was announced, Frantz was finally able to hug his family and rejoice in the fact that he knew where he was going to spend his future. Wearing the same smile that still glimmered with both maturity and innocence, Frantz treated the ESPN crew to an interview. When the cameras stopped filming and the apartment was nearly empty, Frantz took a few moments to sit down and relax.

"I was definitely relieved that I got an opportunity," said Frantz. "For me, it wasn't all about getting drafted. By the time the late rounds come around, it's better to be able to choose where you want to go and put yourself in a better predicament. I'm just going to go in and give it all I got. I'm not trying to make any friends, I'm just trying to make the team. I feel like I'm in the best position possible and I'm very thankful. I'm going to make the most I can out of it and I think I am destined to go this route. Looking back at what I've been through from Pop Warner through high school up until now, I've always been the underdog. That's what God had in place for me and that's the road I'm going to take."

Frantz would sign a two-year deal in which he was set to make the league minimum of $310,000 during his first year and $385,000 in his second year. However, he wouldn't see any of that money if he failed to make the team. He would also receive a signing bonus of $2,500 which was his to keep no matter what.

Morgan would go on to sign a four-year $1.86 million deal that included a $112,000 signing bonus. He was the first of Cincinnati's eleven draft picks to sign a contract. Lydon was held out of his rookie-camp because of a back problem and wound up signing his contract one day before the start of training camp. Lydon signed a three-year $1.2 million contract that included a signing bonus of $40,500.

In Denver, Kenny was trying to make a name for himself amidst a stacked corps of wide receivers. Kenny also signed just before the start of training camp and received a $200,200 signing bonus as part of a four-year $1.95 million deal.

Shortly after the draft, Morgan made good on his promise to pay his former head coach a visit. Morgan was always happy to see Coach Carr and gave him a warm greeting. However, it didn't take long for Coach Carr to get to the main reason why he wanted to see Morgan. It was there that Coach Carr told Morgan why he wasn't drafted until the sixth round.

Apparently, current Michigan head coach Rich Rodriguez had cost Morgan quite a bit of money. Rodriguez had bad-mouthed Morgan to every NFL scout he could. Rodriguez claimed that Morgan was lazy, he had an attitude problem and he was a big reason why the Wolverines finished with a 3-9 record, the worst in school history. In essence, an entire draft season and an entire college career of hard work were decimated by a few petty words. Those words may have meant the difference between a $1.86 million deal and a $2.86 million deal. It may have meant the difference between the sixth round and the third round.

That slight provided Morgan with some extra motivation heading into a new season of his football career. Much like Frantz, Morgan now had a bit of a chip on his shoulder and more to prove. Unfortunately, Frantz wouldn't even get that chance. The Oakland Raiders decided to release Frantz two weeks before the start of training camp. Frantz would not see a dime of that $310,000 nor would he get the opportunity to put on the pads. He had turned down offers from a host of other NFL teams, only to be tossed aside by the one team that seemed to want him the most. The Raiders were unwilling to even take a look and see what he could do. And all Frantz ever wanted was that one chance.

Kenny enjoyed an excellent preseason and went on to lead the Denver Broncos in receptions as well as receiving yards. He finished the preseason third in the NFL in receptions and fifth in receiving yards. Kenny survived the final round of cuts and made the Broncos' 53-man roster. The boy from Atlanta was now blossoming into a man out in Denver. As Kenny was starting out his professional football career, his son was starting out his life with a solid role model to look up to.

When the last round of cuts came in Detroit, Lydon was not so fortunate. Injuries limited his play during the preseason and he wound up being one of the final players released from the Lions' roster. That would mean he would not receive any of the $310,000 he was scheduled to take home. But one day after Lydon was cut, he was offered a spot on the Lions' practice squad. Lydon accepted and was set to receive $5,200 for every week he spent on the practice squad. For the next six weeks, Lydon performed well, prompting the Miami Dolphins to sign him to their 53-man roster a few days before they would play their sixth game of the season. Lydon was set to receive a prorated salary of the $310,000 league minimum. Furthermore, his wish to play professional football in the state of Florida had been granted.

Throughout the preseason, Morgan did more than enough to make the Cincinnati Bengals 2009 roster. He won the team's nickelback spot, which meant he would enter the game during passing situations as part of the nickel and dime packages. While Morgan thrived, Frantz could only watch and wish for one more opportunity to play the game he so desperately loved. That opportunity finally came, but in a different form. Just before the start of the NFL season, the Edmonton Eskimos of the Canadian Football League offered Frantz a contract. Without any NFL teams willing to give him a chance, Frantz signed a deal and headed up to Canada to begin his professional football career.

On his way up to Edmonton, Frantz flew over the state of Ohio where Morgan and Liz had recently settled into a cozy apartment overlooking the city of Cincinnati. Both Frantz and Morgan's situations were quite different as was their journey to this point in their lives. Yet, there was one striking parallel between them. Each of those young men walked through life powered by compassion, humility, dignity and class. Regardless of how many professional football contests either of them would go on to play, both had already become All-Pros in the game of life.